Vered's eyes wide _____ pillars of dark cloud began to swirl and take on human form. Red eyes blazed. Lightning began to jump from finger to finger—and into the ranks of the human guard. The storm warriors marched into battle. To their credit the King's Guard did not turn and flee. Vered knew his courage would not have withstood such an ominous assault. With every pointed finger a soldier died in a blaze of lightning. Sword cuts meant nothing to the inhuman warriors. Lances passed through their bodies, emerging damp with rainwater and not blood. Horses reared and kicked out war-spurred hooves. The horses died, their guts blown from their bodies by billowing gray cloud warriors.

"There is Lorens," cried Vered. "See? In the rear ranks?"

"It is. The rebels might find themselves in control of the kingdom sooner than they thought if the Wizard of Storms' cloud demons kill him now. But why would a wizard remain hidden away for so many years and then suddenly appear *now*?"

The reason had to lie hidden in Santan's rucksack. The Demon Crown had brought forth the storm warriors and the Wizard of Storms, and Vered feared they were invincible.

DEMON 2 CROWN

ROBERT E. VARDEMAN

PHANTOMS ON THE WIND

TOR
fantasy

A TOM DOHERTY ASSOCIATES BOOK
NEW YORK

PHANTOMS ON THE WIND

Copyright © 1989 by Robert E. Vardeman

A TOR Book
Published by Tom Doherty Associates, Inc.
49 West 24 Street
New York, NY 10010

Cover art by Don Brautigam

ISBN: 0-812-55716-6   Can. ISBN: 0-812-55717-4

First edition: October 1989

Printed in the United States of America

0 9 8 7 6 5 4 3 2 1

ONE

"The screams," said Birtle Santon. "It's their awful screams that I cannot tolerate." Even as he spoke, another shriek of pure agony echoed through the corridors of the Castle Porotane, center of power for the kingdom and new residence of King Lorens.

"I think it lends an air of distinction to these miserable, dismal stone corridors," said Vered. The young man lounged languidly on the black velvet-covered fainting couch, nibbling almost daintily at a slice of cheese impaled on the tip of his needle-pointed dirk. "Any castle can be home. I get so tired of simple dripping walls and dungeons that beg for that certain touch of humanity."

"That certain drop of blood, you mean," snapped Santon.

"A drop, a bucket, what matters this?" asked Vered, enjoying his friend's anger. "As long as it is not *our* precious blood being spilled by those butchers of the Inquisition."

Birtle Santon snorted and moved to the narrow window. The view of Porotane's farmlands and the gently flowing, green-hued River Ty from this castle aerie proved deceptive. All seemed tranquil in the land.

Another hideous scream, louder than before, made Santon cringe.

"Is it the Inquisition or merely another of dear King Lorens' interrogations?" he asked of Vered. Santon tapped his withered left arm against the outer stone wall nervously, knowing that it might soon be their screams tormenting the peace of the castle.

For all Vered's apparent ease, Santon saw subtle signs of tension in his friend. The brown eyes darted to and fro at the slightest of sounds. Muscles tensed along his powerful shoulders. The way he ran his hands through the shock of light brown hair dangling into his eyes gave more proof, as if Santon needed it, that Vered grew increasingly apprehensive about their safety. He taunted his friend only to break the boredom—and to relieve the strain they both felt so keenly.

"Lorens owes us much," said Vered, as if trying to convince himself. "Did we not seek him out in the City of Stolen Dreams and pluck him from his cruel master's bondage?"

"I think our young king approved of Patrin."

"Impossible. The wizard was a despot. He ruled the city with an iron hand. He badgered his apprentice. Lorens *must* consider us his saviours. And if that's not enough, we—"

"Gave him the Demon Crown," finished Santon.

They both fell silent at mention of the crown. The simple circlet of gold had been given to King Waellkin three centuries ago by the demon Kalob as restitution for the evil demons had visited upon humans. Only those of the royal line could wear the crown. And therein had been planted the seeds of even more demonic evil.

Civil wars had split the kingdom for years after King Lamost had died mysteriously. Lamost's brother, Duke Freow, had assumed the regency until the twin children of the king could be rescued from a kidnapping wizard.

Freow had proven to be a commoner, a usurping impostor intent on maintaining his own rule over the kingdom. Not until he lay on his deathbed had he sent Alarice, the Glass Warrior, to find an heir to the throne and to restore the Demon Crown to the proper royal brow.

"Alarice," Birtle Santon said in a whisper so low that Vered could not hear. How he had loved her! And how he had wept bitter tears when she had perished rescuing Lorens from the City of Stolen Dreams. Her body had vanished in the sands of the Sazan Desert and they had been unable to pay her the homage due a true hero.

"Very well," said Vered. "Lorens may not approve of our past lives. Who can say that being itinerant thieves is a proper life? But he cannot gainsay our help in restoring him to the throne."

"Was that such a triumph on our part?" asked Santon.

"Quiet, fool!" hissed Vered. His brown eyes grew wide with fear. This startled Santon more than anything Vered might have said. The young warrior feared nothing, and now he showed every sign of outright terror. "Lorens might be wearing the Demon Crown and overhear us!"

Santon sighed. Such was the power of the demonic crown. The wearer could project his senses anywhere in the kingdom, hearing and seeing every word and deed. The intelligence so gathered proved a boon to Lorens in his fight against the rebel factions striving for supremacy in the countryside. It also gave the monarch the perfect method for ferreting out traitors in his own rank.

New screams, higher, shriller, more feminine, raked across Santon's consciousness. He tried to shut out the cries of agony generated in the dungeons and failed. It required no major leap of imagination to picture himself thrust into the wire coffin and having a hooded torturer begin heating the wires. Santon tried not to think of the stench of burned flesh or the pain it would give.

"You think too much, Santon," Vered said. "You dwell on the dark rather than seeking the light."

"You may be right. But there is one point on which we both must ponder. What is to be our destiny? Simply sitting and idly eating until we grow fat and dull, or should we be doing something more?"

"What do you suggest?" Vered had tried to show himself impervious to the agonies being dealt out below them in the dungeons. The new screams visibly wracked him. His face paled and his quick, steady hands developed a tremor.

"Not joining the rebels," Santon said. "There is no profit in being a soldier for even an enlightened commander like Dews Gaemock."

"The name," Vered whispered urgently. "Do not mention it! *He* might be listening!"

"Such fear," scoffed Santon. "Do you think Lorens needs *any* reason for cruelty? Listen well. Let your ears give testimony to the king's generosity with wanton pain."

"He needs no reason to send the innocent

to the dungeons," agreed Vered. The young man sagged in the couch's softness, all pretense of ease gone. A tiny facial tic jerked under his left eye. His nimble fingers stroked up and down the blade of his dirk and one long leg hooked over the couch arm swung constantly. "He needs no reason to send us into the uncaring arms of a torturer, does he?"

"My thoughts match yours, it seems. We have done what Alarice asked of us. We have delivered the true king to the throne and given him the Demon Crown. There is nothing more for us to do here. Let us find safety elsewhere." Again his green eyes turned to the narrow slit in the castle wall and focused on the purpled summits of the Yorral Mountains.

"It has been some time since we travelled across the Uvain Plateau," said Vered. "The wines there are second to none. I can drink no other. The swill they serve in this miserable heap of stone and mortar is certainly not to my liking. And the food tastes of month-old mold and inexpert preparation. Better to endure your trail cooking than this cuisine."

Santon listened to his friend work up trivial reasons for departing the Castle Porotane. The only reason to leave lay in their desire for continued life. Along with the ability to magically cast his senses across the kingdom using the Demon Crown, King Lorens also accepted the penalty: creeping madness.

A sudden rap on the heavy wood door brought both Birtle Santon and Vered to their feet, weapons ready for the fight that would end their lives.

"Vered?" came a muffled voice. "Are you in there? Please. It is Kerin."

"Ah, such a lovely lass. She should not be

kept waiting in the drafty hallways." Vered spoke bravely but his caution in opening the door was not lost on Santon. Vered kept one booted boot planted securely on the floor to prevent the door from being kicked open and his dagger poised for a killing thrust. "It is Kerin!" Vered exclaimed, almost surprised at not finding deception.

The flame-tressed serving maid slipped into the room. Vered closed the door and bolted it, only to find Kerin's slender white arms thrown around his neck. She buried her face in his shoulder and sobbed.

"There, there," he said, trying to still her unbridled sorrow. "What makes one so lovely weep so? Have I not been good to you? Surely, you did not find fault with anything happening last night." He glanced over at Santon and shrugged, as if saying, "Are they never satisfied?"

"Kerin," spoke up Birtle Santon. "What is wrong?"

"It's awful. Th-they came and took her. Rogina."

"Her sister," explained Vered. "Who has taken Rogina? And for what reason? She is only fifteen."

"In the night when I was with you. The king's guard took her. They gave no reason for it. I . . . I just found that they took her to the dungeons."

Another long, high-pitched shriek rose and rattled the foundations of their nerve.

"Can it be Rogina's cries we hear?" Vered asked.

"No," Santon said quickly. "No, it is another's."

Vered knew his friend lied; Santon could not know whose pain they listened to. But Kerin accepted even this small white lie because she wanted to believe.

"There are factions at war within the castle as well as without," said Santon. "Baron Theoll has never accepted Lorens' return. The baron saw the chance to sit on the throne uncontested and did not willingly step down."

"A cruel man, the baron," said Kerin. "But he is not as cruel as Archbishop Nosto."

"Ah, yes, the follower of the True Path with the fanatic's fire in his eyes." Santon had heard the gut-wrenching tales of Nosto's Inquisition against impiety and the holy Inquisitor who tortured until those straying from the path of righteousness confessed—or died before confessing. Luckily, neither Santon nor Vered had occasion to cross paths with the archbishop after Lorens had been crowned King of Porotane.

"Can you find her? Can you save her?" Kerin's plea almost choked in her throat. "I know it's much to ask. After all, we only shared a bed a few nights."

"But those were the best nights of my life!" exclaimed Vered. He shot a glance at Santon to keep his friend silent.

"Then you will find Rogina and save her?"

"Save her?" asked Vered. "From what? We know that a girl so young cannot be a rebel or a conspirator against the king. And what crime could she possibly commit that would require her imprisonment? No, we must look elsewhere."

"Archbishop Nosto?" asked Santon.

Kerin shook her head. Strands of the fiery

hair fell into her eyes. Vered gently pushed them back to stare into her gold-flaked green eyes. For the first time he noticed a tiny island of carmine in her right eye and a circle of black around the iris.

"My sister is devout. She never strays from the True Path."

"Theoll has perverse tastes. Could he have whisked her off to his bed?" Vered clutched Kerin tightly. "There, there," he soothed. "I merely think aloud. This might not have happened at all."

"It might be a better fate than being sent to the king's dungeons," said Santon, not trying to temper the bitterness in his words. He cared nothing for the politics within the castle's walls. He preferred the open countryside with wind in his hair and sun burning his face.

"We need information," said Vered. "And I know the source for all wisdom."

"Harhar?" asked Santon.

"Who else?"

"But he's the court jester! He's a halfwit. Listen to him. And he drools!" Kerin was shocked by the notion that the court fool could provide any information.

"He has astounding moments of lucidity," said Santon. "He listened long to Duke Freow and aided him in his last hours."

"His philosophy is what you would expect of a fool," cut in Vered, "but his eyes and ears are the match of any hunter's."

Kerin stared at Vered in disbelief, but she had no one else to go to for help. Vered seemed competent enough, even if he did think the fool might be of some help.

"You stay in our quarters, my dear," said Vered, "and let Santon and me make a few discreet inquiries. Harhar is easy to find but hard to talk with. He is always near the king."

"Or the baron," said Santon. "He and Baron Theoll spend a considerable amount of time together, or so it's rumored among the house guard."

The two adventurers left the serving maid in their suite and ventured forth. Santon carried his shield of spun glass given to him by Alarice, and Vered sported her short glass sword. They stalked the castle's corridors more like hunters than guests.

"There. The throne room," said Vered. "I hear his silly jape."

Santon pushed aside a hanging curtain of gold beads and peered into the long, narrow throne room. He blinked. How it had changed —and not for the better. The brief time Theoll had occupied the tall-backed ebony throne he had brought in jeweled ornaments for the cold stone walls, fancy carved wood chairs for the court retainers, tapestries both rich and intricate to soften the cold walls, and a magic lantern that emitted a soft, diffuse golden light on everything within the room. It shone on Theoll, when seated on the throne, a single shaft of pure white light.

All that had changed. Gone were the censers burning sandalwood and pine. The heavy, cloying scent from the room reminded Santon of a charnel house. Death was everywhere. Over the jeweled coats of arms on the walls were hung the shriveled bodies of traitors. The tapestries and rugs had been spattered with blood as executions took place at the foot of the throne. Worst of all from Santon's view was the change in the magical light source.

Gone was the golden hue it had once cast.

The single ray of light centered on the throne had turned from virgin white to a sickly green that hinted at corruption and unholy decay.

And King Lorens seemed not to notice—or care.

"The king is in court again," Vered said. He made no attempt to keep his voice down. With the Demon Crown settled upon his temples, the monarch could hear and see anywhere in the kingdom. Those closest garnered the majority of his attention, though, because of several abortive assassination attempts.

Santon tried to hold back the shudder that wracked his body. His distaste for Lorens knew no bounds. The youngling had been apprenticed to the wizard Patrin for too long. He had never learned how to diplomatically deal with others. He had been a slave suddenly released from his bondage and had responded with the same savagery that Patrin had shown him. He knew only master and servant. The word "peer" was lacking in both his vocabulary and experience.

"The crown," said Vered. "See how it glows?"

"I have never seen it radiate that putrid color before. It must be the magic lantern's doing."

"You have it ass backwards, Santon, my friend. The magic from the Demon Crown affects the lantern."

"Infects is a better word," Santon said. The bladder green halo around the crown surged and contracted like a giant muscle flexing. Lorens sat rigidly on the throne, fists clenched and his glassy eyes peering directly ahead.

"He sees nothing," said Vered. "Nothing within this room. He casts forth for traitors in other parts of the kingdom. This is our chance to speak with Harhar."

The two men tried to moderate their pace across the empty throne room but soon found themselves running. The court jester rolled and bounced and shook his rattle at the foot of the dais, as if performing for an audience of thousands.

"Harhar, a word with you," said Vered.

"Ho! My good friends! You have come to see my new act! Listen to my japes. They are ever so much better than the others." Harhar looked around as if imparting court secrets. "I have hired two soldiers to write the jokes for me."

"Fine, yes," said Santon, glancing upward at King Lorens. The monarch's expression had not changed. He might have been one of those impaled along the walls for all the life he showed. Santon knew they were as safe talking in the presence of the king as they were meeting clandestinely—perhaps safer. Secrecy drew the suspicious ruler's attention. But to so openly oppose the young king worried Santon.

"A curious thing happened in the night," said Vered.

"Oh, I've heard this one. It's a joke, isn't it? About the chambermaid and the duke's prize stallion?"

"No, no, not exactly," said Vered, trying to keep his temper. "Rogina, the younger sister of Kerin. You know who I mean?"

"Rogina? Such a brat, but her sister is nice. Fine hair so red that it appears to burn in the sunlight. She has given me food from the royal table. I know Kerin."

"She loves her sister very much and would like to know what has happened to her," continued Vered. "Rogina was taken by guards in the middle of the night."

Santon moved slightly, his shield coming up to protect his side. The motion was pure reflex. The flash of intelligence that had crossed Harhar's face made him doubt the jester's apparent idiocy.

"No reason for Lorens to take her," said Harhar. "He has the pick of any lady in the kingdom."

Santon could not resist asking, "Who does he sleep with? What lady?"

"Or lord. He might sleep with a lord," said Harhar. "But he doesn't."

"Sleep with men?" asked Vered, frowning.

"Sleep with anyone. He might be a cleric for all his escapades."

"Living in the City of Stolen Dreams as a wizard's apprentice might have . . . done things to him," suggested Vered.

"Oh, no, I think not. I think he is frightened. So much power and he is frightened. That is a fine jape, isn't it? More power than any king in our memory and he is afraid." Harhar laughed maniacally and somersaulted to the foot of the throne and peered up.

"Is that it, my liege? Are you scared shitless of the little people like me? Is my wit so barbed that it pierces your lion's heart?" Harhar laughed again and did a double handspring to return to Vered's side.

Santon lowered his shield. The brief flash of intelligence Harhar displayed had passed, the old crackbrained behavior returning. No man taunted a king, much less one as powerful as Lorens.

"What, then, do you make of the serving

maid's disappearance?" asked Vered. "A man of your standing hears all."

"My standing?" Harhar leaped into the air, turned adroitly, and landed on his belly. He began wiggling about like a *poulten* lizard trapped in the Desert of Sazan's midday sun. "I never stand. I lie!" Harhar rolled onto his back and laughed hysterically.

"This is not as good an idea as I thought," said Santon. He stared at Lorens. The king moved slightly, as if shifting his attention from one distant spot to another. Sweat beaded his forehead as if he strained. The obscene pulsations of the green halo from the Demon Crown accentuated the high cheekbones and cast a pallor on Lorens that made him seem sickly.

"We should explore other avenues for our information," said Santon. "Others that take us away from this room." He was not a squeamish man. Being surrounded by the impaled, mummifying remains of so many nobles robbed him of any desire to linger.

The sight of what Lorens had become sickened him even further.

"Harhar, are you sure you cannot tell us who stole the lovely young girl?" Vered tried to coax the information from the jester.

"I lie, I die, I cry, I sigh. It is all too fey for me to say nay or yea."

"Leave him," said Santon. He tugged at Vered's sleeve with his good hand. "Even if he knows, it doesn't seem that he is going to tell us."

"Good day to you, sir jester," said Vered. He performed a courtly bow and backed away, treating the fool as nobility.

Once past the golden beaded curtains,

Vered heaved a deep sigh. "It is difficult dealing with one such as Harhar. I feel the currents of deep thought in him, yet only bubbles of noxious gases rise to the surface."

"The lieutenant of guards who cheated you out of the ten gold pieces," said Santon. "Do you think you might get him to talk of Rogina?"

"Cheated me!" cried Vered. "He did no such thing. I let him take the money in what appeared to be less than fair circumstances. I cultivate him as one cultivates a sickly plant. One day he will bloom and give forth the tempting fruits of information."

Santon started to tell his friend what he thought of such an approach when he stopped and stared. Ahead of them in the hall stood three burly soldiers with swords drawn. Santon glanced over his shoulder. Three more soldiers blocked their retreat.

"We seem to have found the ruffians responsible for poor Rogina's kidnapping," said Vered, drawing his glass sword. "Let us hope they can be convinced to tell us where they've taken her."

"Let's hope we can fight our way out of this!"

Santon lifted his shield in time to deflect a thrust from the soldier in front of him. He whipped a length of chain from around his waist and flailed away with it.

Whoever had stolen away Rogina did not intend for them to find her. Ever.

TWO

Baron Theoll paced the length of his sleeping chambers, one leg dragging slightly from an old wound. He cradled his left arm protectively; that assassin's injury had yet to heal fully. The small, dark, intense man spun suddenly and pointed at Harhar.

"That is all you can tell me?" he demanded of the court fool.

Harhar's head bobbed up and down as if it had been placed on a spring. "Truly, Baron, I know nothing more. How can I when he sits on his throne and stares at . . . places no ordinary mortal can see or hear?"

"He checks on the rebel forces," said Theoll. "That is the only reason he would be so preoccupied."

"Dews Gaemock is a fine man," said Harhar. "I have met him. He gave me sweets and an entire piece of silver for my capers."

Theoll scowled. At times he wondered if anything but maggots infested the fool's brain. At other times, Harhar's observations proved astute. "What of Lorens? His condition. His words. I need to know everything. He has barred me from the throne room."

"A grim place now, Baron Theoll," Harhar

said solemnly. "I can hardly get into the mood for joking with the corpses strewn about. You would think that a king could be neater."

Theoll stared at the jester. Did he mock Lorens—and Theoll—or were the words without sarcasm? Theoll could not tell.

"I need to know everything about our newly crowned king. Tell me of the Demon Crown and how it affects him."

"The ugly green nimbus around his head," Harhar said, as if reciting a litany, "billows and boils. The more he concentrates, the uglier it becomes. It is hard to tell whether he controls it—or it controls our beloved king."

"The crown is dangerous. It is no mere legend that it can seize the mind of a weakling."

"Not like you, O my Lord Theoll?"

Theoll's right hand lashed out. He slapped the jester and sent him tumbling. His hand stung but the jester's face remained untouched. Theoll thought his blow had been robbed of real strength by the fool's quick reflexes.

"Do not taunt me," Theoll said in an icy tone. "I am not of the direct line and could never wear the Demon Crown for the lengths of time Lorens does. But it would sit well on my head for a few minutes a day."

"How goes the spying on the serving wenches? Do you still peer through the holes in the walls at them as they disrobe for their toilet?" The jester scuttled like a beetle to avoid Theoll's weak kick. The baron's injuries prevented him from catching the mocking fool and giving him the thrashing he had so richly earned with that remark.

"I need to know what happens within these walls. Only my constant surveillance can put down dissent."

"Against King Lorens?"

"Against the kingdom. Porotane desperately needs a strong leader. That old fool Freow managed to let the civil war rage for decades." Theoll spun about, pulling his purple silk cape about his small frame. "Lorens is not the leader his beloved father was."

"He's not the leader Duke Freow was," muttered Harhar.

"Even with the crown," Theoll went on, "he is unable to crush the rebels. If anything their power grows. Lorens' coronation has united the strongest rebel bands."

"Dews Gaemock and Dalziel Sef join forces on the other side of the River Ty."

"How did you know that?" snapped Theoll. "Only this morning did my scouts return with that information." Theoll's dark eyes narrowed as he looked at the jester. "Lorens *saw* their alliance using the Demon Crown. Is that how you discovered it?"

"Oh, yes, Lord, yes, yes, of course it is." Harhar hunkered down behind a low table and put up an arm to fend off any further blows directed at him by the baron.

Theoll ignored the fool. The jester had his uses. He overheard tidbits of valuable information because no one considered it necessary to stay their tongue in his presence. Only Theoll had learned to tap this geyser of knowledge. But such an unreliable fount Harhar was!

"Lorens' power extends beyond the crown," Theoll said. "He was not apprenticed to Patrin those long years for naught. But what does he know? What spells does he cast?"

"How badly has he angered the Wizard of Storms?" asked Harhar.

"What?" Theoll swung around, almost losing his balance. His good hand reached out for support. He blanched at the mere mention of the powerful wizard. "What do you know of the Wizard of Storms?"

Harhar shrugged. The fool moved out from behind the table. "I heard Lorens mention him, mayhaps. Or perhaps it was Archbishop Nosto. Someone did. The storms march down the valleys in the far mountains and assault the Uvain Plateau. The Wizard of Storms is upset. That is all that is known."

"For more years than I have been alive, no one has heard from the Wizard of Storms. Why does he choose now to make his power felt?" Theoll sagged into a chair. His rise to power had seemed so simple when he learned that Freow had not been the true brother of King Lamost.

Kill the impostor, assume the throne. Simple. Easy. But Freow had clung tenaciously to life. Too tenaciously. The subtle poisons that Theoll had fed him had been neutralized. But who in Castle Porotane had both knowledge and opportunity? Why save the old faker?

Theoll's teeth ground together as he thought of Freow sending the Glass Warrior to find the royal twins.

"They had been gone for so long. Who would have thought either lived?" he said aloud.

"The twins? Everyone, Lord, everyone knew they lived. Even old Duke Freow."

Theoll glared at the jester. "Lorens lived. His ability to wear the crown as he does proves his royal blood. But nothing has been shown of his leadership. He spies endlessly using the Demon Crown and allows underlings free rein within the castle walls."

"You mean others instead of you, Baron?"

"Is the Glass Warrior truly dead?"

"Alarice perished," Harhar said in a sad tone. "She laughed at my jests. She was a good person. She brought me sweets and gave me money, too."

Theoll reached across the table to cuff the jester. Again his blow missed its target, but Harhar tumbled across the room and crashed into the wall as if it had landed with full force.

"The two who returned with Lorens and the Demon Crown. I need to know their part. I have tried to spy upon them and received—" Theoll abruptly stopped speaking. He had been reaching for the small puncture wound under his right eye. The night after Lorens' coronation Theoll had slipped along his secret passages to open a spyhole into Birtle Santon and Vered's quarters. For his trouble he had received a poke with a pointed stick that nearly put out his eye. Each subsequent attempt to spy on them had resulted in failure. The two petty thieves proved more careful than others inside the castle in both word and deed.

"They are prisoners," said Harhar.

"What?" Again Theoll tried to hide his shock at the jester's words. The baron felt his threads of power breaking. Harhar knew more about movement in the castle than he did.

"The Inquisition, the Inquisition, no one knows when Archbishop Nosto brings his Inquisition!" Harhar turned his words into a shrill chant that set Theoll's nerves on edge.

"Silence!" the baron roared. "How dare Nosto meddle like this!"

"The Archbishop dares to dream. He is a fanatic with a dream. When was the last cleric king in Porotane?"

"There has never been one. Don't be absurd. The people would never tolerate it."

Theoll spoke one way even as his thoughts turned another. Nosto *might* have such aspirations hidden in his putrid heart. With the kingdom torn asunder by the warring factions, who could say that a strong religious leader might not unite Porotane?

"Yes, Baron, the Inquisition is a potent tool," said Harhar. "Are you going to let him keep Santon and Vered?"

"Why not? They are insignificant characters in this passion play." Theoll watched the fool's reaction. Forbidden knowledge, guilty knowledge, revealed knowledge. It all flashed across Harhar's face. "What do they know that can harm me?"

"They travelled with Alarice. She spoke of many things. Maybe they know that the demon Kalob has been banished permanently. To reveal this to Archbishop Nosto might mean . . ." Harhar's words trailed off.

Theoll wiped sweat from his brow. He had used the jester to dupe Nosto into thinking that the demon had returned. It had been a clever piece of stage acting, or so he had thought at the time. Archbishop Nosto had responded in exactly the way Theoll had hoped.

"They cannot know. There is no way that the Glass Warrior could know. Only you and I know, Harhar." From the folds of his cape Theoll drew forth a wicked dagger. He rose and went to where the jester cowered. If Harhar thought to threaten him with this damning information, he could stem the source with a single slice across the fool's throat.

To his surprise, the fool rolled over onto his back like a dog and exposed his privates. When he began barking like a dog, Theoll put the dagger away and turned away in disgust. Harhar was not merely simpleminded. He was demented.

"The guards took them to the dungeons for the Inquisitor," called out Harhar. Theoll looked at the jester and again wondered if insanity or cunning drove him.

"Come along. We must find Archbishop Nosto and get to the prisoners. There might be a way to use them against the Archbishop *and* Lorens."

"Dangerous ploys, my Lord."

"Of course it is dangerous," said Theoll, his mind already exploring possible avenues of intrigue. "Do you think that ruling Porotane is a simple game?"

Theoll started off, his game leg dragging slightly and making a sliding noise along the corridor. At a discreet distance his guards followed. Harhar bobbed and bounced and danced around, showing himself for the fool that he was. Theoll motioned for his guards to hold station when they arrived at Castle Porotane's lowest levels. The Inquisition allowed only a few into the dungeons.

Most departed with neither life nor soul.

The crimson-clad guard at the door opened it and admitted Theoll but tried to slam the heavy wood portal in Harhar's face. The jester began to cry like a small child deprived of his favorite toy.

"Let the fool in," Theoll said distractedly. "He will harm nothing."

"Archbishop Nosto's command—"

"Such an order is meaningless when it comes to a fool. Look at him. He has no soul to contaminate. He has no mind to be swayed from the True Path."

The guard reluctantly allowed Harhar inside the torture chambers. The jester cut capers and danced about until the guard got dizzy watching. He returned to his post at the door to keep unbelievers out—and in.

"Do you come to cleanse your soul, Baron?" asked Nosto. The archbishop had stripped to the waist and wore only tight-fitting red silk breeches and red and black armbands with mystical signs on them. Blood smeared the man's flat, well-muscled belly. Theoll saw no indication that it was Nosto's blood. The archbishop had been converting heretics with knives and branding irons.

"My soul treads the True Path," Theoll said, speaking carefully. "It is yours that worries me, my good friend."

"Mine?" This oblique accusation of impiety affected Archbishop Nosto as Theoll had hoped it would. "I spend so much of my time and effort in this dreary place with heretics. Have they infected me with their evil thoughts? How have I strayed from the Path? My devotions last long into the night."

"The Demon Crown touches us all," said Theoll.

"Yes, the crown. King Lorens refuses my visits." Nosto closed his eyes and muttered what might have been a ward spell. "I feel him not in my presence."

"You sense his scrying spells?" asked Harhar.

"As a higher ranked cleric I wield certain small spells permitted by the saints. The crown's magic does not intrude on my work."

"What of the Wizard of Storms?" asked Harhar. "What of him? Do you sense his magic trundling down from the Castle of the Winds?"

"No." The denial came sharply. The archbishop spun and glared at the jester. "Do not even speak of that one in my presence. He opposes all I attempt."

"How do you know this, Nosto?" asked Theoll. "The Wizard of Storms has not been seen or heard from in decades."

"In my meditations he comes to me with obscene proposals. He sows the seeds of revolt in the land. His storm warriors again do battle with humans."

Theoll reached out and supported himself using the heavy wood table laden with torture instruments. Porotane teetered on the brink of complete war if the archbishop spoke the truth. Few armies were the match for a single magical storm warrior—or so went the legend. Theoll had never seen one of the mythical fighters. He barely believed that the Wizard of Storms existed.

But now? A chill raced up Theoll's spine and embraced his neck. He tried not to choke. Not only did Gaemock and Dalziel Sef disrupt the order of the kingdom, a wizard worked his way into the intricate equations of power. The baron began to doubt his chance for deposing Lorens and assuming the throne once more.

"We have wizards and rebels and a king turned from the True Path. A sorry state for Porotane," the baron said. "What is it that I can do to aid you in restoring order and piety, Archbishop Nosto?"

"Your words assure me that goodness has not fled the people of Porotane, Theoll. I attempt to find the root of festering evil within the walls of our castle. Only when this putrid heart is ripped out and the wound cleansed can we look farther afield and work on those warring beyond the walls."

Theoll slowly scanned the cells and re-
straints used by the Inquisitors. He held back
the shiver of distaste. His methods were more
subtle. He preferred the slow poison to the
branding iron. Many dangled from wrist chains
fastened to hooks driven into the wood ceiling
beams. Others had no chains; the hooks pierced
their bodies. Still others were secured by form-
fitting wire cages awaiting the heat that would
burn the holy wire's imprint into heretical flesh.

"What of her, Nosto?" Theoll pointed out a
red-haired girl chained into a contorted position
across a barrel-shaped torture machine. Theoll
wondered what had been done to her—what
would be done—but did not ask to satisfy his
curiosity. "She seems too young to be seduced
from the True Path."

"She is a special case. Knowledge has fallen
into her hands and she refuses to yield it to me.
The Inquisition must know of every heretic if we
are to succeed. Aiding those opposing me is the
same as opposing me." Archbishop Nosto
walked past a burning brazier. For a brief instant, Theoll fancied that the cleric had turned
into the very demons he opposed. Light shone
upward and gave an inhuman cast to Nosto's
face. Sweat gleamed on his arms and chest, and
the skin-tight breeches showed how excited
Nosto became with his work.

Harhar gestured wildly from the far end of
the dungeon. He pointed to a row of wooden
coffins with holes cut for arms, legs, and heads.
Two of the coffins were occupied. Theoll nodded
slightly to indicate that he understood. These
two were Vered and Birtle Santon.

Theoll tried to put together a plan that
would benefit him the most. Archbishop Nosto
wanted the two freebooters for interrogation.

What did they know that the cleric wanted? What did the serving wench know? Theoll had to believe that the young girl knew nothing. Nosto's reaction when he went to the wheels and barrels over which the redheaded girl was chained convinced Theoll of that.

"It is good that you hear it from another's lips," said Theoll, staring at the girl. He felt a moment of pity for her. Then the emotion faded. He could use her to his own ends without remorse. He had to consider her a victim of Archbishop Nosto's techniques and better off dead, as a result.

"What? Do you know?"

"That King Lorens is . . ." Theoll let his words trail off and entice Archbishop Nosto.

"The king is possessed by a demon!" the cleric roared. The echo throughout the dungeon drowned out the moans of the Inquisition's victims in various stages of dying.

"The Demon Crown has proven too strong for him. This must be the bait attracting the Wizard of Storms." Theoll threw out the name to evoke response. He was not disappointed.

"I knew it! This is proof of my vision! The kingdom has been handed over to demons once again! Heretics rush in to assume secular command and the spiritual is being stolen away by demons. Demons!"

Theoll started to add fuel to the fires of Nosto's fanaticism when he saw Harhar working on the coffins holding Santon and Vered. The baron started to gesture to the fool not to release them.

Too late. Both adventurers rose from their coffins and rubbed swollen and cramped arms and legs. Theoll's mind raced. He dared not bring this to Nosto's attention. The cleric would think him a part of the rescue and brand him a heretic.

The sight of so many lords and ladies dangling from chains and hooks convinced Theoll that his high position in the kingdom would mean nothing to Nosto. Even worse, if Harhar were caught, the fool would reveal the earlier hoax Theoll had engineered convincing Archbishop Nosto that the demon Kalob had returned to Porotane.

Baron Theoll had no choice but to hope that Santon and Vered escaped cleanly. Afterward, he would kill Harhar for putting him in such a dangerous position.

"Archbishop, a word," he said, drawing the cleric away from the serving wench. Theoll had no idea what he said. His lips worked to fabricate lies that would engage Nosto's attention while the two thieves escaped the dungeons. Theoll swallowed hard and almost babbled when he saw that Vered was not leaving.

The man worked his way along the dungeon floor on his belly, obviously intending to release the young girl.

"Tell me of the Wizard of Storms," Theoll said. "I have heard his name mentioned by Lorens several times. Are they truly allies?" Theoll did not listen to the liturgy delivered by the cleric. He had most of his attention focused on Vered cleverly picking the locks on the girl's chains.

She sagged forward and fell to the floor, bent in an arc from being pulled over the wheel for such a long time. Vered urged her to stand. The girl moved painfully, slowly, noisily. Theoll thanked his personal saints for the death sounds from so many others in the dungeon.

"How many Inquisitors do you have working here, Nosto?" he asked loudly. "At this moment there seems to be no one else."

"There is only the Inquisitor at the door and myself. The work must proceed cautiously. When the Question is put to a heretic, those with any doubt about their own belief in following the True Path might suffer."

"Understandable," said Theoll. Harhar and Santon had circled the dungeon and approached the exit from one direction while Vered and the girl approached from the opposite side.

Archbishop Nosto started to turn back to where he thought the girl had been securely chained. Theoll took the cleric's sweaty upper arm and maneuvered him about. "I must confess, Archbishop. I . . ." Theoll's mind refused to produce an appropriate sin for confession. Grasping at threads, he almost babbled, "Dreams. I have dreams inhabited by this Wizard of Storms."

"An evil sign, Baron, but not one to be concerned over unduly. Unless these dreams carry over to your waking moments."

Theoll dared to look over his shoulder. Santon and Vered had taken the girl out of the dungeon. The Inquisitor lay to one side of the door. Theoll felt a small surge of relief at this. His personal guards would capture the trio outside. All that remained was to escape Archbishop Nosto's clutches himself.

"Do your dreams affect you?" demanded Archbishop Nosto.

Harhar came to his rescue. The jester rolled over and over and began to sputter and shout and carry on.

"Him," said Theoll, inspiration upon him. "I dream of the jester being inhabited by demons. He is being seized even as we stare at him!"

Harhar gibbered and danced and ducked under Archbishop Nosto's arms as the cleric tried to restrain him. "Demons everywhere!" the jester cried. "I can see them. Big ones, little ones, they are everywhere! They enter the dungeons and come after me. But Harhar is too fast. He gets away from them before they can harm him!"

"Demons!" Archbishop Nosto reached for his holy book. "Demons have entered these sanctified chambers. Truly, this is the Wizard of Storms' doing!"

"Your Inquisitor," said Theoll, turning Nosto's attention from Harhar. "He is taken by demons!"

"By the saints!" Archbishop Nosto hurried to his assistant's side and knelt, beginning the exorcism rites.

"I will leave you, Nosto. If there is anything I can do to aid you—" Theoll knew that the cleric would deny help from a secular lord. He did. Theoll motioned to Harhar to leave the dungeons. To his relief, the fool did not hesitate.

Theoll closed the heavy dungeon door behind him, shutting off both death moans and Archbishop Nosto's rapid exorcism of nonexistent demons from his Inquisitor.

He had done well planting seeds of doubt about King Lorens and this Wizard of Storms in Nosto's mind. And he had escaped with his life!

Luck went with Theoll. By month's end he would again assume the throne and rule Porotane.

He strode off, his limp hardly hindering him. He wanted to interrogate Vered and Santon. By now his guards would have them safely hidden away in the wing of the castle where even the archbishop's Inquisition could not find them.

THREE

"Guards!" yelled Birtle Santon as the trio escaped into the corridor beyond the Inquisition's dungeons.

His cry alerted Theoll's soldiers. The four men had been relaxing, paying little heed to the ghastly noises coming from the depths of the infernal chamber. When Santon and Vered saw what was happening, they charged.

Bare-handed they fought the soldiers—and drove hard fists into throats and poked fingers into eyes and lifted knees into crotches. The skirmish lasted for less time than four beats of a frenzied heart.

"I'm all cut and bloody," complained Vered. He tried to smooth the wrinkles from his once elegant clothing and failed. Most of his finery hung in tatters from being imprisoned in Archbishop Nosto's coffin for long hours and having nails driven into his flesh.

"Good sirs, this way," Rogina urged. She motioned to a back passage.

"Where does it go?"

"What difference does it make?" asked Birtle Santon. "As long as it is away from the dungeons."

Vered scooped up a fallen sword and tossed

a dagger across to Santon, who deftly caught it in his good hand. Armed again, they felt more confident but neither wanted a fight with armed troopers. Both men found themselves hard pressed to keep up with the fleet Rogina as she climbed the narrow flagstone steps three at a time.

"She was a captive for how long?" panted Vered. "She was drawn on the wheel and stretched backwards over barrels? She's more nimble than any forest fox."

"The resiliency of youth," Santon gasped out, feeling the effect of the hard pace, too.

"You're an old man. Look at you. Arthritic and creaking and always complaining. But me?" Vered wiped sweat from his forehead. "I am hardly a half dozen summers older."

"Hurry!" Rogina was fully two flights of steps ahead of them now.

"It is the distance travelled in life that matters, not the age," said Santon. He sucked in a deep breath and grimly plowed on, refusing to slow or rest even though his body demanded it.

Both men collapsed when they reached the landing where Rogina awaited them. "Here," she said. "In here. No one will search for us if we stay hidden."

Vered's eyes widened in surprise when he saw the glass short sword Alarice had given him. To his right he heard Santon crowing when he retrieved his glass shield.

"You've brought us to the armory," said Vered, eyeing the racks of ready weapons.

"Aye," Rogina said, face flushed. "This is the archbishop's wing. They will seek everywhere for us, but not here. Who would think we would be foolish enough to crawl back into the jaws of the trap?"

"Good point," said Santon, "but then who would have thought we were stupid enough to do it the first time?"

Rogina went to Santon and shyly reached out and took his good hand. "If what you did is stupid, then thank you for being so stupid. You saved my life. The archbishop would have killed me." The young woman shuddered and wrapped her arms around herself.

"If we get word to your sister, can she find a way for us to escape the castle?" asked Vered. "It seems that Kerin is our only hope for leaving these stony walls."

"The walls have eyes," said Rogina. "Baron Theoll spies on everyone. That is well known."

Vered laughed. "He does it cleverly, but I was the smarter. I found his peephole in our quarters. A pity I did not put out his eye with my pointed stick." He made poking motions that produced first a smile, then a laugh from the girl.

"There is another watcher in Castle Porotane," said Santon. His green eyes locked with Vered's brown ones and silent communication passed. King Lorens might use the Demon Crown at any time to find them. If he did, what action would the monarch take? Neither man thought that Lorens supported Archbishop Nosto or Theoll. Both would have his throne. But his own plots and desires became serpentine as he cast his senses out across the kingdom.

"There are many," spoke up Rogina. "The king, aye, he watches." She shivered again at the thought of how the Demon Crown worked its evil magic on the king. "But Harhar sees all."

"And apparently tells anyone who asks in the proper fashion," said Santon. "He might have freed us but I am not certain that the jester wasn't also responsible for our capture."

"The time element is wrong, friend Santon," said Vered. "We had barely left the throne room when Nosto's soldiers captured us. From the looks on their faces, we took them by surprise. They might have thought to find us in our quarters instead of marching along so boldly in the halls outside the throne room."

"Too many seek to oust Lorens and place their own behinds on the throne," said Santon. "It is definitely time we faded into the woodlands and sought the serenity of nature."

"And the fat money pouch of a careless travelling merchant," chimed in Vered. "For all that the war has kept down the number of travellers, there are many who still dare us to rob them."

"You are thieves?" Rogina's eyes grew round. One tiny hand covered her mouth and she stepped back from Vered as if seeing him for the first time.

"It's a living," Vered said nonchalantly. "And it is what attracts your sister to me."

"Kerin prefers a thief to an honest man?"

"Who is honest within these walls?" asked Santon. "Theoll poisons. Nosto tortures. Who can say what Lorens does?"

"But her other lovers. They were all honest men."

"Soldiers, eh?" asked Vered, beginning to become irritated. "Have you ever seen a soldier in an honest game of chance? Or a merchant, mayhaps? Can anyone get an honest measure of grain from a merchant or assurance of not being shortchanged?"

"But—"

"Enough," interrupted Santon. "This is getting us nowhere—and we need to be long gone before the guards begin a systematic search for us. Even such a fine hiding place will come under scrutiny if the full force of the Inquisition is put behind the search."

"Find us or suffer for all eternity," muttered Vered. "A fine problem for the soldiers. We cannot be caught and Archbishop Nosto will damn them for all eternity if they don't find us."

"Let's make sure we are unfindable. Rogina, how do we contact your sister? We must be out of here before midnight."

"Why midnight?" asked the girl. "Oh, the guard changes then and more men patrol the walls."

"Giving Nosto and Theoll more guards to put into the search for us. There is no way we can get down the castle walls from the parapet."

"Not unless we want to end up in the thorny brambles surrounding the base of the castle. We need a special way out, an exit known only to a handful."

"Alarice knew of such," said Santon. Although his tone was neutral, his heart skipped a beat when he mentioned the Glass Warrior.

"She is not with us, except in spirit, old friend," said Vered, laying a hand on Santon's shoulder. "Finding the gate she used would do us little good. We lack the glass key that opens it."

"The postern on the north side?" asked Rogina. "When I was a child I used to play there. A long passage through the wall that opens into the castle? I know it. Not well, but enough to get you there."

"We can force the lock," said Santon. "Or your clever lock picking might again benefit us. Should we try?"

"I have no desire to spend the rest of my life in Archbishop Nosto's armory."

"Then Rogina, go and find Kerin. Bring her here and we will all leave. The Castle Porotane is no safe place for either of you after this day's deeds."

"But it's our home!" The girl almost cried at the idea of abandoning the castle.

"There will be better places," said Vered. "This pile of stone is drafty and rat-infested and reeking of magic."

"I'll find Kerin," Rogina said. "But it might be better if we met near the postern gate."

"She learns quickly," said Santon. "If she is followed, then we are almost free of the castle. Otherwise, she leads the guards back to this hidey-hole and we have to fight across the entire keep."

"The well marked with the statue of the farting cat is near the gate. Let's meet there," said Vered.

"It is a lion rampant," corrected Rogina.

Vered shrugged. To him most statuary looked obscene. The girl ducked through the armory door and vanished.

"It will take us only a few minutes to get to the well," said Vered. "Rogina must find Kerin and go there. We have a goodly hour to waste. Wake me when it is time to go." With that, Vered slid down the wall, pulled up his knees, and rested his head on them. Within seconds he snored loudly.

Santon shook his head. For all the battles he had survived, for all the times he would have given anything to rest for even an instant, he lacked his friend's ability to sleep in the midst of danger.

Birtle Santon stood watch, waiting for the proper time for them to make their escape.

"They betray us, Lord Dews," said Jiskko. "They surround us while we sit on our thumbs doing nothing."

"Calm yourself, Jiskko," said Dews Gaemock. "The meeting is carried out under a peace flag."

"No one but you honors the peace flag, Lord," grumbled the rebel lieutenant. "Remember how the black and gold banners of Ionia worked to cut us off during *those* peace talks?"

"I remember. But I feel that Sef is more honorable. And we knew about the trap in plenty of time."

"Dalziel Sef might be better at springing his traps."

"He might also want to parley."

"I do, Gaemock," came a gruff voice. Striding into the circle defined by the small campfire's light came a burly man with a great sword resting on his shoulder. He twitched a massive wrist and brought the heavy weapon about as if it were nothing heavier than a dirk. Sef drove the point into the dirt beside Gaemock's sword.

"Peace between us," Gaemock said.

"Peace," Dalziel Sef said reluctantly. "My advisors tell me this is a trap."

"You think to murder us!" protested Jiskko.

Sef and Gaemock stared at each other for a moment, then both burst out laughing. Gaemock said, "It seems we have some things in common."

"Untrusting advisors," said Sef. He motioned. A smaller man drifted in from beyond the fire's wan illumination, a nocked arrow ready to fire. "Enough, Asaway." He waited for the man to relax and put the powerful war bow aside.

"Can we get down to discussing an alliance or is there something more we have to endure?" asked Gaemock.

"A spot of brandy?" asked Sef, pulling a flask from his rucksack. He popped the cork and held up the bottle of amber liquid.

"Lord, wait!" Jiskko caught Gaemock's wrist and stopped him. "Poison!"

"Do you want me to drink first?" asked Sef, amused.

"The antidote," Jiskko whispered fiercely. "He may have taken it already."

Gaemock glared at his overly suspicious advisor and took the bottle. He tipped it back and almost choked on the powerful liquor.

"Good, isn't it?" asked Sef. He took the bottle and matched every drop Gaemock had swallowed and more. "The best there is from the shore provinces on the Uvain Plateau. It will be good when this war is behind us and I can return and tend my grapes."

"You're a vintner?"

"Aye. And it's hard for me to believe that you are a dirt farmer, Gaemock."

"Grain. Before Lamost was murdered, the Gaemock clan held the largest farms along the River Ty."

"So I've heard."

The two rebel warlords sat quietly for several minutes, each lost in memory of what had been lost.

Gaemock broke the silence. "Do you wish to ascend the throne?"

"Me? Hardly. I want only peace." Dalziel Sef scowled and peered across the fire at

Gaemock. "What of you? Do you hope to warm your ass on that high throne?"

"I wish to see a monarch able to keep peace in Porotane and nothing more."

"I heard tell that your brother Efran's a royalist."

"He seeks the same end as we, but in other ways."

Sef looked at Jiskko. "I read your lips easily. You think Efran is a traitor, eh?"

"My opinions do not concern scum like you," snapped Jiskko.

Sef rose, his muscles bulging. Asaway came up to stand beside him, hand on dagger.

"Peace. We are not here to discuss the failings of others in my family. Efran thinks Porotane is better off if one of royal blood is on the throne."

"King Lorens puts that theory to the test— and it fails!" Asaway almost shouted this into the night.

"I agree. Jiskko agrees, too," said Gaemock. "My brother is brilliant, but sometimes with brilliance goes a touch of insanity."

"Your battles have been harder fought since he defected to the royalists," observed Sef.

"He is the outstanding tactician of this country," said Gaemock. "I must do his work as well as my own until I can find another to replace him." Gaemock watched Sef carefully, then added, "Your style is much like Efran's. Daring, yet not rash."

"Your grasp of strategy is lacking in my campaign. Even Asaway has commented on this." Sef smiled, showing cracked, yellowed teeth.

"Another reason to join forces. If we, representing the two largest rebel factions, united, the other bands might also add the force of their swords to our cause."

"Possible," said Sef. "We must stand against a powerful wizard, no matter how many join us. The Wizard of Storms will never bend his knee to another."

"It is true, then?" asked Jiskko.

"That the Wizard of Storms has ended his long absence and returned from the Castle of the Winds? Aye, that it is. I have seen one of his storm warriors with my own eyes."

"Lies!" Jiskko sat with his arms crossed. "The Wizard of Storms is a myth, a tale meant to frighten children. What do you take us for?"

Sef shook his shaggy head sadly. "What else do I call a soldier standing half again as tall as you and throwing lightning bolts from his right hand and casting a tornado with his left? Formless he was and within the boiling cloud that made up his body I saw the stuff of storms. No guard from Castle Porotane this one, no. It was a storm warrior—and that can only mean the Wizard of Storms returns to meddle in our war-torn land."

"This is a spell cast by one of the wizards who bedevil us so," said Jiskko. "The wizard befuddled your senses."

"There are those among my rank who can counter spells." Sef glanced at Asaway.

"A sorceror!" cried Jiskko. The man jumped to his feet, his hand reaching beneath his jerkin to pull forth a throwing knife. The leaf-bladed knife flashed twice as it cartwheeled through the air. Asaway's head jerked back at a crazy angle as the knife tip penetrated his eye and sank deep into his brain. Dalziel Sef's lieutenant was dead before he struck the ground.

"Betrayed!" cried Sef. He jumped the fire and pulled his great sword from the ground.

"Wait!" cried Gaemock. "This is all a mistake. Jiskko, why did you strike?"

"He went to place a spell on us. Lord Dews, this maggot admitted that his toady was a wizard. He began the hand motions that would have paralyzed us!"

Dews Gaemock had pulled his own sword from the ground. He stood staring at the burly Dalziel Sef and then at his lieutenant. "Lord Dalziel, I am sorry for this."

"Sorry! This treacherous worm has killed my best spell-sniffer."

"Asaway was no wizard?"

"He had not the power within him, but he had the gift for scenting magic and alerting us to it. Many's the time he warned us of Lorens' probing with the Demon Crown. And now he lies on the ground, foully murdered!"

"*Wait!*" Gaemock lifted his sword. "If we are ever to have peace in Porotane, we cannot continue to war among ourselves. We must unite against our real enemy—King Lorens."

"I agree with you, but honor demands that I avenge Asaway's blood."

"Do so and I must avenge Jiskko's," said Gaemock. "There will be no end of the bloodshed between us."

The two men glared at one another. "So be it," said Sef.

"No, there is another way," said Dews Gaemock.

"I must have Jiskko's blood to appease Asaway's phantom. In no other way can he rest in peace."

"Then my duty is clear." Dews Gaemock

swung around, sword flashing in the night.
Jiskko's eyes widened a split second before his
lord's sharp blade sank halfway through his
neck. Gaemock jerked and swung again. This
time he finished the stroke. Jiskko's head rolled
to the ground and came to rest next to Asaway.

"You would kill your own lieutenant to
forge an alliance with me?" Sef asked in surprise.

"I would. The war has raged too long. If the
Wizard of Storms again walks Porotane's fair
ground, we must be united against two formida-
ble enemies."

Dalziel Sef stared down at the slain advisors. "We must give them a proper funeral. I
won't have their phantoms following us into
battle. I could not bear it."

"Nor I. They deserve a long and peaceful
eternity. They were good and loyal soldiers."

The two warlords began digging the graves
that marked the beginning of their truce.

"Where are they?" Vered asked irritably.
"They should have been here hours ago."

"We've only just arrived," said Birtle
Santon. "Kerin and Rogina might be taking a
more circuitous route to avoid being followed."

"There is that," Vered said, "but my gut
churns. I never ignore that."

"You need food." Even as Santon spoke, he,
too, experienced the uneasiness his friend mentioned. They lived by their wits and relied heavily on instinct. They had forged a fast friendship
because of these shared feelings.

"The postern must lie in that direction.
Let's explore and see if we can't find its entrance
before they arrive."

Vered's nimble fingers worked over the

stone wall seeking evidence of a secret portal.
Santon walked a pace behind, trying to see any
release that Vered might have missed.

"This is the place. I remember that gro-
tesque piece of statuary." Vered pointed to what
he called a farting cat.

"Perhaps the release isn't on the wall but is
some distance away."

"It would give reason for the sculptor to
display such bad taste in his art," agreed Vered.
The pair went to the well and examined the
stonework carefully. But it was Vered who
found the release. "As I thought. All in Castle
Porotane show bad taste, but the locksmith
designing this one wins the prize."

Vered reached over to the lion's posterior
and ran his finger upward. Behind them a loud
snick! signalled the opening of the hidden passage that led outside the castle walls.

"That is solved," said Santon, "but where
are Kerin and Rogina?"

"There. There they are." Vered waved. To
Santon he asked, "Why do they move so slowly?
You would think they didn't want to leave."

"Rogina seemed reluctant," said Santon.
"But she is a young girl and this life is all she has
ever known. Change can be frightening to one
so young."

"Hurry, you two," Vered urged. He pointed
to the dark opening to the passageway.

The two girls exchanged glances, then
Rogina bolted and ran—away from Vered.

"Rogina, this way!" shouted Vered.

"Vered, please forgive us," pleaded Kerin.
"We do not belong outside these walls. This is
our *home*!" She put her hands to her mouth,
then turned and ran after her sister.

"They've betrayed us," said Santon.

"They've exchanged us for indulgences from Archbishop Nosto."

"Preposterous. The girl loves me." Only Santon grabbing Vered by the collar and yanking him aside saved him from being impaled by a dozen war arrows.

The clank of armored guards told Vered the truth of Santon's words. He got to his feet inside the passage and fumbled along the door's stony edges.

"What are you doing?"

"There's got to be a release for the door. If we close it, their pursuit will be the slower."

Santon deflected a sword thrust with his glass shield and kicked another soldier in the groin. A flick of his wrist brought his heavy battle-ax around and cracked a third guardsman's helm open.

"Hurry up. I can't hold off the entire castle guard all night."

"There!" Vered found the release and the door slid slowly closed. But one quick-thinking soldier shoved his shield into the narrowing gap between door and wall. The secret portal ground to a stop a handbreadth short of securely closing.

"Come on," cried Santon. "We've got to outrun them now. It'll be only minutes before they lever open that door."

In the dark passage the two freebooters ran, searching for the locked door that Alarice had once used. Sounds of pursuit behind them grew louder.

The soldiers had opened the secret portal and now flooded into the passage.

FOUR

"It's got to be here. It's got to!" Vered fumbled along in the dark passage trying to find the postern gate leading to freedom. The heavy footsteps of the guardsmen came closer through the darkness behind him. He heard the guardsmen's cursing and saw the sputtering light from a poorly burning torch.

"I'll keep them back," said Birtle Santon. Vered felt the man turning to face the guards. He ignored the sound of Santon's ax singing through the air and cracking still another incautious guardsman's helm. His full attention centered on the cold stone wall moving so slowly under his fingers.

"It's got to be here. This is the proper passage. I know it," he muttered to himself. Before the words left his lips, the stone turned to wood.

"What progress?" asked Santon in a tone appropriate for inquiring about the weather. But Vered knew his friend fought a losing battle from the sounds of sword tips slipping along the glass shield and the louder pounding of more soldiers pouring into the passage now.

"I've found the gate." Vered dropped to his

knees. A sliver of steel slipped from beneath his floppy collar; he applied this flexible metal strip to the lock. The tumblers within worked smoothly but he failed to open the door.

Santon grunted and almost fell over Vered. Vered turned, his knees grinding into the rough, rocky floor. He jerked his dagger free and blindly drove it upward. The point found human flesh; he was rewarded with a cry of anguish.

"Thanks," said Santon, recovering. "But do hurry. I can't hold them back any longer."

Vered's knowing fingers worked across the surface of the door. The lock had opened. Something still held the door.

"A bolt!" he cried. "There is a bolt on the inside. Newly installed, from the feel."

Vered gripped the metal handle and jerked it back. The door opened and a cold autumn wind gusted through. Vered inhaled and felt power returning to his enervated limbs. He jerked harder on the door and slammed it into a charging guardsman. The soldier bellowed and retreated, causing enough confusion among the men behind him to allow Vered and Santon to slip through the door.

"Help me hold it closed," Vered shouted. Birtle Santon pulled on the door, his bulk and the immense strength in his right arm adequate to keep the door closed while Vered's lock pick worked its magic on the tumblers. The lock fastened. Vered dropped back, sitting on the cold ground. He wiped sweat from his forehead.

"That will hold them for a while," said Santon. "They can't have the glass key Alarice used and I'm sure none have your expertise at opening locked doors without a key."

"Let's not tarry," said Vered, getting to his

feet. He looked around. The heavy brambles that protected the base of the castle wall formed a neat arch and provided a passageway out. "I'll feel safer when we have a day's travel and more behind us."

Santon nodded. Together they started through the brambles. Vered cursed volubly every time one of the dagger-long thorns ripped at his clothing. "I spent a month's salary to buy this fine tunic and here it is being ripped to threads."

"You never received a salary in your life. I remember how you stole this from the merchant in the castle courtyard not a week ago."

"Such finery deserves to be worn by someone who can appreciate it. Is it not fit for any prince of the realm?" Vered stuck out one arm and showed the puffed, verdant green sleeve woven with gold threads. Picks and tears in the cloth showed skin equally as battered. Vered bled from a dozen small thorn scratches.

"The end of our safety," said Santon, halting when he came to the mouth of the bramble tunnel. Beyond lay flat lands long since denuded by the tramp of soldiers and the hungry fire of magics misdirected.

Vered walked a few paces beyond and turned to stare at the Castle Porotane. He let out a gusty sigh. "Ah, Kerin. I know you loved me. What a terrible thing having a sister like Rogina."

Vered shook his head and let Santon know that this was not a matter for friendly debate.

"The woods are some distance to the north. Or should we head for the River Ty?" asked Santon, skirting the issue of their abrupt departure from the castle.

"Travel might prove easier on the river," answered Vered, "and I care little for having to walk. But the rebel forces will also seek out water passage. Dews Gaemock's siege last spring failed. The wiser among King Lorens' advisors mumbled about a new siege being laid this fall."

"War engines move more easily on a barge," agreed Santon.

"There must be someone hereabout with a pair of horses he hasn't counted recently," Vered went on. "Even bareback is a superior mode of travel to getting blisters on one's tender feet."

"The night is cloudy. That benefits us and hinders, too."

"Aye, that it does," said Vered. "My eyes are the keener. Let me see if I cannot penetrate the clouds and find the guiding stars." As they walked briskly from the tangle of thorny brambles, Vered craned his head back and studied the occasional clear patches of sky.

"There," he said at last. "There is a constellation I recognize. The Mider Lizard. The three stars forming its tail points a handbreadth from true north."

"We might cross a tributary to the Ty in a day or two," said Santon. "Mayhaps we should change to the north and west and seek the uplift of the Uvain Plateau."

"What we need more than anything else," said Vered, "is a notion of what we intend to do. That will dictate a destination."

Vered fell silent as he trooped along beside his friend. Life had never been easy for him. While still a child, his parents and family had been killed in a rebel raid. He had never discovered which rebel band was responsible; it might have been Duke Freow's troops, for all he knew.

If it had not been for the chance appearance of Birtle Santon, he would have perished.

The older man had taken him along on his aimless wanderings not as an apprentice or son but as an equal. For that Vered owed Birtle Santon much—more than simple coins could ever repay.

He mourned the loss of Alarice in the Desert of Sazan almost as much as his friend. He had loved Alarice in his way, but not as Santon had. The Glass Warrior had given Vered a hint of something more than love. Through her and her quest to find an heir to the throne, he had found purpose. With her dead, with King Lorens on the throne, with the condition in Porotane no better than it had been for all the years of his short life, Vered again lacked purpose. No progress had been made. Or so it seemed to him.

Porotane's wars still dragged on, rebel factions fighting the royalists. Worst of all, King Lorens was rightful heir and proved to be worse for the kingdom than the impostor-duke. Even as the thought crossed his mind, Vered looked around anxiously. He carried a drop of royal blood in his veins, perhaps the result of a long-forgotten foray into his mother's coastal village. He could don the Demon Crown for brief seconds, but the magical gold circlet's effect on him was too potent to bear any longer.

This touch of royal blood allowed him to sense the use of the Demon Crown, however. Hairs rose on the back of his neck and he knew that Lorens cast forth his phantomlike image to spy.

"The crown," he whispered to Santon. Chiding himself for such foolishness, he said louder, "Lorens is exploring magically. I sense the spells controlling the crown."

"Do you think he hunts for us to send troops?" asked Santon.

"The soldiers in the courtyard sported red armbands. They were Archbishop Nosto's guardsmen. What reprieve could Lorens give when Rogina's trouble lay with the Inquisition?"

"He is king."

"The Demon Crown makes him so, but Lorens does not handle the internal affairs of the castle well. He is too busy looking further afield, finding rebels and trying to crush the resistance."

"He might still want us," said Santon.

Vered agreed. They had brought him back to Porotane and they had carried the crown. Lorens might think they possessed power to oppose him. Had they not been with the sorceress who killed his master? The king's suspicions knew no bounds—and grew daily.

What a dangerous dilemma the Demon Crown posed for a ruler. Vered had felt its power and brushed madness as a result. Those of the blood royal who could wear it for long periods would fall under its influence unless they were possessed of a singularly strong will. From all Vered had seen, Lorens lacked such strength of character. His wizard master had not felt it appropriate to develop anything but servility in his pupil. Now that the apprentice became the master, he had few guidelines to aid him.

"What I could do with that crown," Vered said. He ducked, as if a low-flying bird threatened to rake his head with outstretched talons.

"Lorens?"

"Yes. He explores this night. But I sense his probing goes past us and heads to the north."

Vered took a deep breath to steady himself, and inhaled a familiar scent. He turned and homed in on the pungent odor of animals. Pointing, he said, "Horses. Transportation!"

Santon followed as Vered made his way across the rutted plain. Vered came to a corral with a score of horses inside its rough-hewn rails.

"So many horses," mused Santon. "This bodes ill."

"Rebels," said Vered. "But I saw no sentry."

"They might have grown careless."

Neither man believed that. Vered stood outside the corral and stared at the horses. His feet hurt and it offended his dignity to continue walking. If no rebel guard had been posted—and why should not at least one armed guard protect such fine animals?—that meant only one thing.

"Magic," Vered said. "A ward spell protects the horses. We have stumbled across a rebel band led by a wizard."

"Perhaps we would do better to continue without such fine animals," Santon said. Vered heard the longing in his friend's words. Neither of them would easily abandon a remuda waiting to have plucked from it such strong, handsome horses.

Vered walked around the corral trying to get some hint of the spell's power. He leaned against the rail and felt nothing. Cautiously, he reached across the top rail and extended his hand toward a curious mare. Before his hand touched the mare's head a powerful invisible force picked him up and cast him back. Vered landed on his rear.

"So much for that approach," said Santon. "We can dig under and enter the corral in that way."

"Why bother unless you intend to dig a hole large enough for the horses to exit? No, Santon, we need another approach." Vered paced around the corral a second time, keen eyes alert for any weakness. He rejoined Santon.

"Well? How does the master thief intend to pluck the prize steeds from the corral?"

"Above," said Vered. "We can enter from above."

"Insanity."

"Of course. Who else but a master thief would attempt such a foolhardy course?" Vered laughed as he moved closer to the corral. He overturned a bucket and placed it next to the tallest post. He pointed. Santon silently stepped onto the bucket, balanced precariously for a moment, then steadied. He curled his powerful right hand into a hook and waited.

Excitement surged through Vered. This was living. The challenge of entering the corral brought his every sense alive. He backed off a dozen paces, then ran for Santon. He jumped, got his foot in Santon's cupped hand, and launched himself upward. Santon added impetus with a powerful heave.

As he became airborne, Vered heard Santon's grunt. He also heard the air come alive with the hum of magic. Vered soared, gauged his progress, then somersaulted. A new sensation blasted through him: pain.

He crossed the invisible top of the ward spell and came down feet first inside the corral. Horses protested his sudden entry, neighing and pawing at the air.

"Down, old girl, down, easy, yes, it's only

Vered the master thief come to spirit you away!"
He approached one powerful dappled gray, his
voice soothing and his hands outstretched.
When the mare reared, Vered moved to one side
and dashed around. His arms circled the horse's
neck. Buck as she would, she could not dislodge
him. His voice soothed and cajoled as if he spoke
to a new lover. The horse quieted and Vered
relaxed his grip.

"That's all there is to it," Vered said, patting
his new conquest on the neck.

"There is another element to this little play
that has escaped you," said Santon. "How do
you get out? The spell still binds you within the
corral."

"A minor problem for one of my daring and
skill," said Vered. But he had no idea how to get
out with his prize. He mounted the horse and
gentled her once more, patting her frequently
and assuring her that she was the finest horse in
all the world. As Vered rode her around, a
thought came to him.

"Santon," he called out. "Would anyone,
even a wizard, wish to harm a noble steed such
as this one?"

"No. I fail to see what that has to do with
getting out of the corral with your prize."

"The horses don't need the corral fence if
the spell keeps them inside. A touch of pain here
and there and the horses would huddle together
in the center of the spell zone."

"Do horses huddle?"

"Don't cloud the issue." Vered looked up
and saw that the sky cleared. A pale crescent
moon shone down to give him courage. "The
rails hold the horses in, the spell keeps our kind
out."

"So?"

"So I can remove the horse with no trouble. It is only my own skin I need worry about."

"Test your theory. Send out that roan for me."

Vered tugged at the hide thong holding the corral gate shut, then herded what he already thought of as Santon's roan to the gate. A quick swat on the hindquarters startled the roan. It leaped forward, passing the magic barrier with no ill effect.

"I won't say you're a genius," said Santon, capturing the roan as it tried to bolt into the night, "but the word does come to my lips. Only good sense holds it back."

"Luck, skill, what's the difference?" Vered asked. He turned the gray's head toward the gate, then dug his heels into her side. He had sampled the power of the wizard's spell. Only speed would get him free of the corral.

Vered's eyes blinked open. Every part of his body screamed in agony and movement was out of the question.

"The stars?" he asked weakly. "Why are they in front of me?"

"You're flat on your back. The mare got you free but the spell still seized you. Only by hanging on to the horse did you get past its boundaries."

"It knocked me out?"

"And more, from the way you groan. Come along now. Let's ride these stolen creatures for all they're worth. The wizard might have felt some disturbance in his spell when you broke free."

"I can't move!" Vered tried to raise his arms and was greeted with intense pain. When he tried again, the pain diminished. A third attempt, while agonizing, proved possible.

Groaning like an old man, he climbed onto his mare and urged her forward. Every bounce, every change in gait, rattled his teeth and sent lances of white fire into his brain.

"Ride, master thief," came Santon's mocking words.

"Easy for you to say. You had the lesser role in that theft." They rode fast and hard and camped only when pink and gray fingers appeared in the east.

"I feel like death," said Vered. He sank to the ground. "Nay, it is worse. Death is surcease. This is continual misery. There is not a bone or muscle that does not ache abominably."

"Remember the pains, then," said Santon, as he tended their horses, "and become a chirurgeon. It'll save having to cut open your patients to find where all the parts are."

Santon finished his chore and dropped beside his friend. "We have done well this night. Not only did we escape the castle ahead of the Inquisition, we found horses worthy of us."

"We did all that," agreed Vered, "but what now? More of the same? Do we return to the ways that served us well before we met Alarice?"

"Weren't those times good?"

"Yes, but they pale now. I want more."

"Remember how we travelled up and down the coast? We left not a single wine cask untapped or wench untupped."

"The constable of that hamlet—what was it?"

"Landine," said Santon.

"Yes, Landine. The constable followed us for a fortnight before we sneaked into his camp one night and stole his clothing. I swear, he would still be after us if he hadn't been such a modest man."

They fell silent. Vered's thoughts carried on, after the constable, after the brief stint aboard a coastal hugger and being shipwrecked. Their life had been full.

Why did it seem so hollow now?

They had been together long enough for Santon to know Vered's moods. In his uncanny way, he answered the question Vered had only thought. "We know that there can be nothing worthwhile in the kingdom until the war is at an end. Alarice showed us that."

"Alarice," mused Vered. "Would she have accepted Lorens as king?"

"No. Any fool can see that his reign worsens the conditions in Porotane, not betters them."

"What would she have done?" asked Vered. "What would she have us do?"

Silence fell until Vered heard, "There is another heir."

"Of course there is," he said. "There were twins, Lorens and his sister Lokenna."

"What?" came Santon's startled voice. "You awoke me."

"Then you're talking in your sleep. You should stay awake and listen to yourself some night. You speak wisely and well."

"Lokenna can be found to the north. Claymore Pass."

Both men sat stiffly upright. Neither had spoken. And the voice was one they remembered well.

As one, they cried, "Alarice!"

FIVE

Raindrops the size of watery fists beat at the rock and bounced knee-high on impact. Above the barren plateau lightning danced and weaved and formed vivid eye-searing patterns. The actinic glare from the bolts cast an eerie illumination on the land, sending the small animals scurrying for cover from the sudden downpour. On the edge of a sheer precipice towered the Castle of the Winds.

Wind whipped across the plateau and worked airy fingers through the lofty, lacelike spires of crystalline diamond and jade. Aeolian harps sang, their haunting song challenging that of the elements. And on the tallest tower in the center of the castle stood a windswept figure dressed in a robe of grays and soft greens.

Kaga'kalb, the Wizard of Storms, raised his arms and called down lightning from the sky. The mighty lightning strikes touched his fingers and died. He threw back his sleeves and bared his arms and returned the prodigious power to the heavens with a single mumbled spell.

The Wizard of Storms' lightning bolt rivalled anything created naturally. Clouds boiled away and left the sky naked to his gaze. Kaga'kalb reached out with another spell and touched the exposed azure sky. The ring of jet-dark storm clouds he formed began to swirl, trying to close in on the intruding fairness. Faster and faster he let the clouds spin until they formed a tornado with a vortex larger than the Castle of the Winds.

Only when he was satisfied with the intensity of the rotary pattern did Kaga'kalb release his spell. A deafening roar that shook the very mountain on which the castle was built rumbled away. Behind the bull-throated roar of angry elements went the tornado.

Kaga'kalb smiled. He so enjoyed playing with his toys. He dropped his hands and let the long sleeves cover his hands. He rubbed them against his robe to bring back circulation. He was growing old. Frostbite set in more quickly now whenever he commanded the storms. Many years ago he had been able to summon blizzards and never feel their wintry bite. No longer.

And tiredness turned his sprightly step into one less energetic. Kaga'kalb cared little about this. The power he controlled from the Castle of the Winds was so immense that no wizard in Porotane could withstand his full attack.

Or so it had been for many decades. Kaga'kalb went inside the tower and walked slowly down the spiral staircase fashioned from huge blood rubies to the comfortable living quarters in the center of the keep. Porotane had changed after Duke Freow died.

Kaga'kalb settled into a well-cushioned chair and lifted his feet to a table. "I would view the kingdom and the petty warlords," he said aloud. Tiny white clouds formed in the corners of the room, hardly more than misty patches. They swirled and hardened and became dark balls of water vapor stretching out tendrils that touched in the center of one wall. At first all Kaga'kalb saw was water droplets trickling down the wall. Then a tiny lightning bolt crossed the wall. Following quickly came smudges that solidified into figures of men and women.

"The warlords, not the castle," ordered Kaga'kalb. The spells controlling his scrying wavered from time to time. He might have to recast. He noted some lessening of clarity and blurring of detail in the lifelike picture growing on his wall.

As if they shared the room with him, Dews Gaemock and Dalziel Sef popped into view. Their mouths moved but no sound came out.

"Full scrying," Kaga'kalb ordered. A flash of purple produced a sharper image of the rebels and their voices. Sef turned as if someone had tapped him on the shoulder, then frowned and returned to his discussion with Gaemock. The Wizard of Storms listened to the two rebel leaders forge their alliance. He shook his head. He had seen such unification in the past end with bloody murder. He doubted Dalziel Sef and Dews Gaemock would avoid that fate.

"Give me Lorens," he ordered. The small clouds expanded and turned mistier. Kaga'kalb frowned. He pulled back his sleeves and began the chant to intensify his spell. When this did not work the Wizard of Storms started making small gestures in the air before him. Tiny purple streamers of magical energy flowed from his thumbs. Each finger left a red and green trail in the air that shot sparks in all directions before dying. As quickly as the aerial trail vanished, Kaga'kalb replaced it.

Over and over, faster and faster the Wizard of Storms wove his potent scrying spell. The air in the room cooled and clouds formed along the ceiling beams. Kaga'kalb began directing the clouds like a general marshalling his forces. In precise ranks, the miniature thunderclouds floated across the room as if driven by unseen winds, merged, parted, and retraced their storm track.

"Damn him!" cried Kaga'kalb. "Damn Lorens!" The wizard worked even more intricate magic spells and found it impossible to penetrate the barrier the new monarch built around himself.

Kaga'kalb settled back, a pass of his hand dismissing the potent magic clouds he had summoned. "So Lorens dares block my view of him. The Demon Crown gives him false confidence."

The Wizard of Storms scowled and pondered the subject of the wizard-king on the throne of Porotane. He had not meddled unduly in Porotane's internal affairs when the Demon Crown had been inactive. Freow's death and Alarice finding Lorens upset the careful balance of nature that gave Kaga'kalb his power. With the crown becoming a force to be reckoned with in the kingdom, Kaga'kalb sensed his own power diminishing.

Not much, not yet. He scowled so hard that deep furrows creased his forehead and turned his handsome visage into something hideous. Lorens knew so little of the powers locked within the Demon Crown. His continued and constant use would only result in disaster for wizard and peasant alike.

Kaga'kalb shoved down hard on the arms of the chair. He shot to his feet as angry with his own inability as he was with Lorens' magical blocking. The crown's gift of knowledge had already pushed Lorens past all reasoning. The young wizard-king would never relinquish his

magical aid now. The lure of seeing and hearing
and tasting and feeling anywhere in the kingdom had proven too great a freedom for a youth
imprisoned by a harsh master most of his life.

Steps long and sure, he walked outside the
keep and into the empty courtyard. A single
gesture of his hand blew open the ponderous
opalescent gates of the Castle of the Winds.
Onto the barren plain he strode, the natural
storm raging around his mountaintop.

Kaga'kalb stopped and stared at the underbelly of the clouds. His left hand pointed. Searing white lightning shot to the cloud. Riding
down this scintillant trail came a puff of cloud,
swirling and uncertain of form. With his right
hand, Kaga'kalb gestured at another cloud. A
second misty patch detached itself and came
sliding down the jerking rope of pure energy.

The two cloud segments stopped just above
Kaga'kalb's head. He clapped his hands. A peal
of thunder louder than anything produced naturally by the storm rolled across the windswept
plateau. With it, the two clouds merged into one
huge pillar.

Swirling tendrils shot forth. Within the dark
cloud a dull red core formed that began a slow,
rhythmic pulsation. The wisps of tendril hardened into arms and legs. A head without a neck
formed. Twin beacons of red formed where
human eyes would be had this cloud creature
been born of woman.

Kaga'kalb stepped back and watched the
final stages of transformation of his storm warrior.

"Pass in review!" bellowed Kaga'kalb, his
voice almost lost in the violent winds whipping
across the plains.

Lightning sizzled at the fingertips of the

huge storm warrior. Each spark produced a
smaller version of the towering magical creature. Ten storm warriors taller than Kaga'kalb
fell into step. From each of their misty fingers
came a new warrior equal to Kaga'kalb in
height. The hundred saluted as they passed their
master.

They reached the precipice, wheeled, and
came back. Each storm warrior in this legion
reached out and produced ten. A thousand
storm warriors reaching almost to Kaga'kalb's
shoulder marched by, the impact of their misty
feet on the rock sounding like a fierce rain-
storm. Kaga'kalb smiled. The ten thousand
waist-high warriors who returned from across
the plains filled his vision.

"An army to be reckoned with," Kaga'kalb
said. "No ragtag rebel band can oppose them!"

The Wizard of Storms uttered the magical
command of release. His vaporous army
marched in step over the edge of the cliff. They
did not fall. Their substance dispersed, then
whipped around and got caught in an updraft.
Long columns of mist soared to rejoin the
lightning-wracked cloud above.

Kaga'kalb turned to his giant storm warrior
and smiled. No human army could fight his
warriors. Rebels meant nothing. The full might
of a kingdom dwarfed next to his cloudy minions. And neither could any wizard hope to
defeat him, not even a wizard-king possessing
the potent magic locked within the Demon
Crown!

SIX

Birtle Santon and Vered turned and stared at one another in disbelief. Both opened their mouths to speak, then clamped them shut, as if doubting their senses.

Finally, Santon took the initiative and said, "It was Alarice. I know it."

"No," said Vered, shaking his head, "not Alarice—but it was her phantom."

"We never found the body in the Desert of Sazan to give her a proper burial. We should have searched harder."

"Patrin's magic and the destruction of the City of Stolen Dreams kept us from doing many things," said Vered. "How I would have loved to loot that city. The fine dreams, all locked away in tightly sealed jars. The price those would have fetched in a decent market!"

"She died and we didn't bury her. Alarice's phantom now walks the land."

"It was a faint and misty phantom. I barely heard her. At first, I thought it was you."

"And I thought it was you who spoke." Santon smiled slightly. "I knew it could not be, though. The words I heard made sense."

"You're saying I never make sense?" Vered snorted indignantly and settled down, his arms pulling in his legs and his chin resting on his knees as he stared into the campfire. "The other twin. Lokenna. We can find her and replace Lorens on the throne."

"Just like that?" asked Santon. He snapped his fingers. The sound was that of dried twigs breaking—or dreams falling apart. "Lorens has the Demon Crown. He is a wizard of small ability, true, but a wizard nonetheless."

"His sister might reason with him. She might moderate his wild swings of mood. She might introduce some humanity to his purges."

Santon shook his head. "You no more believe that than I. The crown is as much at fault as what Patrin did to the youngling in the name of apprenticeship."

"But Alarice spoke of the twin sister. Can we deny her shade?"

Santon had no answer for that. He had not been swift enough to look around at the sound of his beloved's voice. If he had, he might have caught a shifting form of white gauzy air, a small disturbance and nothing more. Would this brief glimpse of her phantom have assuaged his heartache—or made it worse?

They should not have left the Desert of Sazan until her body had been located and properly buried. One so valiant should not have to endure the uncertain fate of being a phantom, trapped between worlds, communicating only with difficulty to the living and not at all with the other dead who roamed as spirits.

"What do you know of Claymore Pass?" asked Vered. "Alarice said that Lokenna was there."

"The pass," Santon said with no enthusiasm. "That stretch through the Yorral Mountains has cost more men their lives than any other. The pass is deadly, even during high summer. The battles fought there have been even worse."

"I remember none."

"They were before your time. I was barely your age when I served with King Lamost's troops. We were attacked front and rear while we marched through Claymore Pass. Brutal. Slaughter. Five hundred entered the pass on patrol. Only fifty left."

"Rebels?"

"Not in those times. Not while Lamost reigned. No, Vered, those were brigands."

"Some band of petty cutpurses," Vered said. "I cannot believe you would march with troops ill-equipped or untrained."

"They called them brigands. Although I never knew for certain, I believed the rumors that they were mercenaries outfitted by a wizard living far to the north and desiring Porotane for his private domain. Whoever they fought for, it was a war of blood and iron and not of magic."

"This Wizard of Storms everyone is abuzz over? Was he the one?"

"No name was ever placed on him. It is possible. All that matters is the large graveyard in the pass. I cannot even guess how many bodies were never buried. On any given night you can hear the moans of the phantoms as they desperately seek their bodies and beg and cajole mortals for proper consecration."

Vered shuddered. "An unlikely place to find the heir to the throne of Porotane. Mayhaps we mistook a casual gust of wind for Alarice? We might have imagined hearing the name Claymore Pass."

"I imagined nothing. It was Alarice's phantom. We must do something."

"I agree," said Vered, "but am at a loss to decide what. We were going to the Uvain Plateau to sample their fine wines and . . . other delicacies. Should we delay this small holiday to the wine country and join with a rebel band?"

"To what end? I am not convinced that any want a true heir on the throne. Gaemock might. There have been rumors about him. But Dalziel Sef? He seeks power for himself."

"But he is a strong leader and his cavalry is second to none. Gaemock is an able strategist but he fails to carry out his fine plans."

"And Dalziel Sef executes well and gets nowhere because his reach is too short for his ambition. No, Vered, we began this mission with Alarice. We must finish it."

"For her?"

"For ourselves," Santon snapped.

"And I worried about purpose to life," said Vered, sighing. "Now I worry about dying for a cause." He let out a gusty sigh. "We ride north for Claymore Pass in the morning?"

Santon fell silent, his mind turning over the complex problem facing them. Rebel bands cared little what mission sent riders across Porotane—if they did not pay allegiance to the particular rebel leader, they were fair game. A temporary truce with Gaemock might give Vered and him safe passage to the north.

Or they might run afoul of other rebel bands. He had heard of the small but vicious groups headed by wizards. Most were rumored to be roving along the River Ty in the northlands and across to where the upthrust of the Uvain Plateau relieved the flatness of the river flood plains.

Santon's mind worked on, dismissing the

obvious. The rebels would be under continual observation by Lorens. The Demon Crown allowed the monarch to look and hear anywhere within the realm. As a pair of travellers, he and Vered posed no threat. They might never even come to Lorens' attention as he scanned the countryside. If they rode as emissaries of Dews Gaemock, they would definitely attract unwanted notice. Since their hasty departure from Castle Porotane he did not relish the prospect of once more falling into the clutches of those nobles.

Santon's green eyes locked with Vered's brown ones. The older man shook his head to deny that they both had come up with the same ridiculous, insanely dangerous idea at the same time.

"What other course is open to us?" asked Vered. "You see it, just as I do. We cannot move through Porotane in search of Lokenna without pulling Lorens' spying onto ourselves like a decaying carcass draws flies."

"If we return to the castle, Archbishop Nosto will seize us."

"If Baron Theoll doesn't find us first."

"Or," Santon went on, "the king himself. There is nothing Lorens wouldn't do to keep us from such a mad venture."

"Ah," said Vered, smiling broadly. "Therein lies the genius of such a plan. Who in their right minds would *ever* return, much less return to steal away with the most potent tidbit of magic in all Porotane?"

Birtle Santon leaned back and stared at the sky, trying to find a flaw in what Vered proposed. He couldn't. The same thoughts had taken a different road in his own mind but had still arrived at the same destination. They could never find Lokenna and place her in a position of power while the Demon Crown allowed her brother free access anywhere in Porotane.

"She might not be any better than what we've got as king," said Santon.

"True. But can she be worse?" Vered countered.

"There is always room for things to grow worse. Such is the nature of the universe."

"Pah!" snorted Vered. "You always look at the dark side. You should consider—" The two argued the proper philosophy of the world as they mounted their horses and retraced their path to Castle Porotane.

They had a crown to steal.

"Guards!" hissed Vered. "They will have thousands of guardsmen waiting for us if we try to reenter the castle through the same postern gate."

"How else can we get inside?" demanded Birtle Santon. "This is the only secret way we know. We can hardly go riding up to the main gate and proclaim that we have returned to steal the Demon Crown and to please let us in."

The two stood at the entrance to the tunnel through the thicket of brambles. Vered looked around nervously, sure that a scouting patrol would see them and bring the full armed wrath of the castle guard down on their heads.

"What a time to die," he moaned. "My clothing hangs in tatters and it's been forever since I've had a decent bath."

"You won't die. Not even from the stench of your journey."

"The horses should never have run through the golden velvet stinkweed. Lorens need not use the magic of the crown to find us. He need only sniff the air."

Santon had long since grown used to the odor. They had crossed a tributary to the River Ty and had washed off most of the lingering scent, but Vered needed something more than his sorry apparel to complain about to feel right.

"We go in here. If we find guardsmen, then we fight. If we don't, we press on to the throne room and steal the Demon Crown."

"You make it sound simple."

"Aren't we the greatest thieves in all Porotane? For us it *will* be easy."

Vered shook his head, wanting to believe the high praise but having to weigh it against common sense. The castle contained factions warring politically. No one slept with both eyes closed. Constant danger of assassination produced a society of fitful sleepers—and swift daggers.

"We may be the greatest thieves in the kingdom," said Vered, "but I fear that the Demon Crown might prove to be the greatest thief catcher."

"You chide me for being negative. Come and let's explore. Let's see if Kerin awaits you with open arms."

"That one?" Vered sniffed haughtily. "I had forgotten her until you mentioned her traitorous name. By now she has been in the bed of a dozen others—and not a one as good as I!"

"She'd been in the beds of a dozen before you," taunted Santon, trying to get his friend's mind off the thorns clawing at their flesh as they made their way toward the hidden gate.

"But I was the best. She told me so. What good is it finding a virgin? How can one with no experience know you are the best? Kerin compared me with the most famous lovers who have ever tramped the halls of the castle and named me best!''

As he bragged, Vered worked with his steel slivers on the lock. Tumblers fell into place with a well-oiled *snick*! and the door opened to darkness.

Santon strained for traces of guardsmen waiting in ambush. Vision gave him only blackness deeper than any moonless midnight. Smell was out of the question. His and Vered's pungent aroma overwhelmed this fragile sense. But Santon listened intently, for breathing, for movement, for the clank of swords against armor. Only the frightened scurrying of a rat came to his ears.

He motioned for Vered to follow. Glass shield on his withered arm and battle-ax ready for an overhead stroke, Santon walked the length of the unlighted passage.

''Here,'' said Vered. ''Here's the doorway out into the courtyard and that hideous statue.'' The door slid open as he leaned against it. Vered stuck his head out and looked around. The courtyard was empty. ''When we return, *you* have to open the door. I am tired of being humiliated by that farting feline.''

''Whatever is necessary for our escape,'' Santon answered. He followed Vered. They had chosen the time of their assault well. They had waited until four hours past midnight when most of the castle's residents slept their uneasy sleep and the guards had begun to flag in their attention after having assumed their posts at midnight.

''What now? Do we just walk into the king's chambers and rip it from his head?''

"He cannot keep it on his head forever. When he removes it, we strike."

"I've known you most of my life, or so it seems, Santon, and never have I heard you spout such nonsense. Lorens is a *wizard*. Do you not think he protects the crown with a ward spell when he isn't wearing it?"

"Then we will have to be crafty."

Vered shook his head. A quick smile curled Santon's lips. He had no idea how they would steal the Demon Crown, but he knew that his taunts would put a dozen wild schemes into Vered's head. One would work. All he had to do was listen to the young thief and pick the one with the best chance of succeeding.

"He knows all his personal guards," Vered complained. "We cannot impersonate them and hope to get away."

"But Theoll's soldiers. They patrol everywhere," Santon said. They entered a long corridor that led back toward the wing where their quarters had been. Santon briefly wondered if others had moved in or if superstition kept out squatters. To occupy the sleeping chambers of those executed or otherwise in disfavor and in the dungeons was seen by some as bad luck.

"We dare not impersonate them, either. Lorens' guard would question them instantly. But consider Archbishop Nosto's holy soldiers!" Vered stopped talking for a moment as they crept past a sleeping guardsman. Once past, Vered picked up his thought. "The Inquisition is feared by all. I doubt even King Lorens challenges the archbishop openly."

"Then we get Inquisitors' uniforms to steal the crown," said Santon.

"If we are seen, who would dare to look us

in the eye? They all drop to their pitiful knees and beg not to be taken away and put to the Question."

"A good plan," said Santon. They stopped outside their former quarters. Santon pressed his ear against the panel and heard nothing. As thick as the door was, he had not expected to overhear anyone talking unless they shouted at one another.

"Here," said Vered. "This must be the entrance to the secret passage where Theoll spied on us." The young man ran his knowing fingers along the sides of a mahogany cabinet until he found the door catch. No sound went along with the cabinet swinging away from the wall and revealing a crawl space.

Santon quickly looked up and down the hall and followed Vered into the secret passage. They went only a few feet before finding the spy holes looking into their chambers. Both men squinted through the tiny slits.

"Empty," said Santon.

"No, not so. I see someone moving. It . . . it's Kerin! She is robbing me!"

"Quiet, you fool, or she'll hear you. Let her take what she wants. We will not need it."

"What could she possibly want with my fine clothing?" Vered scooted around and found another spy hole. "Ah, she's left that. She's taken only that which might be of worth if she sells it in the market."

Santon almost laughed. Vered did not understand that he'd just proclaimed all his supposedly stylish clothing worthless.

"She's gone now."

"Then let us enter and change clothing and bathe," said Santon. "I see the tub is still filled from when we left."

"The water will be cold."

Santon grabbed Vered's leg and dragged him back to the corridor. They waited until Kerin vanished around the corner before slipping out and going into their chambers. A half hour of bathing made them feel better. A change of clothing turned them into intrepids thinking they could challenge the world.

"We cannot stay here forever," said Vered, eyeing his remaining wardrobe with regret. He did not want to leave such finery. "What do we do? Go hunting for Inquisitors?"

Santon smiled without humor as he looked through the partially opened door. "No need. Luck is with us. A pair of the red-dressed ruffians are coming by. Get ready."

Archbishop Nosto's two guardsmen had just passed the door when Santon and Vered jumped out behind them. Vered used his dagger, driving it directly into one Inquisitor's kidney. Santon took aim and swung the glass shield, catching his victim on the back of the neck with the rounded edge. The impact knocked the Inquisitor's head forward. The crunch told that Santon had broken the man's neck.

Within minutes they had the pair dragged within the sleeping rooms and stripped. Vered's red uniform, even worn over his clothing, hung in folds. Santon had taken the larger and his was almost skin-tight, restricting movement as he swung the glass shield to and fro.

"Cut the seams under my left arm," he told Vered. "I might be able to fight then."

"The need for personal combat will not arise," Vered said with renewed bravado. "We have come this far. We will finish this job and none will be the wiser."

It was Santon's turn to worry. How long would it be before Archbishop Nosto missed his two Inquisitors? An hour? Five minutes? There was no way of telling. He felt the need for haste. Together, they almost ran to the king's chambers.

Santon lifted his shield and restrained Vered. In the corridor stood a pair of indolent guards. One looked as if he slept on his feet. The other stared out a window toward the rapidly flowing River Ty.

"We dare not attack them," said Santon. "There might be another pair inside the king's chamber."

"Doubtful. What monarch would want such ruffians watching him sleep? But you are right. They must be distracted."

"What is it?" demanded Santon. "I know that tone in your voice. What are you planning?"

"I'll be back in a few minutes. Stay here." Vered reached up and flipped forward the crimson hood on Santon's uniform so that it hid the man's face. He pulled his own up and forward so that his face vanished into shadows and soft folds.

Santon almost cried out when Vered returned in ten minutes. Dutifully following two paces behind him was an almost naked Kerin. She wore only the flimsiest of nightgowns and looked upset.

"There, my daughter," Vered said, his voice almost an octave lower than usual. "Those are the guards you must cause to stray from grace. Do as Archbishop Nosto commands."

"Must I?" she said, her voice almost breaking with fear.

"How long can you resist the pincers—or the Inquisition's branding iron on your fine body?" Vered reached out a crooked finger and pulled away what little cloth veiled the woman's body. He let it drop back into place. "Go!"

She scuttled into the hall, looked back, then cast her eyes down before going to the guards.

"What did you tell her?" asked Santon.

"She'll keep the guards busy—and happy —for an hour. It eludes me why this charity toward such uncouth guardsmen is ordered, but the archbishop feels this is penance for her sins." Vered shrugged. "You were the one who said that she'd bed a dozen others after me. Now she need find only ten."

Santon motioned to Vered. Kerin and the two soldiers had vanished into another room. Santon stopped before the door leading into the king's quarters. Vered gingerly touched the door latch. It moved easily. He pulled it back and ducked into the room. Santon followed, his heart beating wildly.

Lorens sprawled across the massive bed, still clothed except for one boot, which had been kicked off. Santon's nose wrinkled. The king smelled as bad as they had after going through the stinkweed patch. He had not bathed in many days—or weeks. The haggard look on his face even while sleeping showed the strain he endured.

"Can it be this simple?" Vered asked in surprise. Lorens had tumbled face forward onto the bed while wearing the Demon Crown. It had fallen off and lay near the monarch's head.

Santon gestured for Vered to carefully lift it from the soft bed. He saw the glass box in which Alarice had carried the dangerous magical artifact for so many years and picked it up. When he turned Vered had already scooped up the crown.

"My drop of royal blood stands me in good stead," Vered whispered. The crown glowed green between his fingertips. He dropped it into the glass box. Santon quickly closed the jewel-hinged transparent lid and glanced back to where Lorens stirred restlessly on the bed.

His hand held the box with the Demon Crown. He could use the edge of his glass shield to kill Lorens as he had killed the Inquisitor. It would be so easy and would solve so many problems for Porotane.

"Out. Hurry!" Vered stood at the door and gestured. Santon quickly joined his friend and saw the problem. Four of Baron Theoll's soldiers marched down the hall toward the king's sleeping chambers.

"Leave him," said Vered. "We must get out of the castle with all our parts in working condition." Before Santon could say a word, Vered slipped back through the door and into the corridor in front of Theoll's approaching guardsmen.

Santon joined him, keeping the glass box hidden behind his shield. He stretched slightly and felt the tight fabric give way.

"Give way for soldiers of the Inquisition!" boomed Vered. He strode forward, head high and hands hidden in the voluminous folds of the Inquisitor's uniform.

As he passed the leading guard, his dagger flashed out and up, entering under the man's lowest rib and cutting upward to pierce the heart. Before the man had fallen forward, dead, Vered slashed viciously and cut the second guard's throat.

Santon dropped to the floor and kicked out, his feet engaging the third guard's legs, one foot behind the guard's heel and the other snapping hard into the kneecap. The man went down in a jumble, too surprised at this sudden attack to do more than croak weakly. Santon rolled over and brought the shield down squarely on the man's throat, almost decapitating him.

The final guard made the mistake of attempting to draw his sword. Vered moved inside the arc of the man's arm and drove the hilt of his dagger into the guard's sternum. He let out a sick gasp and fell retching to the floor.

"Leave him be," said Vered when Santon started to kill him. Santon stared in surprise at his friend. Vered said loudly, "We have accomplished what Archbishop Nosto sent us to do. Let us hurry to his chambers with our prize."

Santon understood then. Confusion to their enemies! Let Theoll accuse Archbishop Nosto and Lorens suspect them both.

SEVEN

Lorens, King of Porotane, former apprentice to the wizard Patrin, son of Lamost and blood heir of Waellkin thrashed about on the bed and moaned loudly. His dreams had grown steadily worse. His eyelids fluttered but did not open as unseen terrors rose from the quagmire of his mind to torment him.

"No," he muttered, arms waving about to chase away the dark and unsettling dream figures. "Not me. You want someone else. Take my sister. Get away."

Lorens shrieked as the dream turned into nightmare. Talons raked at his face and eyes. Pits opened under his feet, threatening to plunge him into pools of burning sulphur. Boils sprouted on his arms and leaked yellow pus. And no one came to aid him. No one.

That was the worst punishment of all. Around him in a circle stood his advisors and none offered any help. No one grabbed his outstretched hand. No one cautioned him. No one even looked in his direction as the nightmare figures began their ghoulish tortures.

Lorens gasped and sat upright in the soft bed, drenched in sweat and heart pounding at

twice its natural rate. A shaking hand wiped the
perspiration from his face. He missed a few
drops; the sweat got into his eyes and stung.
Lorens leaned forward, head sagging. The nightmare had been so real. He had been tortured,
yes, but worse than this was the betrayal of his
closest advisors.

"I need to be more wary. Trust no one.
That's the lesson Patrin taught. He was right. By
the saints, he was right!" Lorens' throat con-
stricted as he thought of his dead master. The
wizard had been a harsh taskmaster and required every lesson to be learned exactly, but
the discipline now stood the lonely king in good
stead. He overlooked no detail. He suspected
everyone. They all plotted against him. All of
them.

Lorens' head came up and he straightened
his shoulders. This was no condition for the
ruler of the strongest kingdom to be in. He had
to look regal and command with authority. A
king needed a crown. Lorens' lips twisted back
in a feral smile. His crown was enough to
guarantee loyalty of his treacherous subjects.

Lorens reached out for the crown. His
groping hand found only the soft down comforter on the bed. He spun around, bunching up the
fabric under his legs. Panic again surged within
him. He pawed frantically at the comforter as he
searched for the Demon Crown.

He kicked himself free of the bed and
dropped to hands and knees. "It must have
fallen onto the floor. Under the bed. Somewhere!"

King Lorens sought the magical crown and
failed to find it. He sagged, his back against a
stone wall.

"It's here. Don't show fear. Weakness like

that will kill me. They'll all come swooping in like carrion hawks. I need the crown. I *need* it!"

Another feverish search failed to reveal the Demon Crown. On shaky legs Lorens stood. He quickly found that he had to lean against a table for support. The thought of losing the only protection he had against rebels outside the castle walls and insurrectionists within robbed him of his strength.

"Guards!" he shrieked. He swallowed hard and tried to compose himself. No weakness. Don't show fear, especially to guards. They were in the pay of others and would report his lapse to their true masters. "Guards," he called in a lower, more controlled voice. When neither of the men posted outside his chamber entered, Lorens flung back the door and peered into the corridor.

No guards. As if winter had come early to Porotane, Lorens felt a cold wind blow across his spine. He had no experience with palace politics, but he needed little to know that assassinations occurred in situations like this. The guards were either traitors or paid to leave at the proper time. The assassin quietly walked in, dagger drawn, sword ready, garrote looped for dropping over an unsuspecting head.

Lorens' hand touched his throat. Would the assassin try to choke him to death? He could not bear that thought. Better a slow poison or a foot of cold steel through his guts. To die slowly, the air gusting from his lungs and nothing coming in to replace it. The pressure in his chest. Encroaching blackness at the edges of his vision. His heart threatening to explode.

Lorens shrieked again in fear, hands tearing at the hair on his temples.

"King," came one guard's voice. The man

hurried down the corridor from the direction of a suite of empty bedchambers. The dead duke's whores had lived in those chambers. Lorens had ordered them all from the castle after his coronation. He need not share the bed with a woman who would slit his throat when he slept after making love to her.

"King Lorens, what's wrong?" The guard fastened his breeches as he ran clumsily. He dropped his sword, bent and retrieved it. By this time the second guard emerged, more unclad than in uniform. He held his dagger poised for an attack.

Was he the one? The thought blasted across Lorens' mind and exploded like Spring Festival fireworks.

"Him," he said, pointing a shaky finger at the guard with the dagger. "He wants to kill me!"

"Lader? But he's completely loyal to you, Majesty, as I am." The guard dropped to his knee, head bowed. Lorens sucked in several deep breaths in an effort to calm himself. The guard paid this small obeisance only to cover the act of fastening his sword belt and keeping his trousers from falling down.

"Where were you? Both of you?"

"We . . . I . . . we heard strange noises and went to explore. It was nothing, Majesty."

Lorens had lived an isolated existence but he was no fool. Patrin had tried to school him in human foibles that a wizard might exploit. He had learned of these from books and grimoires, not from experience. It took Lorens several seconds to piece together what he saw.

"Are you two lovers?" he asked, incredulous at the idea.

"Majesty, no!" both men protested in unison.

"It's as Deprry said," explained the one called Lader. "A noise. We went to investigate a strange sound."

Lorens pushed past the two guards and went to the door where they had emerged. Inside, cowering on the bed, was a redheaded serving wench. Lorens' hands clenched into fists. Power rose within him, magical power fostered and schooled by Patrin. But the proper spells to form the searing death bolt did not come to his lips. His anger blotted out the skills needed.

"Emotion has no place in wizardry," he said over and over to himself. Patrin had tried to teach him this and had failed. A simple spell would have boiled the blood of the serving wench who had seduced his guards—and he could not remember it.

A headache grew to torment him. A dull pulsation began at the back of his neck and worked up to fragment on the top of his head and send fiery knives deep into his skull from all sides. Lorens spun away from the naked woman. He stalked back to the guards, who had finished readjusting their uniforms.

"You abandoned your posts."

"Majesty," started Lader. He glanced at Deprry, then lowered his head. "Majesty, it is true. We were weak and throw ourselves on your mercy."

Lorens could barely stand. The headache turned the world red with pain. To Lader, he said, "Get me the jester. Harhar. Roust him from bed and get him here immediately."

"Th-that's all, Majesty?" asked Deprry, wor-

ried about his punishment for abandoning his
duty post.

"Do it now!" he roared. Lorens went into
his sleeping chambers and slammed the heavy
door. He leaned against it, again wiping the
sweat from his face.

Lorens yelped when a faint rap came at the
door. He jerked open the door. Standing in
the light cast by the guttering torch at the end of
the hall was a strangely dressed figure. Lorens
backed away, fear clamping icy fingers around
his throat. He struggled to breathe and could
not.

"You sent for me, King Lorens," said the
court fool. Harhar dropped to his hands and
knees, then kicked into a headstand. From this,
he pushed to a handstand and flopped over,
rolling easily and coming to his feet. He shook
his rattle at the frightened monarch.

"Oh, this is wonderful!" crowed Harhar.
"You are such a good actor, my king. You are
doing such a *fine* job of looking scared at my
pitiful act!"

"Yes, of course, that's all. Just an act. An act.
Come in."

"I am in, Majesty. All of me," Harhar said,
using both hands to check his backside.

"Close the door."

Lorens used this brief instant when
Harhar's back was to him to stumble to a chair
and drop heavily into it. The jester turned to see
his king seated in a sedate pose, apparently at
ease with himself and his world.

"What can I do to make your burden easier,
Majesty?" Harhar made a mocking bow that
ended with him unbalanced and teetering precariously. He bumped into a table and fell over

it, coming to his feet on the far side as if nothing had happened.

In spite of himself, Lorens smiled. "What crushing burden is this, jester?"

"The burden of rule. Duke Freow spent long, sleepless nights worrying over this and that in Porotane. Do you do less?"

"Of course not. I am content." Lorens held back the tension that made his nerves twitch like the strings of a bull fiddle.

"Yet you desire my company in the middle of the night. Better the serving wench down the hall, eh, Majesty?"

"What of her?" Lorens demanded sharply. "What do you know of her and the guards?"

"Only that Kerin is lovely and would make a fine consort. A drop or two of royal blood flows in her, methinks."

"No." Lorens dismissed the idea with a pass of his hand. He dared not share his bed with a woman capable of cutting his throat. That this red-haired witch sported a drop of royal blood was something Lorens had not known. That made such a dangerous coupling even less likely. He dared have no one challenge his rule. They all conspired against him now. To have one that close to him would only make their schemes the more likely to succeed.

"A joke then, Majesty. How do you keep a barrister from drowning?"

"What?" Lorens asked, startled at the sudden turn in the conversation. "I don't know."

"You take your foot off his head!"

"That's not funny."

"It's not funny, if you are a barrister," said Harhar. "For the rest of us, it is a fine jest." Harhar did a cartwheel across the room, smashed into the wall, and then did a hand-spring to show that his clumsiness was all part of his act.

"You hear much in the castle," said Lorens. He wiped the sweat from his upper lip. The harder he tried to control his emotions, the more obvious his distress became. Would the fool notice?

"Ah, it's gossip you desire, then. I know much. Did you know that the second assistant chef is . . ." Harhar's voice trailed off. Lorens' anger mounted.

"I need information about those who con-spire against me!" the monarch roared.

"Your power is supreme, Majesty," said the jester, his ebony eyes locking with Lorens'. "Use the Demon Crown to spy on your enemies. Such fine magic will show more than a simpleton such as I could."

Lorens wiped another river of perspiration from his face and neck. He had revealed the secret he wished kept—and he had done it to the court jester. He cursed himself for such carelessness.

"Unless," Harhar said slowly, "unless you no longer possess the Demon Crown. Could this be the heart of your melancholy this night?"

"I'll cut your tongue out and cram it up your nose if you tell anyone. *Anyone*! Is this clear?"

"Majesty, I am your humble and obedient servant." Harhar fell and began banging his forehead against the floor. "I would never betray your best interests."

"The crown is gone. Stolen. The guards were lured away and the Demon Crown was stolen from my very chambers. Who in the castle has committed this foul deed?"

"Not I, Majesty!" declared Harhar. "I am as innocent as a newborn babe in arms suckling at its mother's fine, shapely, firm breast. I am even *more* innocent. I—"

"Silence, fool. I am not accusing you. I am asking advice."

"From a fool?"

The headache blasted white-hot needles into Lorens' skull. He could barely focus his eyes. Never had such headaches assailed him— not until he wore the Demon Crown. But its power! The lure of knowing every spoken word in the kingdom, seeing every covert action, being anywhere his magical senses could reach. How could he relinquish the crown for even a few minutes when so many plotted against him?

Harhar rocked back onto his heels and stared up at the King of Porotane. "Majesty," Harhar said, "if your guards are innocent, then others must be guilty. Who can walk the halls of the castle unchallenged at this hour?"

A pounding on the door kept Lorens from answering. Harhar tumbled backward and came to his feet. He opened the door. The guard pushed him aside and hurried into the room.

"Majesty, we have information you must hear," Lader said. He motioned. Deprry dragged in a soldier clad in the uniform of Baron Theoll's service.

"What can he know?" Lorens asked. The headache had become a steady throb worse than the shooting pains. He could not concentrate.

"He and three others attempted to stop two men coming from your quarters."

Lorens blasted to his feet. He wobbled slightly and recovered. Of Theoll's guardsman he asked, "What men? Describe them."

"Majesty," the guard choked out. "They attacked me. I am in pain."

"Add to his pain. Get him to speak." Lader and Deprry twisted the poor wight's arms into a double hammerlock and applied pressure. The guard went white and stammered incoherently.

"Less pressure, more talk," suggested Harhar. Lorens motioned for his guardsmen to relax their grips.

"Majesty, they were Archbishop Nosto's Inquisitors," the captive gasped out.

"You recognized them? Their names. Be quick about it."

"I . . . do not know them, Majesty." The guard turned even paler. Lader and Deprry now supported him as he weakened. "They were dressed as Inquisitors."

"What did they look like? Describe their faces. Were they tall or short? Heavy or thin?"

"They . . . were Inquisitors."

Lorens motioned for his guards to again apply their grip. Theoll's soldier gasped and fainted from pain.

"No," said Lorens when his men started to drag out the unconscious soldier. "Revive him. I must know more of this. Can it be true that Nosto plots against me?"

"It is rumored that he is of the royal blood," said Harhar.

"What?"

"All rumors, only rumors, some rumors. Who can say what is true and what is only jest?" Harhar shook his rattle and smiled as if his wits had left him.

Lader shook the soldier awake again. "No more," the guardsman moaned. "I hurt so. They broke something within me. I cannot breathe without pain."

"They killed the other three, Majesty," said Deprry. "This one is in sorry shape. They might have thought him dead."

Lorens sat on the edge of his chair. He leaned forward so that his face was only inches from the guardsman's. "These red-clad Inquisitors killed your comrades."

"Yes," the soldier gasped out.

"They carried something with them. What was it?"

"I saw nothing, but . . ."

"But what?" roared Lorens, spittle running down his chin. Spells swirled in his head. He tried to sort out the proper words of magic and summoning chants, to find the invocation that would drag the truth from this dying soldier.

"Th-they said that Nosto awaited them. That they carried something to him. I saw nothing, but . . ." Again his words drifted away as pain worked its debilitating magic on his body.

Lorens gestured to his guardsmen. They broke one of the soldier's arms in their attempt to force the truth from him.

"A box. I saw a glass box. That's all. I—"

"What else?" Lorens reached out and grabbed the soldier by the throat and shook. The guard's head flopped loosely.

"Majesty, he is dead," said Lader. "We didn't mean to kill him."

"Get him out of here. Bury him in the gardens. Let no one see you."

"Sire," spoke up Harhar, "should both of your guards leave your side at this hour?"

"What are you saying?"

"Why did the good baron have a squad of men patrolling the corridor in front of your living quarters? Is he empowered to protect you in such a fashion?"

"The fool thinks more clearly than my personal guardsmen!" Lorens leaned back, hands on his head as if this would hold back the pain. It didn't.

Archbishop Nosto's Inquisitors had stolen the Demon Crown. Baron Theoll had a squad of soldiers in the hallway outside his quarters— while his own men dallied with a serving wench. Nosto had royal blood in his veins; he could wear the Demon Crown he had stolen. The Inquisition's brutal power spread and Theoll sent men in the middle of the night and his own were away from their post and he knew nothing about it because the crown had been taken. Lorens could no longer keep his emotions in check and broke down, weeping uncontrollably.

Life had been so much simpler in the City of Stolen Dreams under his master's tutelage.

Lorens turned and buried his face in Harhar's tunic and cried. The jester gently patted him on the head, as if he were a small child instead of king of a powerful and rich kingdom.

EIGHT

Birtle Santon watched silently as Vered drew the dagger and slipped it between his own clothing and the tightly fitting red Inquisitor's uniform. A quick motion parted the fabric and Santon wiggled out of it like a snake shedding an unwanted skin.

"I feel better," he said. "It cut off my circulation."

"And I feel better for being out of Castle Porotane once again," said Vered. He glanced over his shoulder at the bramble-arched tunnel leading to the postern gate they had used so many times. "When will Lorens post a guard there?"

"Does it matter if he ever does? Neither of us will be returning by this route. If the saints are with us, we go in the main gates or we never return."

Vered nodded. What his friend said was true. They might find Lokenna. If so, putting her on the throne in place of the demented Lorens might prove impossible. If they succeeded, it would not be by riding through the huge southern gate at the head of an army.

And if Lorens caught them before they found the royal twin sister, the monarch would

never return them to the castle for trial. He
would behead them on the spot.

Santon awkwardly shucked off the remaining sleeve of the crimson uniform and kicked
the tatters under a rock and out of sight of a
casual searcher. He moved so that starlight
shone off the glass box tucked under his arm.
Santon saw Vered's sharp interest. He used his
good hand to hold the box at arm's length.

Resting within the container lay the Demon
Crown. Starlight caught on the points of the
crown and magnified so much that Santon had
to look away. When they had carried the crown
before, it had glowed a subtle shade of green.
Now the verdant radiance was more insistent—
and the blazing white tips of the metallic gold
circlet showed that the magic once dormant
within the crown had been awakened.

"It has changed," said Vered. "The brief
moment I touched it, I felt the new power."

Santon's attention turned fully to Vered.
Something in the way the man spoke seemed
different.

"Isn't it lovely?" asked Vered. The young
thief moved closer, his eyes on nothing but the
crown. "It offers so much. A touch is hardly
enough."

"What did you see when you put it in the
box?" asked Santon. He moved away so that
Vered had to trail along. He looked around,
thinking that they were still too close to the
castle. They had to find their horses and ride
once more. Lorens would send out every soldier
in Castle Porotane when he awoke and learned
of the theft. Their small deception might put the
monarch on the wrong scent, but he dared not
count on it. Let Archbishop Nosto and Baron
Theoll try to explain their doings this night.

How long this diversion would work, Santon could not say. Not long. A day? A pair of
days? He doubted that. Even if Lorens believed
the Demon Crown was still within the castle
walls, Archbishop Nosto and Theoll would
know that it wasn't. If Theoll did not send forth
men to capture them, Nosto would.

The crown was a prize to each of them.

"I saw nothing unusual," Vered said. "Only
hints of what might be. There are so many
people in the castle worthy of my attention.
Rogina? She is cunning. More so than her
sister. And what of Nosto? His Inquisition
makes corpses and enemies. Who? We can find
them with the crown and turn them to our
side."

"Why do we need them?" asked Santon. His
worry over Vered's behavior increased. It was as
if the Demon Crown had infected him with the
disease devouring Lorens' mind.

"We know little of Claymore Pass," said
Vered. "Such ignorance means danger. If I just
touch the crown to my head, I can send out a
reconnaissance unmatched by rebel or royal.
We can learn the location of every rebel trooper,
every ruffian, every cow in all Porotane!"

"Lokenna," said Santon. He used the box
containing the crown like bait to draw Vered on.
Their horses neighed and pawed the ground
nervously. Santon caught the box between
shield and body and used his good arm to swing
up onto the horse's back. He almost slid off the
other side. They needed saddles for proper
mounting and riding if they were to make good
time.

"Yes," hissed Vered. "What a fine thought! I
can use the Demon Crown to find Lokenna. Why
spend fruitless days hunting her when I can

spend only minutes with the crown and locate her?''

"Do you remember what Alarice said?" Santon used his knees to turn his horse. The roan tossed its head and sniffed the air. Finding the crisp autumn night to its liking, the roan trotted off. Behind, Santon heard Vered curse and get his own dappled gray mare onto the trail. It took only seconds for Vered to catch up and ride apace. His face shone in the pale moonlight with his enthusiasm for once more donning the Demon Crown.

"You lack enough strong arms to carry it easily," said Vered. "Let me tend to the box. I have two good arms and my balance on bareback is better."

"The Glass Warrior warned us of the insidious pull exerted by the crown. She had to use her magical abilities for over twenty years to keep from succumbing."

"What do we care of Alarice?" Vered snapped.

Santon jerked around, eyes blazing. He said nothing. Vered's expression changed from one of lust to utter confusion. The man touched his forehead, then stared at both hands as if he had never seen them before.

"Birtle, what did I say?"

"You know."

"I . . . yes, I know. But I did not mean it. I couldn't help myself. The words just slipped out because of—"

"The Demon Crown spoke for you," interrupted Santon. "Alarice warned us of its evil. If I don it, I die. Your fate would be even worse. You would become its slave."

"As Lorens is." Vered rubbed his eyes and said, "How our king must be suffering without it. I only brushed my fingertips across it and it almost possessed me. How diabolical the demon Kalob was, giving this to King Waellkin."

"For three hundred years the Demon Crown has been the focus of conflict. Porotane might be better off if we rode to the ocean and cast it in."

"No!" Vered's denial worried Santon anew.

"Please, Santon, it's not like that. I . . . I know its power over me now. I am warned. But we cannot destroy it."

"Why not?"

"This is a powerful legacy, a relic of our empire. It can be evil, yes, but if the monarch is aware and strong, it can be an even greater tool for peace and prosperity."

"The ruler's burden would be too great."

"That is not for you to decide," said Vered. "Nor is it for me, although I carry a drop of royal blood in my arteries. Think for a moment. If destroying the crown is a proper solution, why didn't Alarice do it in the two decades she was custodian?"

"She gave her promise to King Lamost— and to Duke Freow."

"A promise balanced against the peace of a kingdom? Do you think a decent, caring woman like Alarice would hesitate to dishonor herself for the good of uncounted millions of people? She would not consider only those caught up in our paltry civil war—she would think of unborn generations."

"She didn't destroy this demon device, did she?" Santon pulled his shield around and balanced the glass box containing the Demon Crown on its rounded surface. The magical brilliance of the crown shone undimmed and reflected like starlight from the glass shield.

Birtle Santon stared at it, and his thoughts turned to lovely Alarice, her white hair flowing as she rode, her trim figure that of a young maiden and not a woman years older than he.

She had ample reason to destroy it. And Alarice was a sorceress with power enough to deal with the crown's magical component. She had kept it for twenty years and had not destroyed it. Had she tried? Santon could not answer.

Perhaps she had. Perhaps she had tried and failed. If this were true, Santon knew they had no chance to destroy it. Both his and Vered's talents did not turn to magic. A strong arm in battle, a deft move resulting in a stolen money pouch, those were their talents.

"Do you think pursuit has begun?" asked Vered.

"We have an ample lead, if it has. They have to find our trail, though you might be right in thinking we should begin confusing pursuers. The River Ty lies a few leagues to the east."

"Why divert from our path north if I could just touch the crown and *see* if there is any pursuit?"

Santon's left arm had withered after being struck in battle. Over the years his right arm had grown immeasurably strong to compensate for the infirmity. He turned and put the full power of his shoulder and upper body behind the blow that landed on Vered's chest. The younger man was lifted up and off his horse by the force. He landed heavily beside the trail in a pile of leaves.

"Does that clear your head or should I bash it in and see if anything oozes out?" Santon hefted his battle-ax and spun it in a circle that could easily end at Vered's skull.

"You didn't have to knock me off my horse,"

complained Vered. He shook his head and winced at the pain. "My whole body hurts."

"What of this?" Santon tapped the glass box holding the crown.

"You keep it. I don't want to risk another fall. You could have crushed my chest." Vered rolled onto hands and knees, then forced himself up to his knees, breathing as difficult as standing. From this way station he got to his feet. His gray mare pawed at the ground impatiently. He remounted.

"I fear this journey might be our undoing unless you can control your urge to wear the Demon Crown," said Santon. "I cannot watch over you night and day."

"Mayhaps a change of clothing and some decent food will change my perspective on life. Why do I need to spy on others if I am content with my lot?"

"We have no money, we have no tack, an army might be following us, and everywhere across the land there are bands of rebels willing to slay us without even inquiring of our names. You think that a fine meal and fancy clothes are *all* you need?"

"They are a start," said Vered. "And you must admit that it's better than crowning myself."

"You carry it for a while," said Santon, handing over the glass box. He studied Vered's face as the man's eyes glowed with anticipation. But the look died as reason prevailed. Vered knew the danger of even a brief touch. That knowledge replaced the eagerness for the supreme power offered by the Demon Crown.

"Let's ride as if we meant it instead of dawdling. The stream feeding the River Ty is a good place to start losing any pursuit," Vered said. He put his heels into the gray's flanks. Santon had to gallop to catch up with his friend.

A war arrow whistled through the air and stuck into a tree trunk just beyond Birtle Santon. Reflexes caused the man to duck long after the arrow had sunk into the wood.

"You're slowing down," accused Vered. The young man's quick eyes scanned the terrain behind. They had ridden out of a thin forest and onto a plain, only to find themselves ringed by Lorens' troops. A clever retreat had gained them a few minutes and the cover of the forest once more. But the arrows arching into the air from the plain fell into the forest and drove them like cattle.

"They'll close in on us again unless we do something," Santon said. He shifted his weight in the saddle. They had stolen tack and food a day out of Castle Porotane. He wished that they had stolen a better quality of leather goods. The saddle's seat peeled and resulted in chafing after more than a week of perilous riding. All that faded into insignificance. They had eluded Lorens' soldiers until today.

"The Yorral Mountains are pretty this time of year," said Vered, his eyes focused on the horizon to the north. "The purple haze is offset so well by the first winter snows. See how the tallest mountains are capped with snow lit by the dawn's light? And is that a new storm forming around yon peak?"

"The soldiers, dammit!" flared Santon. "They will have our heads if we don't do something besides mooning over nature's beauty and the damned mountains."

"You anger so easily these days," said Vered. "Is the trip wearing you down?"

"Yes, it is," Santon said from between clenched teeth. "And if you had a whit of good sense, it'd be reducing you to the same condition."

"You want me to get mad?"

Santon sucked in cold air and exhaled, silvery plumes from his breath hanging in the chilly morning. He knew what drove Vered to this extreme. On the trip they had learned of the Demon Crown's power over the man, even though his royal blood was slight. By refusing to acknowledge his emotions, Vered had kept the crown's fatal attraction at bay.

"Claymore Pass is another two days' travel," said Santon. "We dare not let the troops know that is our destination. They can block our way too easily since they are between us and the mountains."

"Then let us go west, as if we are trying to reach the river. They might think we seek a barge to take us down the River Ty and back into the relative warmth of the southlands."

"Fine plan," said Santon. "But there are hundreds of them. How they got ahead of us I'll never know."

"They might have been on patrol," said Vered, hooking one leg across the saddle pommel and leaning forward. "A wizard's message might have alerted them about us. Or even something more common. The semaphore towers might be working once more."

Santon snorted derisively. "The rebels haven't allowed them to operate for more years than I can remember. They know the power of the royal army. The rebels' most potent weapons are speed and keeping the king in ignorance of their movements."

"All the more reason for our desperate

King Lorens to want to recover his precious crown," said Vered. Without another word, he pointed into the distance.

Santon shook his head. Attempting a ride west was out of the question. A thin column of cavalry trotted from the north, effectively cutting off travel in that direction. The flights of arrows had stopped, but the archers maintained their position to the north. They had no idea about the east and they had just ridden from the south. For all the need to succeed, Santon disliked the notion of retreating.

"No, friend, we need not backtrack," said Vered. "I have seen what your blurred vision has missed."

"My eyesight is fine." He stood in his stirrups and carefully surveyed the land gently rolling toward the river. It took several seconds before he made out a second longer column of cavalry, between the king's and the Ty.

"Rebels, aye," said Vered. "The horsemen cannot last long against the rebel troops. Unless I miss my count, they outnumber the royalist troops five to one."

"There's no way you can tell that from this distance. You're guessing."

"Perhaps," Vered said smugly. Santon cared little whether his friend knew the exact composition of the rebel band. As long as they drew the royalists' attention, that was all that counted.

"There, smoke," said Santon. The rebel forces touched the leading edge of the battle line formed by the king's men. "And dust. The archers are turning to join the battle."

"That is the only way they will drive off the rebels. It is time for us to be off for Claymore

Pass. We must slip past before anyone notices us."

"The rebels are as likely to kill us as the royalists," agreed Santon. They had been lucky in their forced ride to the north. Although they had seen several companies of rebel troops, they had avoided them easily. Most seemed intent on gathering materiel for the renewed siege of the castle and not on individual riders.

"Do you think they are Dews Gaemock's men?"

"They ride under a green and black banner," said Santon.

"Ionia again meddles in the northlands. If Gaemock learns of this, there might well be a three-way battle on those plains." Vered pulled his leg off the pommel and settled down. They rode out of the woods and onto the plain once more. Santon instinctively found the path through low, rolling hills that would shield them from prying eyes. Even though the soldiers fought on the west, they might have sentries watching for a flank attack.

"How do you stand on the rebel forces?" asked Santon. "If we are unable to find Lokenna, who would you see on the throne?"

Vered shrugged. "I never paid attention to politics. What matters it to me who collects the taxes when I pay none? Any trying to separate me from my hard-won coin is my enemy."

"We've seen how poorly Lorens has ruled."

"The crown has added to his woe. Without it, he might have been a weak but decent monarch." Vered rose in his stirrups again. "Be quick about it, Santon. Ride like the wind. The battle is nearing an end and I fear the rebel troops are withdrawing!"

Santon did not ask how Vered knew. His ears were keener and, as much as Santon hated to admit it, the young man's eyesight was better than his own. He had lived many summers and the penalties mounted, gathering like barnacles on the hull of a ship. His joints cracked and his senses failed. Santon tried not to think of the time when his strength would slip away like sand through an hourglass.

Better to die in battle.

"Ho, friend Santon, we have outdistanced any possible pursuit!" crowed Vered. But neither slackened their breakneck pace. They knew that the royalist troops might not have been hunting for them specifically—but they would hunt for them as rebel scouts now that Lady Ionia's forces had given them battle.

Birtle Santon stared ahead as his roan picked its way along the partially frozen plain. The Yorral Mountains rose as majestically as Vered had described them. And in Claymore Pass had been a battle the likes of which had not been fought in over thirty years, even in the worst years of the civil war. Hundreds, perhaps thousands, had died there and he had almost been one of that number.

The pass held bad memories for him, but what lay beyond? Where would they find Lokenna? To that he had no answer.

NINE

"The horses can't go on much longer," said Vered. The young man leaned forward in his saddle to relieve the pressure on his behind. The cold wind blowing off the steep, jagged slopes of the Yorral Mountains chapped their lips and burned their cheeks, but it was the steepness of the poor road that took its toll on their strength.

"We've got to," said Birtle Santon. "Lorens' guardsmen have found our trail again."

"Too bad Ionia's rebels couldn't have occupied them longer. I never cared much for that woman. All brag and no do."

"She's kept this section of Porotane in an uproar for over six years," said Santon. He stretched to get the kinks out of his tired, knotted muscles. His left arm throbbed dully, more annoying than painful. The withered hand flopped bonelessly and above his wrist along his forearm the tight straps on the glass shield Alarice had given him cut brutally into swollen, numb flesh.

"An alliance with Dews Gaemock might suit her. But there were rumors around the castle that she had approached him under a truce and attempted to kill him."

"I heard similar rumors," said Santon. "She was partly responsible for him lifting his siege of the castle in the spring." Santon's thoughts turned to those turbulent days. During Gaemock's siege Alarice had crept into Castle Porotane and left on Duke Freow's mission to find the royal twins. It had been shortly after that he and Vered had come across the Glass Warrior in the forest.

Santon slipped from the saddle and landed heavily on the loose stone in the roadway. He led his roan to give the noble steed a rest. The going got harder when the road appeared to climb straight up the side of a cliff. But such was road building in the Yorral Mountains.

"Where do we go? Claymore Pass is long, if I remember my geography aright," said Vered.

"It goes through to Ionia's fiefdom on the far side of the mountains," said Santon. "But we need to find villages, towns where someone might have heard of Lokenna."

"She might not be known by that name," said Vered. "We have a long and difficult search ahead of us. Damn all wizards!"

"Tahir stole the twins, but it was Patrin whom we should blame."

"I blame them all." Vered turned up the collar of his jacket as cold winds whipped down from the highest peaks. To the north and west gathered storm clouds of prodigious size and impenetrable blackness.

Santon had noticed those clouds as soon as they reached the foothills. No normal storm formed in that fashion—or no storm he had ever seen. The Wizard of Storms hid somewhere to the north of the Uvain Plateau. Santon had a feeling in his gut that the reclusive wizard was responsible for the towering columns of jet black clouds and the turbulence that overflowed into the Yorral Mountains.

"It is cold for this time of year. Cold for any time of year," complained Vered, lowering his head even more to shield himself from the wind.

Santon said nothing about his suspicions regarding the source of the fiercely biting wind. It might be the harbinger of an unusually early winter—or it might be wizardry.

"Hold for a moment. Let an old man rest." Santon watched Vered sink to the hard ground for a precious minute of not walking uphill. Santon did not sit. He looked back along their path for signs of pursuit. No dust cloud could rise from that rocky road, but he saw suspicious glints off shiny metal. Estimating distances in the clear, cold mountain air was difficult but Santon thought that Lorens' troopers were several hours behind them. Weighed down with armor and battle gear, the guardsmen made slower progress through the foothills and lower mountain slopes.

He considered several courses of action. They might take the time to lay an ambush. Rocks rolled down from the heights were devastating and easy to find, but he didn't want to use this ploy. Not unless there was no other way. Although a few large boulders might eliminate the entire force, if they didn't, he and Vered would face angry survivors. Better to keep ahead and tire out the soldiers.

"We can hide and let them go past," spoke up Vered, again uncannily reading his friend's thoughts.

"I don't think that would work. Our trail is faint on rock, but there are too few good places to hide. The steep walls keep us bottled up like cattle in a chute."

"So we ride ahead of them like corks bobbing on a tidal wave."

"Something like that," Santon admitted. He surveyed their route ahead. For an hour they would be going downhill but Santon saw that this was the last such stretch they would find for days. Only when they reached Claymore Pass would the terrain level out, and even this was small help for their straining lungs and aching muscles. The floor of the pass was several thousand feet above the level of the castle. Any exertion would tire them quickly. Riding would help but their horses would weaken without frequent rests.

Trying to cross the Yorral Mountains and not using Claymore Pass was impossible for a man on horseback.

"When do we encounter the checkpoints?" asked Vered. "I cannot believe Ionia allows anyone through the mountains without a fight."

"She knows that Porotane is ill-equipped to attack, even through the pass. She might not guard the way well."

"It wouldn't take many men. A few companies would make her fiefdom invincible."

"That's Ionia's trouble. She has no population on which to draw for her army. The few farmers working their poor, rocky lands protest losing their sons to Ionia's army. Her constant forays into Porotane do not please many at home. She must watch not only Lorens but those in her own country."

"Why bother, then?" asked Vered. "She could stay at home and tend to her vassals."

Santon laughed. "Vered, Vered, I'm surprised at you. What does lust for power have to do with practicality? Ionia desires control of

Porotane even though she has no reasonable chance to conquer a country ten times the size of her own and with a population a hundred times greater. But the lure of power and wealth has infected her, and *that* drives her on, not good sense."

"She would have done well to ally herself with Gaemock," Vered said. "She could have carved out a moderate kingdom on the far side of Claymore Pass and defended it well. From there she could have turned against Gaemock and sallied forth against him when he least expected it.

"Again, that is reasonable. I do not think she is any saner than Lorens—and he has the excuse of wearing the Demon Crown."

"Is there any way we could enlist her aid in finding Lokenna?" asked Vered. "Even if she has only a few hundred soldiers in the area, that magnifies our chance of finding her by a few hundred."

"We do not want to alert Ionia of our search." Santon started down the long incline, leading his roan. Ionia was treacherous, of that there could be no doubt. What would the mercenary would-be queen do if she found Lokenna before they did? Kidnapping? Murder? Santon didn't know. Whatever course benefited Ionia most would be followed. And did Ionia carry royal blood in her veins? Santon knew little of countries beyond Porotane and how their rulers were related, if at all, to those in Porotane.

The lure of the Demon Crown would be too great for a power-hungry ruler to refuse. Ionia would subjugate Lokenna, if possible, kill her if necessary—and she would try the crown for herself no matter how great the warnings.

"Secrecy serves us best in our search," Santon said as they reached the bottom of the incline and faced the steady climb up to the floor of Claymore Pass.

"Why do I always feel abandoned?" asked Vered.

Santon had to laugh at this. "It's because you always have been. The bastard offspring of some noble, rebels burning your village and killing your mother, constables in a hundred villages longing to cut off your ears and nail them to their punishment posts—where in all that is anything but abandonment?"

"I can always count on you to cheer me up," Vered said sourly. He, too, looked up the steep slope ahead and asked, "Can we ride? For a while?"

Santon answered by remaining afoot. The horses would be needed later. He knew. He had been in Claymore Pass before.

"With so many deep ravines, it's a wonder that water is so hard to find," said Vered.

"With so much rock, you wonder?" responded Santon. They had found a small, scraggly stand of trees in a level spot and had camped here. It took some digging before Santon had found a tiny trickle of water. "Rain runs directly off. It can't soak into the ground."

Vered swung his glass sword and scraped the ground, revealing nothing but solid stone beneath a thin layer of dirt. "I see your point." He looked around and shook his head. "Is there nowhere else to camp? I don't like this place."

"There's nothing wrong with it. We have a good view of the road. Should Lorens' men begin to narrow the distance between us we will have ample warning. And there is even some small game to be had around here trying to find water."

"Fresh meat is worth the risk," admitted Vered.

"What risk? Other than being in the Yorral Mountains?"

"You said that battles were fought throughout Claymore Pass. This is the mouth of the pass, isn't it? I feel a lingering *presence* that bothers me."

"There will be phantoms," admitted Santon. "We cannot do anything about them. But I did not know you were so sensitive to their presence." He frowned as he looked from his friend to the glass box containing the Demon Crown. Had such a brief encounter with the potent magical device imparted some measure of sorcerous power to Vered? As far as he could tell, the Demon Crown had lain quiescent in its beveled-glass case since being taken from the king's chambers. The brilliance of the crown's points remained but the putrescent green glow had subsided and returned to the more familiar verdant green before Lorens had donned it.

"We'll keep a sharp lookout," Santon said. "We don't want the king's troops sending a scout ahead to find us."

"It would take only a few to do us in," said Vered. He danced from foot to foot to keep warm, rubbing his hands together and then slapping himself on the shoulders. "I might have been more exhausted in my life but I cannot remember when."

"It's the altitude," said Santon. "And the cold. And the idea of being constantly chased."

"All that," said Vered. "And more."

He did not go into detail and Santon did not press the issue. They prepared a small meal from their trail rations. Santon vowed to hunt for game in the morning, but now, like his friend, he was too tired to do more than unroll a blanket and sleep.

Vered took the first watch. Two hours into the night he shook Santon awake. The older man shivered in the cold and wrapped the blanket more tightly around his shoulders. He found a rough-barked tree trunk to rest against and drew up his knees. The smaller the target for the biting wind, the better.

Santon strained to hear sounds in the night. Vered snored. He ignored that. The wind blowing through trees mostly shorn of their summer foliage produced an eerie whining. No animal sounds came to him. More important for his peace of mind, no sounds of approaching soldiers could be heard.

Santon walked around their tiny camp occasionally to keep awake, but he began to think the effort wasn't worth it. He craned his neck back and studied the constellations in the pure black sky. By their slow wheeling he kept track of the time.

He nodded, jerked awake, and began to nod off again when a distinct voice said, "I need your aid, fellow soldier."

"Are you dreaming, Vered?" Santon mumbled. "You were never a soldier." It took several seconds for Santon to come fully awake. Vered had not spoken. Across their low campfire he still snored away contentedly.

"I am a soldier. I was," the voice came again. "Sergeant of Scouts Ruirik Kulattian begging for your aid."

Santon's hand flew to his dagger but he did not draw. He had heard no one approaching camp. He got to his feet and turned about slowly. Nothing.

The voice came again.

"Please help me. It is so lonely in this terrible cold nothingness. I cannot even talk to my own kind. They drift just beyond the range of my voice and hearing."

"A phantom!" Santon saw a misty white patch weaving in and out of the wind-bent tree limbs above him. The mist took on a form he almost recognized as human before the strong, gusty wind carried thin tendrils downslope.

"Wait!" Santon called. "Ruirik Kulattian, wait!"

The phantom's torso became more substantial. Santon swallowed hard. There were no arms or legs—or head.

"Will you aid me? After all these years, are you the one who can deliver me to my deserved rest?"

"How long have you roamed these hills?" Santon asked. "Did you fall in Claymore Pass?"

"I did. For King Lamost I gave my life."

"I was a private in the army. Only fifty escaped Claymore Pass alive."

"Many still roam these mountainous trails," said Ruirik Kulattian. "Before I joined them, I pitied them. Then I died." The torso firmed until it glowed an eerie white. No legs touched the ground but faint hints of long, thin arms and a head appeared until a sudden gust of wind whipped them away.

"It's been more than twenty years," said Santon.

"So many," the phantom said sorrowfully.

"I guessed but did not know. There is no way to measure the passage of time. The seasons change but often confuse me since I am without sensation other than the coldness that invades my ectoplasm. Without true form or sensation, the world around me is all so vague."

"What's going on?" came Vered's sleepy voice.

"A visitor. A phantom late of King Lamost's army. A comrade in arms of mine, though I never met him."

Ruirik Kulattian solidified even more. Santon thought that the spirit forced himself to materialize. The set of the body and the determined expression on the indistinct face showed the importance of being seen to Kulattian.

"I tire of endless roaming. There is no death for me, only half life. Take me from this nothingness. I beseech you, as a comrade in arms, as a warrior, as a man, I beg you!"

Santon and Vered exchanged glances. Vered said, "How many other phantoms drift through Claymore Pass?"

"I do not know," said Kulattian's ghost. "I cannot talk to other phantoms. It is my curse to be trapped between worlds, neither alive nor dead. Others such as I are beyond my reach."

"What can you tell us of our world?" asked Vered, hunkering down and pulling his blanket around his shoulders.

"Do we barter?" asked Kulattian. "Have you no humanity and make me beg for release? Find my body and bury it properly!"

"Tell us of other humans in the area. King Lorens sends his soldiers after us."

"King Lorens? But Lamost is ruler of Porotane. There is no King Lorens."

"His son."

"Lamost has no children."

"You died before the birth of his children — twins," said Vered. "We seek his daughter Lokenna."

"A queen on the throne of Porotane," murmured Ruirik Kulattian, as if the concept lay far beyond his credulity. Santon had difficulty remembering that the phantom had been born in a different time and had died before the civil war wracked the country. When so many died, ability replaced consideration of gender.

"Lamost was foully murdered. A poison, though it was never proven. We have his crown and seek his daughter. We would crown her as Queen of Porotane."

"The Demon Crown," Ruirik said, his voice thin and reedy like the wind in high branches. "That is what draws me to you. Such power. I . . . I feel it. I actually *feel* it. It gives me warmth."

"The demon power is strong," said Vered. "We must be wary that wizards might sense it and be drawn to us."

Santon glanced into the dark night toward the distant peaks to the northwest. He was unable to see the gathering thunderstorm but knew the Wizard of Storms summoned his forces. Did the wizard know where they travelled? Did the Demon Crown serve as a beacon for those able to use—or misuse—its power? Birtle Santon had no easy answers.

"You cannot see other phantoms," said Vered, "but you can detect other humans. What of those following us?"

Ruirik Kulattian's substance thinned to a white streamer that twisted skyward and became so transparent that stars shone through. As quickly as the phantom had left, he returned, his appearance subtly different. Santon saw more character in the face now. Sergeant Kulattian gained in ability every time he reformed his body.

"A squad. Clumsy men. They know little of mountain warfare. They are burdened by useless armor. They sleep two leagues behind you, downslope and in a dry camp."

"That will slow them even more on the morrow," said Santon. "Their horses need water as much as the men." He straightened. "Thank you, Ruirik. This is important to us."

"Service for service," the phantom said, his tone pleading. "Find my body and bury it in a consecrated grave. Take me away from this senseless half-existence."

"You helped us, but there is no way we can aid you," said Vered. "Claymore Pass is long and the battles you speak of were fought long ago. Unless you can pinpoint your corpse, we have no way of finding or identifying it."

"I cannot locate my own body. Such power is denied me."

"I am truly sorry," Santon said, trying to lay his hand on the phantom's shoulder. His good hand passed through thin white fog and disrupted Ruirik Kulattian's body for several seconds. The phantom reshaped himself.

"I cannot locate my own body," Ruirik said. "Such is denied to a phantom. But you seek another."

"Lokenna, daughter of Lamost," said Vered. "Do you know of her?"

"Find my corpse and properly bury it," said Ruirik Kulattian, "and I will tell you where to find the royal heir. *I know where she lives in these hills.*"

TEN

"He might be lying," said Vered. "He might say what we want to hear simply to be free of his half-world existence."

"That is so," said Birtle Santon. To the phantom, he said, "How do you answer such a challenge? Do you lie only to win free of your current condition?"

"I would, if it benefited me. You cannot know the pain I feel. Not physical," Ruirik Kulattian hastened to add, pieces of his insubstantial body getting caught up in small eddies as the wind curled around the mountaintops and gusted downward into the Ty Valley. "I suffer psychic pain. I can talk only to those who still live."

"Other phantoms ignore you?" asked Santon.

"There is a barrier between the others and myself. I do not know if I have been singled out for this punishment or if it is universal. I can talk to those who live, not to those who are in transition—or beyond."

"Do you know what lies . . . beyond?" asked Vered.

"No. If it is total oblivion, I will greet it with

gladness. If it is more or less than I endure now, that will be its own reward. There is no change in this state. None. And it is so lonely."

"Most mortals want nothing to do with phantoms," observed Santon. "With good reason, too. Why should we be reminded of the slow march of days toward our own death?"

"Although I lack substance, I can drift from village to village much faster than you can travel. My search will be tireless. I have nothing else to fill my days."

"So you really don't know where Lokenna is," accused Vered.

"I can find her. I know of a village where one with this name lives."

"But?" urged Vered. "There is more. What is it?"

"I do not know how long ago she lived there. It might be a moment, or it might be a decade. In my phantom's existence, time is meaningless." Ruirik spread his vaporous hands in a gesture of helplessness.

"You'll do this searching in exchange for our finding your body and burying it?" Vered shook his head. "It seems our mission changes. We hunt for Ruirik's corpse while he looks for Lokenna. One search is as difficult as the other. If anything, our finding Lokenna might be the easier. She is alive and must have contact with others. If those others speak with still more, we can trace back the threads until we find the tapestry, if you get my meaning."

"What he says is true, Ruirik. It will be simpler for us to hunt for Lokenna on our own."

"Speed," the phantom said. "I can move more quickly. You have little time before the soldiers overtake you."

"They have followed us for long days. We can continue to elude them," said Santon.

"Claymore Pass is narrow and treacherously rocky. Dodging an enemy between those stone walls is impossible. If you were there as you claim, you remember."

Santon nodded. He remembered too well. They had tried to outflank the brigands and had failed. That move cost them fully half their fighting force. Any maneuver other than outright retreat or frontal assault had been thwarted easily.

"The soldiers follow us whether we hunt for Lokenna or your body," said Vered. "We gain nothing by adding this new complication."

"Not so," argued the spirit. "I can find Lokenna and lead you directly to her. If they dog your steps, you take them to her even as you search. The longer you hunt, the closer they get to you."

"A good point," said Santon.

"And if the soldiers overtake us when we find your body," continued Vered, "you can plead with them to bury you in a proper grave. They might take pity on you."

"That is so. They have no quarrel with Sergeant Ruirik Kulattian who died before many of them were born and who served the same throne."

"That poses a dilemma for us," said Santon. "Your honesty. We carry out our part of the bargain—but what keeps you from leading Lorens' guardsmen to Lokenna?"

"Why should I do this?"

"Our only hold over you is not burying your corpse. You might find a better deal with the soldiers."

"In all my dealings, I was honest."

"But you've admitted you would do any-thing to escape your current fate. Lying is a small price to pay."

Ruirik Kulattian said nothing. And Santon had little else to add. They either trusted one another or they didn't. The spirit's argument about their search leading the troopers directly to Lokenna carried much weight. The barren mountains did not offer much in the way of shelter. After only a few inquiries, the officer in charge of the squad would be on their trail.

"Where did you fall in battle?" Santon asked.

Kulattian's phantom asked, "We have an agreement?"

"We need more information. If we are to search these saints-deserted hills, we need a starting point."

"I am sorry. I cannot tell you. I was struck in the back by a war arrow. The poisons on the barbed head put me into a coma. I have the impression of being carried for hours—perhaps days or even weeks—before dying. All I know is that I died in Claymore Pass."

"A long stretch of rock," muttered Santon. The task appeared impossible. Louder, he said, "Very well. We will seek out the bones of all those fallen and bury the ones we can identify. You realize that if we cannot properly identify your body among the others, we cannot conse-crate the grave and release you?"

"I will take that risk. Do what you can and I will find Lokenna for you."

"Agreed," said Santon, holding out his hand. A tendril of white vapor curled out and placed itself atop the man's good hand. Vered inched closer and placed his hand over the misty patch of phantom flesh.

"Agreed," Vered said.

"For all eternity will I search to carry out my promise. Agreed!" Ruirik Kulattian spun about his glowing core so rapidly that pieces of his substance spun off into the night. Within seconds nothing remained of the phantom.

"I hope we're doing the right thing," said Vered. "How can we trust a spirit?"

"You must," came a low voice.

"Easy for you to say," said Vered. Then he stared at Santon. "Your lips didn't move."

"That's because I didn't speak." They turned, hands on weapons. Less than a dozen paces away another phantom hung in a vaporous column.

"Finding you has been hard," the phantom said in a voice that brought a tear to Santon's eye.

"Alarice!" he cried.

"There is so little time." Santon paid no attention. He rushed forward, arm reaching for her. His mighty forearm passed through the phantom, scattering its gauzy substance. The ghostly figure reformed more quickly than Ruirik's had. "I must not waste energy," Alarice chided gently. "You must listen."

Vered gripped Santon's shoulders and held him in place. "Go on," Vered said. "You sent us here. Where is Lokenna? You can find her. We don't need the other phantom now."

"You do. I must not linger. I cannot. There is a magic coming alive in Porotane unlike any in my experience. The Wizard of Storms meddles once again. He is drawn to the power of my phantom."

"Your body," asked Santon. "Where is it? Still in the Desert of Sazan? We'll find it and give it a proper burial. I swear on my sacred honor!"

"That is nice but unnecessary. Let Ruirik find Lokenna. You must avoid Lorens' soldiers. They are almost upon you."

"We can outrun them."

"Take care!" Alarice warned. "Claymore Pass holds more than memories. Dalziel Sef's troops return from parley with Ionia."

"They're ahead of us in the pass?" Vered turned and looked, as if he could see them in the darkness. "That means we're caught between two war parties!"

"Alarice, there's so much you must tell me." Santon reached again for the Glass Warrior's phantom but she had dissipated, another victim of the strong wind blowing across the rocky slopes. He stood, his good arm futilely reaching out for her.

"She's gone again," said Vered in a soft voice. "She'll return."

"How she must suffer. You heard what Ruirik said. What must the existence be like for one as vital as Alarice?"

"She has powers Ruirik doesn't. She must have heard him tell us his tale of woe. She might be able to communicate with other phantoms. If not, she can at least eavesdrop on them. She was more than a doughty warrior, Santon old friend, she was also a sorceress of considerable ability."

"She fought Patrin to the death and he was supposed to be the strongest wizard in the kingdom."

"No longer," said Vered. "She fears the Wizard of Storms. We should, also."

"We should fear what the soldiers will do to us if they catch us. Let's get our gear ready. We must ride like the demon-cursed wind or we'll be trapped between them!"

"Wait, Santon. You're always telling me to make haste slowly. We should consider our next move with great care, or we might end up like Ruirik."

Santon said nothing to this, but the thought crossed his mind that it might not be a sorry fate. He might be able to again touch Alarice. No matter that they would both be phantoms. Just to be together with the lovely woman once more. . . .

"They ride early. Dawn has barely ignited the eastern sky." Vered shifted in the saddle as he peered down the valley at a single-file line of riders.

"Morning comes late in the mountains. The peaks block the sun until almost midday," said Birtle Santon. "A good commander would have had his men ready for the trail long before first light."

"Definitely Dalziel Sef's troops. Even though I see no banner, look at the way they stagger their line. No one is going to drop rocks on them from above and do much damage."

Santon studied the formation that Vered commented on. The rebel commander had his men spaced so that rock slides might kill a few but most fighting men would escape. He had either fought before in Claymore Pass or he had imagination.

Santon hoped it was the former. Any show of intelligence on the part of their enemies might mean their deaths.

"Lorens' troopers are less than an hour's travel behind us," said Vered, turning in his saddle to look backward.

Santon didn't listen to his friend's description of troop placements and their relative strengths. He concentrated on the jagged terrain. It had been many years—decades!—since he had been here, but the memory refused to fade. It had been brutal slaughter along that narrow trail. For weeks his troops had dealt bloody death to the brigands, only to have it returned when they encountered a force too strong to break with a frontal assault.

Somewhere in that valley lay Ruirik Kulattian's body. But where? The elements would have bleached the bones after the insects and mountain hawks had stripped the flesh from the skeleton. Or had Ruirik been left in the pass at all? He had said he was injured. The wounded men had been carried until suitable shelters could be found.

He began scanning the sheer cliffs for signs of caves. If his commander had discovered a small cave, he would have dispatched the medical team there with the wounded. Ruirik might have died in a cave. Santon shuddered. He could deal with chalky bones left twenty years in the sun and wind. A body placed in a protected cave might have mummified. He chided himself for such morbid thoughts. He had no fear of the dead. Phantoms did little more than annoy the living; they had no substance to do real harm. But the soldier's ancient fear of the dead and dying came back fully to him.

"Both sides have sighted us," said Vered. "We are in for a busy day."

"What? Already?" Birtle Santon snapped out of his reverie. A lone scout raced back along Claymore Pass to alert the rebel captain. He craned his neck and saw that a royalist soldier also galloped to inform his leader. Whatever they had planned was now past changing.

"Are you ready to lead them into one another's arms?"

"Neither has seen the other side?"

"How can they? Both scouts ran like the wind to report our presence. If they had waited even a minute before reporting, both would know. But not now."

"Let's hope that is so," said Santon. He had no stomach for deadly games such as this.

He urged his roan down the stony slope of the hill and into the valley that was Claymore Pass. He waited for Vered to join him. The younger man seemed to be enjoying his ruse.

"Which side do you want?" asked Vered. "Rebel or royalist?"

"What does it matter?" Since Santon's horse faced the rebels, he put his heels to the animal's bony flanks and shot forward. Behind him he heard Vered laugh. Then only the echoing clatter of the gray's hooves against flint could be heard.

Santon adjusted his shield and jerked at the thong around his wrist holding his battle-ax. It would not do to lose his most deadly weapon in the heat of combat.

His heart rose and clogged his throat when he saw that he faced not a lone scout but three. He had come too far to rein in and turn his horse. He continued to urge the steed forward. Attack might mean survival. Retreat meant only death.

A battlecry rose in his throat as he charged. A flick of his wrist brought the heavy ax up and into his grip. The thick shaft reassured him. The *thunk*! as an arrow glanced off his shield reassured him. The fear on the scouts' faces reassured him. He was again in battle!

His ax flowed in an arc level with his shoulders. He felt the impact as the well-honed blade struck the first scout's sword blade and snapped it off at the hilt. The scout tumbled backward from his saddle, falling heavily to the ground.

Well past him, Santon ignored the fallen rebel and turned to the second and third. Between them he rode, shield protecting him on one side and his ax finding a fleshy berth on the other. The wounded scout doubled over but stayed in the saddle. He turned and trotted back toward the main force.

Santon let him go. That was part of the plan.

And he found himself fully engaged with the remaining scout. The man did not fight well but fear and desperation gave him added strength. The tip of his sword raked along Santon's forehead and opened a shallow, bloody gash. Santon spurred his horse into a full gallop.

He had been wounded like this before and knew the danger. Blood gushed from the scratch and blinded him. The world turned red as the blood worked its way beneath his tightly shut eyelids. Santon dropped his ax and let it dangle from the wrist thong while he wiped away the blood.

He blinked rapidly and cleared his vision. As he had hoped, the scout had not pursued. The man had been so surprised that his feeble attack had driven off the warrior who had severely wounded one and downed another that he had failed to take advantage of his lucky sword stroke.

Ahead Santon saw Vered waving his arms.

Santon lifted his shield in acknowledgment. His friend had not found it difficult chasing the royalist scout.

"What happened?" Vered demanded.

"A lucky cut, nothing more. Let's ride. We don't want to tarry. There are three scouts behind."

"Only one on my side. I had to work to let him escape. What a fool!"

Santon and Vered rode hard back up the hill from which they had sighted the two opposing forces. By the time they reached the summit, their horses gasped and stumbled. There would be no more running—for a time.

"Let me tend that cut. It's leaking again."

Santon winced as Vered plucked a weed from the ground and applied its astringent to the wound. It took several seconds before the sides of the cut began to pucker and close.

"Hurts like a demon spitting on it," said Santon.

"Be glad that lucky cut didn't land a bit lower. You might be grinning from a new mouth." Vered touched Santon's neck to show where such a slash would have been.

They turned to see how their plan progressed. Santon forgot about his minor cut. Dalziel Sef's rebel force charged forward in a fan-shaped battle formation. Lorens' troops moved more slowly. They had already fought their way up steep slopes from the valley of the River Ty. Their horses and men were tired.

"This is like watching a boulder plunge from a cliff. It seems to move in the air so slowly," said Vered with some glee. "No real motion at first, then it picks up speed and goes faster and faster." He smiled broadly when the two forces spotted each other.

"Then the rock hits the ground and shatters," finished Santon. The rebels had the advantage of position and formation and used it. He watched with no real pleasure as the rebel forces let out a battlecry and charged. The royalist troops had an inferior position, lesser numbers, and the disadvantage of exhaustion.

But still they fought well. To the last man they fought well. Birtle Santon watched, thinking how similar this had been to the slaughter he remembered so vividly from more than twenty years ago.

ELEVEN

"A rider just reported sighting Lorens' troops in Claymore Pass," said Dalziel Sef. "I am at a loss to understand why the king would have such a large force there."

"A better question," said Dews Gaemock, "is why you had troops in the pass when we concentrate our forces in the south for another siege of the castle."

"It wasn't a *large* company," Dalziel Sef said, smiling broadly and holding out his hands to show his innocence. "They merely returned from negotiations with Ionia. They had been sent before our, umm, agreement to join forces for this new attack on Lorens."

Gaemock said nothing to this. The timing was poor. Dalziel Sef might have sent his representative to Ionia before the parley began, but Gaemock doubted it. Sef played his own game and thought to align himself with Ionia to control the northern reaches of Porotane. Cut off Claymore Pass and an important escape route could be denied to the rebels. It took little effort to get a fleeing army aboard barges and take them up the River Ty. From shallow-water ports near the foothills of the Yorral Mountains it was only a short journey into the pass and to freedom—in Ionia's fiefdom.

Cut off the pass, and such an interdiction would take only a handful of men, made a retreating army fair game for royalist troopers.

"How are preparations going for the siege?" asked Gaemock.

"Well. We have the design for a new siege engine that can throw boulders so large that five men cannot reach around them."

"Getting ammunition for this mighty catapult will prove chancy, won't it?"

"The basket is large for such a boulder. However, we think to throw in burning debris. Perhaps lighted pitch torches. We can burn them out." Sef smiled even more. "If nothing else, we can burn away the brambles surrounding the castle and give ourselves good ground for lifting ladders to their battlements."

"Such an assault will fail. It always has. We must break their will. Only surrender works, not attrition."

"With Lorens able to observe our every movement the siege might last a long time. We must show great strength and determination if we are to cow him."

"The Demon Crown gives him courage," said Gaemock. "We must break the will of those on the battlements."

"We will." Sef's confidence proved contagious and Gaemock felt himself believing such an attack could work. Gaemock watched the other rebel warlord saunter off to inspect his troops. Gaemock waited until Dalziel Sef vanished from sight, then slipped past the inner ring of sentries and started walking toward the distant castle.

Darkness enveloped him like a shroud. The

northern winter winds came early and their siege would be costly in lives if it did not end soon. They had been unable to find adequate food for their troops; it would not do having his freezing, starving men staring at the warm, well-fed royalists patrolling the castle's battlements. Gaemock felt an obligation to try the siege now but would lift it within a month in favor of a new siege before spring planting. If he could prevent foodstuffs from reaching the castle next year, he had a good chance to win by attrition.

His only hope for ending this attack was a poor harvest and lack of larder to feed those within Castle Porotane.

Gaemock stopped, turned to his left, walked a few paces, then retraced his path, every sense alert for anyone tracking him from the rebel encampment. Satisfied that he was alone, he continued toward the castle. The sound of the rushing river died behind him and the land turned loamy beneath his boots. An hour's walk brought him to the edge of a large field.

Castle Porotane loomed large and menacing, deep black against the lesser black of the nighttime sky. Again Dews Gaemock checked to be sure that he was not followed from the rebel camp. He dared not let anyone see who he met this night. They would brand him a traitor, in spite of his fine record against the royalists.

Gaemock grinned without humor when he thought of Sef's reaction if he blundered on this nocturnal meeting. He did not trust the other rebel leader, and he was sure Dalziel Sef did not trust him. This would be proof of duplicity.

No one followed—or if someone did, they were a better woodsman than Gaemock. He doubted this was possible. Much of his life, after leaving his fine grain farm to royalist tax collectors, had been spent in the forests as a hunter and scout. With a sureness in his stride, he went directly to the edge of the farm where a stump had been blasted by lightning. He settled on the blackened seat and waited.

Ten minutes later he heard a faint jingling noise.

"Bells? You have bells announcing your entrance? You have truly spent too much time in the castle. You have been seduced by their decadent ways."

From the direction of the faint jingling bells came a booming voice. "Dear brother, you are never suspicious enough. You have vision but no fear."

"I leave that to tacticians such as yourself. I can plan grand, sweeping campaigns. Only the details bog me down."

Gaemock rose and turned. Before him stood Harhar in his jester's costume. The two embraced, then held one another at arm's length.

"It's been too long since I saw you, Dews."

"Nonsense. It's been less than a month."

"Much has happened in that time," said the jester. He stripped off his peaked hat and tossed it aside. He carefully removed the threads from his fingers. The bells behind them jingled as he tugged on the invisible cords.

"Efran, leave this playacting. Return to camp with me. We don't need you risking your life inside the castle. We know all there is to know of those fools."

"You don't include me with the fools? I play the fool, yes, but like me none within Castle

Porotane really *are* fools. Ambitious, cunning, dangerous—but no fools. Those who were slow to learn have long since been executed."

"Lorens continues his purges?"

"Lorens has run out of people to put to death, but Archbishop Nosto finds new heretics to put to the Question every day."

"Can we use this to create a rebellion from within?"

Efran Gaemock—Harhar—shook his head. "Nosto blends faith and fear too well. Many go to their death praising him."

"Theoll? What of the baron?"

"He tasted a moment on the throne after Freow died and before Lorens came from the Desert of Sazan with the crown. He has become addicted to that high position, but he is not careless in his pursuit to regain it. Even after it became apparent that I was giving Duke Freow an antidote to his poison, Theoll did not panic."

"Does he know you were aiding the old duke?"

"He might suspect, though I doubt it. I have become confessor to both Theoll and Lorens." Efran Gaemock laughed a deep, rich laugh. "What a position! Both consider me an idiot— and safe."

"A dangerous position. Take care, my brother." Dews Gaemock settled down on the lightning-struck stump. "But I must know of the castle supplies. Can they withstand a siege if we begin immediately?"

"The larder is full. Theoll and Nosto have seen to that. Lorens spent all his days wearing the Demon Crown and spying on other parts of the realm. Without the baron and archbishop, the castle would be ripe for the plucking."

"There is something in your words that tells me you hide an important fact. What do you hold back, Efran?"

"There might be much to gain by restraining your soldiers for a few days. Perhaps a week would suffice."

"Why? Does Theoll plan to assassinate the king?"

"I am sure he has such a scheme brewing, and if he knew the truth he would strike immediately. King Lorens no longer wears the Demon Crown."

"Its magic has finally worn him down?" Dews Gaemock considered what his brother had said. His dark eyes widened. "The crown is stolen! Is that what you're telling me?"

"I cannot be sure who stole it. The pair who accompanied Lorens back from the Desert of Sazan, perhaps."

"Why would they steal it? They installed him on the throne."

"These two, Vered and Santon, play their own game—or that of the Glass Warrior."

"She is dead? Truly?"

"She is. Or Santon and Vered so believe. They are not good enough posers to feign such sorrow. I was unable to discover what happened when they found Lorens, but the battle must have been awesome and left the Glass Warrior a casualty."

"So they have no loyalty to Lorens?"

"None. I have watched them carefully and their disgust at him and his purges has grown. It is for this reason I feel they are responsible for the crown's theft."

"We can attack immediately. Why should we hesitate now that Lorens is not able to watch our every move?"

"He has confided to me that his forces in the north have located the pair. He is contemplating leading a few companies of men personally. He is desperate to regain the crown and does not trust any underling with the mission."

"We can capture or kill him on the way! Where have his men bottled up Santon and Vered?"

"Claymore Pass."

Efran's words shocked Dews Gaemock.

"What is wrong, brother?"

"Perhaps it is only coincidence, though I doubt it." Dews explained succinctly how Dalziel Sef had patrols roaming in the Yorral Mountains and along Claymore Pass.

"This alliance might end quickly, Dews. Be on guard."

The rebel leader pushed such problems aside for the moment. "When Lorens leaves, who will be in command of the castle? Theoll?"

"Whoever Lorens puts in control will quickly fall to the baron, so, yes, let us assume he will be in charge. However, he will be robbed of full control by Archbishop Nosto and the power of his saints-cursed Inquisition."

"Turmoil," said Dews Gaemock. "They will rot from within. Castle Porotane will be ours very soon!"

"And with it the power base to control the kingdom. Even with the Demon Crown, Lorens cannot retain power without the riches and safety offered by the castle."

"He would still be a thorn in the side—a dangerous one. We must capture him as he goes to retrieve the crown."

"Good. I will signal when he leaves. A thin red banner from the northwestern tower battlements."

"Be careful, Efran," Dews said. "The castle becomes more dangerous for you with every passing day."

"How? The baron loves to tell me everything. Lorens has no other confidant. And I am beneath notice for the Inquisition. I come and go and who listens to a fool?"

"Who cares if a fool is killed?" countered Dews.

"You worry too much. You must admit that this little spy mission of mine has given us the edge in the rebellion. Without me inside the castle, Lorens and the Demon Crown would have been too powerful a combination to overcome."

"It is a shame that he hasn't proven to be the ruler his father was. I would gladly bend my knee to one such as King Lamost."

"We will see a good ruler on the throne, dear brother." Efran clamped his hand firmly on Dews' shoulder. "Wait for my signal."

"I will." The two again embraced. And Efran Gaemock vanished when he put on his peaked cap and smoothed his motley; in his place stood Harhar, the royal jester.

Dews Gaemock watched his younger brother slip back into the night, a feeling of loss overcoming his excitement at the information Efran had given him.

TWELVE

The hard blow to the center of Birtle Santon's forehead opened the sword gash once more. Blood ran down, dammed on his eyebrows, and then flooded into his eyes. The world turned red around him as he blinked and fought to wipe off the blood. He found it hard to use his shield against his attacker and let his heavy ax swing free on the thong to do so. He backpedalled and almost lost his balance.

"Vered!" he called. "Lend a hand!"

Santon's vision vanished entirely when a fresh spurt of blood came gushing down from his wound. He lifted his glass shield and cowered behind it to ward off unseen blows.

None came.

He dared to use his right hand to wipe away the blood, then dabbed gently with his sleeve to clear his eyes. He blinked. The salty burn of the blood caused a flow of hot tears that washed away the last of it.

Vered stood over the fallen rebel soldier, his glass short sword dripping gore. The thief bent over and wiped the weapon on his fallen foe's tunic.

"Have you had enough or can we find shelter? They will follow us all the way into the

jaws of a demon. Never have I seen such mindless enthusiasm for dying."

"They have a gusto for fighting that the
royalist soldiers lack," admitted Santon. "But I
would not want to meet with either at this
moment."

He stood on shaky legs. Vered helped him
back up the slope to where their horses were
tethered. The animals cropped at the sparse, dry
grass. When their masters settled for a rest, both
horses glared at them, as if accusing them of
being responsible for such a lean meal.

"How many of the royalists survived Sef's
attack?" asked Vered. "Everywhere we turn, we
find another pocket of them. Searching these
mountains is becoming hazardous."

"Time works against us," said Santon. He
carefully smeared a paste made from several
plant stalks and roots along his cut. It puckered
shut, but Santon began to worry about it ever
healing properly. Twice since he had been cut it
had opened to blind him. The first time had
been during the night. He had rolled over and
the wound had ruptured. This time was more
understandable. The rebel had stuck him in the
forehead with the butt end of his sword hilt.

"We do not want to be trapped in these
miserable, barren passes when winter begins to
cover the ground with snow," said Vered. "Why
doesn't Ruirik Kulattian report back of his
success? That demon-cursed phantom has been
lying to us. I know it! He has no intention of
finding Lokenna. He might be unable to."

"It does appear that all he wants is for us to
find his corpse and give it a burial."

"There's nothing wrong with such charitable work," said Vered. "It's just that we have so

little time to do it. Rebels and royalists everywhere! Why won't they leave us alone?"

Santon glanced toward the rucksack containing the Demon Crown. That single magical ornament drove the troops from Porotane. The rebel forces had other goads—unless the word had spread that Lorens had lost the crown. Santon shuddered at the idea of being the target for every petty rebel warlord and wizard in Porotane.

"Alarice said that we could trust Ruirik. What other choice do we have?"

"There is always another option," said Vered. "At the moment, the one I desire above all others is peace and quiet. To sleep undisturbed for an entire day, to have enough food to fill my belly, to find enough water to keep my mouth from feeling like desert sands—those are worthy goals for us to attain."

"I share them," said Santon. "How do we realize any of them? Game is sparse in the autumn. Water is always a problem in mountainous areas, and sleep? That is something I have long since given up on."

Vered mounted his gray mare and peered downslope. "Lorens' troopers march up to meet the tiny knot of resistance we stumbled across. The rebels will retreat, but that doesn't help us." He slowly scanned the countryside. He pointed to a narrow canyon leading westward. "There. Let's seek a spot there to rest."

"These side canyons were the sites of many massacres," said Santon. "Troop elements entered, only to find themselves boxed in. We don't wish to repeat previous mistakes."

"The royalist forces keep the rebels busy enough for the time being so that they forget all

about us. We will never find Ruirik's body if we
don't explore side canyons. There is little
chance of discovering his carcass in well-
travelled areas."

Santon sighed. His friend spoke the truth.
But it made him uneasy to ride into canyons
such as the one Vered indicated.

Santon climbed into the saddle. His roan
protested and tried to shy. His strong legs
guided the animal downslope and to the canyon
entrance. Again his horse protested. Santon had
come to depend on the horse's instincts. More
than once the roan had alerted him to an
ambush set by one side or the other.

"Vered, my horse is skittish."

"Mine is, also. That might mean anything.
We haven't seen troop movement in this direction."

Santon paused just inside the canyon
mouth, head cocked to one side. The sound that
had spooked his horse now became audible.
Santon settled his shield into a more comfortable position on his left arm and then swung his
ax up and into his hand.

"Birtle, wait," said Vered. The young man
frowned. "That isn't the sound of an army."

"But . . ." Santon's voice trailed off. His
friend's keener hearing had properly identified
the noise. And it was more chilling than if they
did face Lorens' entire army.

Phantoms.

"The entire valley must be filled with
them," Vered said, almost whispering.

"We seek Ruirik's body. What better place
than this?"

"We seek bodies, not more phantoms. None
of those can help us. Let us choose another

canyon to search. There are more promising ones to the north. I saw them from the hill."

"No, Vered. We look here." Santon put his heels into his roan's flanks. The horse reared and then settled down. The animal did not want to enter the canyon filled with the spirits of dozens—hundreds—of fallen warriors.

They rode forward slowly. Santon's head turned from side to side, studying the steep canyon walls. He tried to shut out the eerie, soul-searing wails that came from deeper within the canyon. He could not. Santon found himself shivering, in spite of the increased temperature in the valley.

"The rocks still hold summer warmth," said Vered. "That feels good after enduring so many chilly gusts coming down Claymore Pass. But that is all that feels good."

Santon lifted his shield and indicated a sparsely forested area ahead. He had seen low, long-limbed trees in swamps burdened with heavy hanging mosses. These tree limbs appeared to be infested with white moss—but the moss shifted position constantly. The lack of wind in the canyon contributed to lifeless heat.

"What moves the moss?" asked Vered.

"It is not moss. Those are phantoms."

Santon's guess proved correct. As they neared the stand of trees, they saw the gauzy white, insubstantial forms of scores of phantoms tirelessly shifting position, flowing upward and then collapsing back through the limbs and surging toward the ground. The ever-shifting array of spirits made Santon blink. He tried to focus on them and failed.

"They whine so," said Vered. "Never have I heard such a forlorn sound."

"They cry out for surcease," said Santon. "They might not even realize that they do."

He rode closer, keeping his horse under tight control. The animal jerked and tried to buck. Santon soothed it. He forced himself to remain calm when a thin sheet of white mist rose up from the ground and fell toward him.

He closed his eyes as the phantom passed through him. A tiny tingling at his fingertips and the end of his nose gave the only sign that the phantom even existed.

"They like you," Vered said uncomfortably. "They move toward you."

"I hope they don't sense that I will soon join their rank."

"Don't joke," Vered snapped. His discomfort was etched on every line of his wind-burned face. He sat stiffly on his horse, hand clenched on his sword hilt.

"You are the one with the flippant attitude. Come now, Vered. Don't you see any humor in this?"

"None."

Santon pulled his horse around and skirted the edge of the small forest. He halted at one point and dismounted. Santon silently motioned for Vered to remain mounted and on guard. He did not have to plead with his friend. Vered's tenseness showed that he was poised for instant flight at the slightest sound.

Santon walked slowly into the copse. The phantoms rose around him, like mist from the ground. The swirling obscured his vision but Santon pressed on. He stood and stared when he rounded a small pile of rocks. In the small depression lay a jumble of bones. He tried to restrain himself but failed. He began counting skulls as a way of estimating how many valiant men had died here.

Santon stopped at thirty.

"Please," came a soft plea. "Bury me. I was Hoaslare."

Other voices rose in chorus, each begging for surcease. "I was corporal of sentries. Wobare was my name."

"Imblade. Bury Imblade."

"Seek the body of Lespage."

"Give me grace. By the saints, bury Nicuner."

Santon backed away. The phantoms billowed around him. He stepped as if they might trip him. His substance proved more than enough to dissipate the ghostly spirits and tear them into tiny streamers. Some coalesced once more. The weaker ones vanished.

But there was no lack of new phantoms to replace them.

Vered swallowed hard and blanched when he saw Santon. "What did you find?"

"More than we can bury. At least thirty died here. My estimate is twice that number."

"So many," Vered said in a low voice. "Is there nothing we can do for them?"

"We do not even know if they were brigands or royalists."

"Does it matter? They were men. They deserve better than this damned, endless existence, if you can call drifting forever without body or companionship an existence."

"We cannot help them. We must identify and bury each. The consecration frees them from this . . . nothingness."

"Were there no nametags?" asked Vered. "Any way of identifying them would help."

"The phantoms we see might not even belong to those bleached bones. The spirits might be attracted to this spot out of hope that their bodies are here."

"Ruirik said he cannot tell which is his corpse. They are unable to identify themselves in death?"

Santon nodded sadly. "After all these years of exposure to winter cold and summer heat, there is no way we can be certain of their identity, either. Even if they carried engraved plates, who is to say we would get the proper arm bone with the skull? Such a mistake would doom them forever."

"They are already cursed," said Vered. "Can we do worse for them?"

"They give names."

"I hear their pleas." Vered shivered. "If we can do nothing, let us continue on our way. But how can we be sure that Ruirik is not among these?"

"We can't, but small deduction hints that he is not. King Lamost did not approve of leaving his dead in the open. He was not a gentle man, but he cared deeply about his troops and maintained a high level of morale. If possible, bodies would not be left in the open. Such a pit as the one I saw was the trademark of one particular brigand captain." Santon took a deep breath. "Bechadror was a beast."

"Why did he not care for those under him?" Vered's question was as sincere as it was shocked.

"Why did he doom them?" Santon laughed without humor. "Fight and win for Bechadror, or die and be forgotten. That gave a powerful incentive to his followers. I had seen his men crawl into our ranks and beg for clean death and burial."

"Did you give it to them?"

Santon laughed, this time with bitterness. "Seldom. But those we could save, we did. We found in them dedicated recruits."

"What happened to Bechadror? I remember hearing nothing of him as a power in this region."

"Who can say? My personal belief—and this was rumored widely—is that one of his own men killed him. Those were not days of mercy and justice."

"What days of war ever are?"

"Let us look along the cliff faces for caves. If Ruirik Kulattian's body is to be found, it might be there." Santon mounted and stared back toward the open pit with the bones of so many in it.

Phantoms weaved in and out of the trees, making their plaintive presence known to any of the living who passed. What had sounded like the wind whining through an Aeolian harp had been the massed cries of the phantoms.

Birtle Santon wished he could help them, give them the release from the trap between worlds in which they found themselves. But he could not. If Alarice had been here, with her special sorcerous powers, she might have aided the phantoms.

But Santon did not think so. These were the lost and nothing could be done for them except offer a moment of pity.

He prayed to the saints that he and Vered did not join these sorry ranks of floating, gauzy white, lost phantoms.

THIRTEEN

Rain pelted down and parted just before touching Kaga'kalb's face. The Wizard of Storms stood on the tallest tower of the Castle of the Winds and stared intently into the tempest raging around him. Eye-searing bolts of green and blue lightning crashed and sent waves of thunder rolling down the slopes of the mountain and across the Uvain Plateau. Winds whipped his garments and caused them to outline his thin, strong body. But Kaga'kalb paid no attention to the wind or the raging storm that had been his most recent creation.

He had played with it, orchestrating its progress across the Yorral Mountains. It had grown in intensity, then died down. A glissando, a softening, a gradual building to full-blown storm. The elements of nature became his musical instrument and he played them well.

Kaga'kalb ignored his creation to peer into a cloud overhead. Its lead-colored belly lit with an inner glow not of natural lightning but of sorcerous fire. The Wizard of Storms enticed the tiny glow, made it grow, watched intently.

Pictures appeared. Men moved. The cloudy frame of his potent scrying spell billowed and boiled with the storm feeding his wizardry. Kaga'kalb studied his larger-than-life picture and saw Dews Gaemock and another speaking. He could not hear their words over the rumble of his storm. It mattered little. Kaga'kalb knew the players in this little drama well. He had seen Efran Gaemock leave the rebel camp to become the court jester for Duke Freow. Kaga'kalb nodded in approval. Efran had courage and intelligence.

That made him more dangerous than his brother, Dews. The elder Gaemock led men well but lacked the ambition to rule. That drive burned like an ember inside Efran Gaemock. The slightest fanning of those smoldering coals would cause a conflagration that would envelop all Porotane.

Kaga'kalb watched and waited and followed Efran's winding path back to Castle Porotane, noting his secret entrance and the hidden ways built into the massive stone walls. Kaga'kalb shifted his magical focus a small amount and spied on Baron Theoll, who continued to plot against Archbishop Nosto and Lorens.

The thought of the new king caused the wizard to seek him out—but cautiously. Lorens lacked the developed sorcerous power of his former master, but Kaga'kalb still respected the bits and pieces of magic under the king's control.

Most of all he respected the awesome power locked in the Demon Crown.

Kaga'kalb frowned when he failed to find Lorens easily. The Demon Crown should have provided a pivot point around which everything in the castle revolved. The axle was gone. The Wizard of Storms summoned more power, gave himself a refreshing blast of cold rainwater in the face, and then cut off the torrential down-pour before it drowned him. He stared into the underside of the cloud, watching the movement of those within the castle—and still not locating Lorens.

Kaga'kalb worried that the wizard-king had found a way of blocking out even this potent scrying spell. With the full force of a thunder-storm powering his spell, Kaga'kalb knew that he would be unable to summon any more energy. He had reached the limit of his ability. And Lorens blocked him.

Or did he?

Kaga'kalb spread his magical search out, looking not for the Demon Crown but for the spark of Lorens' magical ability. He found it, a tiny, wavering speck hardly worthy of his notice. But the crown was not on the king's brow. Nor was it in his chamber. Kaga'kalb searched fur-ther. No cranny in Castle Porotane went un-checked.

"The crown is gone! He has allowed it to be stolen!" The shock of this knowledge rocked Kaga'kalb. How could any wizard allow such a prize as the Demon Crown to be taken?

Kaga'kalb threw out his arms and caused the storm above him to expand. As the dark cloud billowed and boiled, the scrying picture also changed scope. No longer content to view only the castle, the Wizard of Storms studied the countryside around the castle. He saw Dews Gaemock and Dalziel Sef in camp. Further. He cast further afield.

The Yorral Mountains rushed past him. The Iron Range grew in his magic picture on the churning underbelly of the cloud. The ocean beat against its shoreline and the swamp where Tahir had been imprisoned showed its scummy water and strange beats. But he failed to detect the Demon Crown.

Panic gripped him. What had happened to the most powerful relic of this empire? Kaga'-kalb again magnified the range he viewed. This time the bright dot of the Demon Crown appeared.

"Them again," he said. "What power do they possess that they can so easily make off with the crown when it is protected by Lorens so well?" Kaga'kalb reduced the energy outpouring and concentrated only on Birtle Santon and Vered. They carried the crown in the same case that the Glass Warrior had used. Kaga'kalb's fingertips danced with electrical discharges from the lightning held prisoner within the dark storm clouds. He longed to direct just one searing blast at the pair of freebooters to see what their response would be.

He did not believe that they were wizards, yet they bested those capable of intricate major spells. They carried a demonic artifact that meant death to any not of the royal line.

"They must know its power. They *do*. Then where do they take the Demon Crown? Why do they rush to Claymore Pass?"

Wild thoughts rushed through Kaga'kalb's head. Ionia? He doubted the petty tyrant commanded the resources to make use of the crown. She had no chance of even touching the Demon Crown. She was not a descendant of King Waellkin, no matter what claims she made publicly. Only her own death would result if the crown fell into her hands.

"Another," muttered Kaga'kalb. "They seek another. Why give the crown to Lorens, though, and then steal it back to seek another?"

The Wizard of Storms did not understand

all that happened. But he would. His magic controlled the storms and through them he could watch any spot in Porotane afflicted by rain.

When he learned as much as he needed to know, he would finally put things right in the kingdom. No more would petty rebel warlords disturb the serenity. No more would inept wizards vie for power that was not theirs for the taking.

But how did those two adventurers fit into the storm track of Porotane's history?

FOURTEEN

Birtle Santon shifted suddenly in the saddle, the movement almost throwing him off his roan.

"What's wrong?" asked Vered. The younger man rode up beside his friend and eyed him critically. The wound on Santon's head had not begun to heal, and this worried Vered. He was no wizard and produced no magical healing potions, but the herbs and roots he had blended into a paste should have worked. They hadn't. The ugly red gash across Santon's forehead did not bleed; it oozed constantly.

Something about the way Santon moved also bothered Vered. It looked as if Santon grew increasingly stiff. For a man as powerful as Santon, that could mean more than physical problems. He might begin to doubt his own ability, and when he did, that spelled death.

"Pain in my joints. Comes from the altitude and being too long asaddle."

"You're getting old," Vered taunted, but he hoped that Santon's explanation struck closer to the truth than his own worry about magic-induced diseases. "Any head pain?"

"What? None." Santon reached up and lightly touched the gash on his head. "You fear the soldier poisoned his sword blade? No one's done that for many a year. No reason for him to start now."

"But it was done before, back when Claymore Pass was patrolled constantly. You just said so, even though I had not known it. We should look for a potion that counters poisons."

"What poison? If he did it intentionally, there are thousands of assassin's brews to select from. More likely, he had failed to keep a clean edge. See the jagged edges of the wound? He hadn't sharpened his weapon in many a day. You worry too much, Vered."

The man snorted and shook his head. It was not his way to worry needlessly. This did not seem to fall into that bin, however. Reason for concern existed. He did not want to lose his good friend to an insidious drug. There were too many phantoms loose in these mountains without adding another to their rank.

"See the rock structure?" spoke up Santon, trying to change the topic. "Wind whips along and cuts through the softer orange and yellow rock. Like cheese, that stone. Treacherous to climb. We tried. It crumbles under your fingers."

"Still, it forms interesting statues to the saints," said Vered. "See that one? It looks like a face."

"It looks more like a knob sitting on top of a pyramid."

"You lack imagination, Santon," exclaimed Vered, warming to his topic. "Turn your head to one side and peer at it. See? Doesn't it change and become the face of King Lorens?"

He watched Santon carefully as the grizzled man canted his head to one side. The brief flash of pain mirrored on his features told Vered that the wound bothered Santon more than he admitted.

"Let's rest for a bit," Vered suggested. "My rear end feels as if all the king's chefs have been hacking and slashing at it for their ground meat specials."

"A rest would do me. I feel tired after so many hours travelling." Santon climbed down wearily and looked around. "And I must admit it, the sight of so many phantoms wears on me, too."

Vered glanced back up the sheer canyon wall at the softstone formations Santon had pointed out. Through the smaller apertures soared gauzy white streams, like water forced from a drinking bag. The phantoms rose until strong updrafts caught their substance and pulled them skyward in long, thin streamers.

"The sight of even one phantom bothers me," said Vered. "So many make me wonder if there will ever be peace in the kingdom. So many souls lost and never redeemed. So many more who will be."

"Where's the old cheerful Vered?" asked Santon. "You are becoming much too morose."

"It comes from being around you too much. We should find ourselves a nice-sized city. Not too large, but large enough. Too large, they tax their citizenry unmercifully and spend overmuch on constabulary. Too small and there isn't enough diversity."

"What do we do when we find this mythical city?"

"Ah, then we begin to enjoy ourselves. I remember a woman with hair like spun sunlight and the scent of spring. She knew tricks that amazed even me. We should hunt for her."

"After we've finished our mission," said

Santon. He gathered up the rucksack containing the Demon Crown and tucked it under his withered arm. The glass shield he had gotten from Alarice protected it and helped hold it firmly. The way he sat so forlorn and defensive made Vered sorry he had tried to shift topics to something lighter.

Santon was obsessed with duty—and the Glass Warrior. Vered had seen his friend's love for Alarice. It could not be denied, even though Alarice lay dead in the Desert of Sazan.

"Is there any hope of finding Ruirik's body in this canyon?" asked Vered, giving up on banter.

"Some. I wish he could have given more information about his company. I remember several squads splitting off and seeking out positions in side canyons. They sought areas that might be fortified and held against the brigands."

Vered looked around. "They should have built a shoulder-high wall across the mouth of this canyon. A handful of bowmen could hold back a major assault."

"Or a few archers could bottle up an entire force in this place," countered Santon. "That is the treachery of the Yorral Mountains. What is a good position suddenly turns into a death trap when a commander a tad cleverer enters the fray."

"That is always the way."

"Not so. I have been in battles where a position was defensible by any fool—and just about any fool commanded to a victory. No, Vered, the king lost his best in these canyons."

"What's that?" Vered shot to his feet, head slowly turning to locate the source of the mysterious noise.

"Another phantom wailing out his misery. Think nothing of it."

"No, it was something more. I've almost gotten used to the phantoms and their incessant wailing." Before the words left Vered's mouth, the deep rumble of thunder rolled down the canyon and echoed off the softstone walls.

"A storm."

"The sky is clear. That was thunder but there is not a single cloud to be seen." Vered's hands shook slightly. "Look to the Demon Crown. Tell me what you see."

"I . . . I don't have to look," said Santon. "The sack glows. The crown responds strongly. But to what?"

"Magic plays along these rocks." Vered turned slowly, eyes closed. A soft, warm, secure feeling came to him. He spun until he faced in the opposite direction. He groaned. His heart missed a beat and his mouth turned to desert sand.

"What do you sense?"

"Tremendous magic is at work in the direction of the canyon mouth. We might be trapped, though the spell does not seem to be directed against us. It . . . it is directed against another."

"Do you know this for sure?"

Vered nodded. "My brief moments with the Demon Crown awakened something within me. I sense magic around us now, even if I am unable to do anything about it." He smiled slightly. "If I could cast a spell, I'd lift us out of here and all the way to Blisoic."

"Why to a smelly seaport like Blisoic?"

"That's where the girl with golden hair and delicate scent lived. I remembered even as I nattered on about decent-sized cities."

"Blisoic," muttered Santon, shaking his

head. He touched the wound on his brow, winced slightly, then stood. "We must ride. If the magic envelops the canyon mouth, we might be trapped, no matter who the spell is against."

The pair rode deliberately, retracing their path. Vered grew more and more nervous as they neared the canyon entrance. The phantoms who had once swirled about through the wormholes in the rocks had vanished, as if this magic threatened even their tenuous existence.

Santon cried out, "Look yonder. Lorens' troops. A full company of them."

"Your eyes grow old and weak, Santon," his companion said, studying the more than one hundred riders on the Claymore Pass trail. "Those are Lorens' personal guardsmen. See the golden fringe on the royal banner?"

"The king rides after us personally? He wouldn't dare leave Castle Porotane with Gaemock readying a siege."

"What is the castle to him without the crown? He gambles everything to regain his legacy." Vered glanced over at Santon. The man had stowed the Demon Crown in a sling that jostled behind him as he rode. Desire rose within his breast. How easy to reach over and pluck the magic crown from his friend.

Vered closed his eyes and forced down the feeling of emptiness. How filled with power he was when wearing the Demon Crown—how fulfilled. He transcended his petty existence. No longer a vagabond wandering aimlessly, he became the single most powerful man in Porotane. In the world! With the gold circlet around his head, he aspired to godhood. He rivalled the saints and demons in power. And more.

Nothing would escape him. His senses

would sharpen and his power would be absolute.

Vered bit his lower lip until blood flowed. The pain prevented desire from becoming fact.

He wiped sweat from his forehead, even though the cold wind whipping through Claymore Pass threatened to freeze him in the saddle. The Demon Crown's pull was great, and he had to keep fighting it.

"What's wrong?" asked Santon.

"The magic. Someone uses a potent spell against Lorens."

"Are you sure he's not using it to track us?"

"Look at his troops. They are milling around like small children at play. Lorens' commander is trying to form them into a defensive position. If he knew we watched him from less than five minutes' gallop, he would have every single soldier in full flight after us."

Another thunderclap left their ears ringing. Vered's eyes rose to the sky. A single dark cloud formed above Lorens' position. Streamers of mist flickered with lightning and drooped until they dragged foggy fingers along the ground.

"Lorens is a wizard of small power and no judgment. He had not finished his apprenticeship under Patrin. Mayhaps he practices his conjurations."

Vered turned cold inside when he saw the truth before his eyes. King Lorens did not summon these clouds. Not when red-eyed warriors of swirling fog and lightning-tipped fingers marched toward his battle array with destruction their obvious goal.

The yowls of fear from the king's personal guard drowned out the thunder. Vered turned even colder inside. The king's guard prided itself on fearless defense of their monarch. Now they whimpered like frightened children.

Vered did not blame them. The magical warriors that had descended from the clouds began to move inexorably toward the front rank of Lorens' personal guard. A flight of arrows arched up and over the heads of the leading guardsmen and dropped with startling accuracy into the storm warriors.

The poison-tipped missiles passed harmlessly through the lightning-wracked warriors.

"The Wizard of Storms sends *his* personal guardsmen," whispered Santon.

"They are not human. They are not even flesh," said Vered, in a voice hardly louder. He patted his gray's neck to keep the horse from rearing. The frightened animal sensed the powerful magic behind the storm warriors and wanted nothing more than to be away from it.

Vered's eyes widened in astonishment as the five pillars of dark cloud began to swirl and take on even more human form. The red eyes blazed. The lightning began to jump from finger to finger—and into the ranks of the human guards. Five mist-shrouded legs stepped out in unison. The storm warriors marched forward into battle.

"Look, Vered. See how it rains around them?"

"They aren't human. They are clouds. The Wizard of Storms has called down pieces of cloud to fight soldiers."

"To kill soldiers," corrected Santon.

The five storm warriors walked into the front rank of Lorens' guards. To their credit the men did not turn and flee. Vered knew his courage would not have withstood such an ominous assault. With every pointed finger a soldier died in the blaze of a cast lightning bolt. Sword cuts meant nothing to those inhuman warriors. Lances passed through their torsos, emerging damp with rainwater and not blood. Horses reared and kicked out war-spurred hooves. The horses died, their guts blown from their bodies by billowing gray cloud parodies of humans.

"There is Lorens," cried Vered. "See? In the rear rank?"

"It is. The rebels might find themselves in control of the kingdom sooner than they thought if the Wizard of Storms' cloud demons kill him now."

"Gaemock and the others might find themselves facing an adversary even worse than Lorens," said Vered. "Why should a wizard remain hidden away for so many years and then suddenly appear?"

Vered swallowed hard when he silently answered his own question. The reason had to lie hidden in Santon's rucksack. The Demon Crown had brought forth the storm warriors and the Wizard of Storms and magic unlike anything that had embraced Porotane for all the years of his life. Could he prevent untold deaths and suffering for the men and women of Porotane by grabbing the sack and throwing it downhill to the storm warriors? Would the Wizard of Storms accept the Demon Crown as a peace offering?

"No!"

The sharp word startled Vered. "I said nothing."

"You," accused Santon, "considered turning over the crown to those *things*." He lifted his withered arm and indicated the storm warriors. Even at this distance the magical beings' red eyes glowed with inhuman lust. The storm warriors killed because of the spell powering them, giving them form and substance—and because it was a basic part of their infernal magical existence. Like the mindless storms that wrecked incautious ships against the rocky shoreline, the cyclonic winds that blew away entire villages, the high waters that flooded farmlands, these warriors were implacable and uncaring.

And, Vered feared, they were invincible. How could anyone fight against the elements? Especially if they carried within their stormy heads the spark of intelligence?

"They are looking in our direction," said Vered, beginning to tremble. "See how they turn and point?"

"It's your imagination," Santon said uneasily.

"No, no, see?" Vered watched the storm warriors break off their attack on Lorens' soldiers and begin to wheel about slowly, as if listening—or seeking.

"They might sense the presence of the Demon Crown," said Santon.

"We can't get past them. They're blocking the mouth of the canyon."

Santon jerked at the reins and got his horse headed back into the canyon. Vered wasted no time in following.

"What can we hope to accomplish?" asked Vered, fear clogging his throat now. "We cannot outrun the wind. Better that we try to stop the rains from pouring out of the sky."

"They might not be after us. The Wizard of Storms might have sent his minions after Lorens alone."

Vered did not believe that. The now-ineffectual king had lost his power. The reclusive wizard could want only one thing. And Birtle Santon carried it.

Vered looked at the Demon Crown's sack. It glowed the same ugly green that it had when Lorens wore it.

FIFTEEN

Baron Theoll flexed his leg and twisted it around. The stiffness had passed and he might be able to walk without a limp. He stood and put his weight on it. The assassin had been careless and had missed his target, but Theoll was not sure that maiming him had not been worse than an outright kill. Who would follow a deformed ruler?

He practiced walking without the limp or slight hesitation that had developed. As he strutted back and forth in his chambers, he studied himself in a full-length mirror of polished steel. Posture. He had to work on posture to make himself seem taller. Boots. Thicker soled boots would elevate him, too. And never let the leg drag along behind. Theoll smiled slightly at his success.

Only his left arm still bothered him, sometimes giving enough pain to make him wince visibly. He would have to exercise it, test it, perhaps even find someone who would practice swordsmanship with him and not rush out telling everyone of the baron's true infirmity.

Theoll stood for a moment beside a decorative panel of carved woods and inlaid pearls. Behind it lay the entrance to the secret ways that

ran throughout the castle walls—his private
kingdom. He had learned much from his spying.

   He felt his heart beating faster at the
thought of again watching Lady Anneshoria
trying to seduce her way to power. Even if he
had not watched her working her considerable
wiles on the commander of the castle forces,
Theoll would have known soon after. Commander Squann was a loyal supporter.

   "As loyal as any gets in this madhouse,"
Theoll muttered aloud. He turned from the
secret entrance and started for the door. There
was so little time for pleasure now. He had work
to do. Because of a sudden unexplained cooling
by the king toward him and the Inquisition,
Archbishop Nosto slackened his efforts to find
heretics among the ranks of the castle lords and
ladies. This encouraged them to renew their
efforts to overthrow Lorens.

   Before he reached the door, a hesitant
rapping came. Theoll flung open the door.
Harhar crouched in the hallway, weakly shaking
his rattle and trying to smile. The effort looked
more like a grimace.

   "May the demons take him," grumbled
Theoll. Louder, he asked, "What's wrong with
you?"

   "Oh, mighty Baron, it is a tragedy. It is, it
is!"

   Theoll grabbed Harhar by the collar—he
used his left hand to test the strength in it—and
yanked the jester into the room. Theoll slammed
the door behind them.

   "What are you blithering about, fool?"

   "The king, it's terrible, the king, the poor
king!"

   Theoll puffed up and looked around, hating

himself even as he did so. King Lorens could spy
on anyone in the castle at any time using the
Demon Crown. Had the monarch sent Harhar to
squeeze an unsuspecting confession from his
lips? Theoll pushed the idea aside. Harhar had
shown no true love for the ruler. If the jester's
sympathies lay anywhere, it was with Theoll's
attempts to sit once more on the throne.

"What are you saying about Lorens? Has an
assassin's quick blade robbed us of our dear
king?" Theoll did not try to keep the sarcasm
from his voice. If the king eavesdropped, let
Lorens impale him for his disloyal thoughts. He
cared little at the moment.

"He suffers so. I cannot bear to see him like
that. No matter how I try, I cannot cheer him.
His loss is too great."

"What loss?" Theoll cuffed Harhar to loos-
en the knave's tongue.

"The crown. His precious crown is gone."

Theoll stood and stared at Harhar, wondering if the fool lied. Nothing about the simple
face showed deception. Harhar believed that the
Demon Crown was gone.

"Stolen?" Theoll did not wait to see
Harhar's head bouncing up and down. He
locked his hands behind his back and began
pacing. The movement let him think better. So
much that had occurred within the castle walls
took on new meaning—better meaning.

His troops had been ambushed outside the
king's quarters. They had patrolled this section
of the castle for no good reason. He liked the
intelligence they ofttimes stumbled across. But
they had been put to death—or so Lorens had
told him.

"The guards lost the other night. What of
them?"

"Three were killed. The fourth died after torture."

"What did he reveal?"

"Archbishop Nosto sent thieves to steal the king's crown."

"Nosto?" Theoll was stunned at this revelation. He knew every move made by the archbishop and his Inquisitors—or so he had thought. How could the archbishop steal the Demon Crown without Theoll learning of it instantly? The baron went over his network of spies and informants and slowly shook his head. It was not possible. Therefore, Archbishop Nosto had not stolen the crown.

"The king believed this until he spoke with the archbishop. Our cleric convinced him of his innocence in the theft."

"The crown would be a magical beacon. Nosto could never hide it from the king. I don't see how anyone could."

"The crown was spirited out of the castle and is now . . . elsewhere."

"Damn you!" roared Theoll. "Stop giving me the information piecemeal. Tell me everything. Now!"

Harhar babbled. Through the torrent of words Theoll puzzled together the curious story. Thieves had stolen the Demon Crown and left Castle Porotane with it. The king believed them to be in the Yorral Mountains, travelling through Claymore Pass. Strangest of all, Theoll had not felt the slightest tremor in his spiderweb of agents posted throughout the castle.

He went to the door and called to the guard stationed at the junction of two corridors, "Summon Squann immediately."

He slammed the door. "There is more. Tell me."

"There is nothing else to say," said Harhar. "You already know that King Lorens has left the castle and is galloping to the Yorral Mountains to retrieve his crown."

Theoll's legs turned weak under him. He wobbled and sat down heavily in a nearby chair. How could this happen and he remained ignorant of it? The king's crown was stolen? Lorens had left the castle?

Commander Squann silently entered the chamber.

"When did Lorens leave?" demanded Theoll. The contemptuous expression on the officer's face started a slow fire of anger burning within Theoll. Harhar had lied! If Squann knew nothing of the king chasing after the thieves who had stolen the Demon Crown, then it was not true.

"Put him to death," Theoll said, his emotions barely under control.

"At once," said Squann. "I've never liked his jokes."

"That's because they were always at your expense," said Harhar. The jester rolled into a tight ball and eluded the commander's groping hands. "You are a joke, a big one, a tall one. Look at your big, fake medals dangling and banging against your thin chest. How many did you award to yourself?"

Squann roared and whipped out his sword.

"Stop that," ordered Theoll, leaping to his feet. "Do not kill him in my chambers. Do it elsewhere."

"Baron Theoll, the king is gone. The crown is stolen. Does the truth offend you so?"

"He is lying," said Squann. "I saw Lorens an hour ago at his dinner."

"What? Wait." Theoll held out his hand to stay Squann. "You saw Lorens eating?"

"Like the pig that he is."

Theoll sat down again, no strength remaining in his legs. "The fool is telling the truth. But how? Lorens hasn't done more than peck at his food since he began wearing the crown night and day. It robs him of all appetite."

"But who was it I saw?"

"The king has a double. Why let yourself be assassinated if you can let a double die in your stead?" asked Theoll.

"True, true," babbled Harhar. "The king's double sits on the throne with a fake crown. He brought him here from far-off Linder."

"Find out for certain," Theoll ordered. "And be quick about it."

Commander Squann sheathed his sword and glowered at the jester. The soldier spun and stormed from the room. Silence fell as Theoll stared into space, his mind working over all the possibilities.

Lorens would not alert many to his absence, not when Dews Gaemock prepared another siege of the castle. Lorens might find himself trapped outside if the siege lasted very long. Such a position would cut him off from his most powerful allies. Losing Castle Porotane might prove a blow that he could never recover from.

No, the young wizard-king would not advertise his departure. Theoll smiled thinly. He would not want even his few allies within the castle walls to know. Allegiances shifted daily. If the king and his powerful crown vanished, new treaties would be forged. Lorens would quickly find himself without a castle—or country—to rule.

How could he profit by the king's absence?

Lorens would take his personal guard. With Squann in control of the castle guard, Theoll might launch a coup. His rear warmed again to the thought of being on the throne.

Caution prevented the baron from ordering Squann into immediate rebellion. Dews Gaemock still threatened a siege, but something more made Theoll hold back. Archbishop Nosto had been used as scapegoat for the ruffians who stole away with the Demon Crown. Theoll had no desire to see his own execution order signed should a coup fail.

Let Nosto take the blame. Theoll smiled wickedly as a plan formed in his fertile brain.

Stride firm and confident, Theoll left his quarters. Behind him he heard Harhar scurrying along, trying to keep pace. Theoll gestured at his guards at the end of the corridor. They fell into step behind to protect him from assassins sent by his enemies. Lady Anneshoria might have learned of his spying on her most intimate and calculating moments. He had to protect himself from her.

Theoll almost laughed aloud. If his scheme worked as it should, he could take Anneshoria for his consort. But he would never take her as his wife. That would make the conniving bitch his queen and place her on the throne beside him. Better to keep her out of the line of succession but where he could benefit from her skills—all her skills, in bed and out. Theoll admitted reluctantly that Anneshoria's plotting had been elegant, even brilliant, and would have brought her considerable power had she but known Squann's true master and Lorens' absence.

"Harhar," he barked. "Who else knows of the matter discussed in my chambers?"

"Only Squann, Baron. And you told him."

"No one else knows. Good. Keep it that way."

"You're not going to have me put to death?"

"Not today. Tomorrow is another day, however. Be sure you keep on my good side."

"Is that your right side or are you still pretending your left is whole again?" asked the fool.

Theoll bit back an angry response. The halfwit had given him the key to ultimate power. He could be charitable and not beat him for his insolence.

"Hold your tongue while we are in Archbishop Nosto's presence or I'll have it cut out and feed it to you for supper. Do you understand?" Theoll sneered when he saw Harhar grab his tongue with both hands and pretend to tug at it.

The baron rapped loudly on the door leading to the archbishop's audience chamber. Several minutes passed before a crimson-clad Inquisitor opened the door. The man wore a long silk cape, tight black breeches, and no tunic. His hairy chest was dotted with beads of sweat. As Theoll turned he saw rivers of perspiration run down the cleric's torso. The Inquisitor had been hard at work. Theoll did not want to know the nature of the work.

"I seek Archbishop Nosto's blessing," he said. "I have come to report a heresy." Theoll ignored Harhar's frightened gasp.

"Wait here. The archbishop will attend you soon." The Inquisitor closed the door in Theoll's face.

The baron let out a deep breath he had not known he was holding. Dealing with fanatics always made him uneasy. Better to treat with the greedy or ambitious. He understood their motives. Never had he gotten a clear picture of Archbishop Nosto's motives. It might be just as the cleric so loudly proclaimed. A desire to rid the kingdom of demonically inspired heretics might blaze within his breast. But what man's faith ran so deep and pure?

Baron Theoll simply did not understand such altruism. He thought that Nosto used it only as a ploy to gain power. If he was right Nosto would be unable to turn his back on what Theoll told him.

"Where's Squann? Hasn't he returned yet? How long does it take the man to go to the king's chambers and back?"

"There, Baron, there he comes now. See how he runs?" Harhar did a handstand. Theoll pushed him over and hurried to the guard commander's side.

"Well, is it true?" he demanded of Squann.

"Baron, it is incredible. The man is an almost perfect likeness of King Lorens."

"So the king *has* left the castle." Theoll smiled broadly. Success lay within his grasp. So soon, so very soon, he would be the true power in Porotane.

"I also checked the guard barracks. All the king's personal guardsmen have departed. Not even the stablehands know where, but they left over two days ago."

"Two days!" exclaimed Theoll. How had Lorens maintained this secret for even two minutes? It had to be wizardry.

"The crown is not the real one, either," said Squann. "The double wearing it is no wizard."

"Better and better." Theoll spun when the door to Archbishop Nosto's audience chamber opened to reveal the archbishop. The man toweled off bloody hands and threw the rag back into his rooms.

"You wished an audience with me, Theoll?"

"I have found a heretic, Archbishop. This is not a matter to discuss openly. May I present my case inside?"

Archbishop Nosto bowed and ushered Theoll, Squann, and Harhar inside. The jester perched on the edge of a straight-backed chair in the corner of the sparsely decorated room while Squann and Theoll stood before the cleric.

"There is a great need for speed, Archbishop Nosto," Theoll said without preamble. "Our beloved monarch has been deposed and an impostor has taken his place."

Nosto stared at Theoll as if the small lord had lost his mind.

Theoll kept from grinning like a fool. Disbelief now, gradual belief later, and then unthinking obedience in the end. That was his route along which to lead Nosto.

"I believe that Lorens has been kidnapped. A military coup in the rank of his personal guard resulted in the imposter taking the throne."

"Commander Squann, is this so?"

"Sire, all the king's personal guard left mysteriously two days ago. I learned of this only minutes ago."

"You? The commandant of all castle guards?"

"This is the horror of it, Archbishop. The king's true supporters have been left in the dark. I do not know who has done this vile deed, but it must be demon-inspired." Theoll watched Nosto's reaction. He had duped the man once before into believing he spoke with the demon

Kalob. The cleric's thoughts had to return to that charade now.

"Why do you think this is a demonic matter?"

"I cannot find what has happened to the Demon Crown," said Theoll. "The imposter—the heretic occupying the throne—does not wear the magical symbol of our monarch."

"Both crown and king are missing?"

"Taken by the king's personal guard," repeated Theoll. "If you so deem, this is a matter for the church and you must investigate immediately. I fear the worst."

"Why is this? Granted, the matter is serious, but it might be purely secular."

"Harhar, tell Archbishop Nosto of what you saw."

"What?" The jester's dark eyes shot open in surprise. "But I saw nothing."

"Sire, he saw a demon conversing with the impostor on the throne," cut in Squann. "He is too frightened to speak. The fool fears for his soul."

"Well that he should," said Archbishop Nosto. The cleric made a vague protective gesture in the direction of the court jester. His thoughts were obviously on the Demon Crown's absence from Castle Porotane and the impostor on the throne.

"Is this not a matter for the Inquisition?" asked Theoll.

"Heretics must be put to the Question, no matter what their rank," said Nosto. "There is no error? Lorens has been kidnapped?"

"Spirited away. I believe the renegade soldiers have taken him to Claymore Pass," said Squann. He fell silent under Theoll's dark look.

The baron did not want his minion revealing too much to Nosto.

The archbishop would believe it all the more if he discovered the details for himself.

"Heretics must never rule Porotane. Such is blasphemous to those of us treading the True Path. We must purge this impostor of his demonic influences." Archbishop Nosto motioned to his silently waiting assistant. The Inquisitor drifted away like a phantom. "We will go immediately to interrogate this ersatz king. Thank you, Theoll."

"I wish only what is best for Porotane," said Theoll. He hastily added, "And those walking the True Path as I do."

Theoll tipped his head slightly, motioning Squann and Harhar from the archbishop's chamber. In the corridor the baron allowed himself a wicked smile that lit his features with evil intent.

"The machine is put into motion. There is no stopping it now," said Theoll.

"But, Baron, the archbishop will get credit for unearthing the impostor."

"He will torture the impostor. By the time the Question is put to him, the heretic will say whatever soothes Nosto and his fellow Inquisitors and prevents them from inflicting still more pain on his fragile body and tormented soul. After the heretic has repented, we might find that Porotane is riddled with demonic influences that only a cleric-king can root out."

"Nosto as king? But that's . . ." Squann's voice trailed off. The commander's grin matched that of the baron's.

"Yes, Commander, that would place unacceptable strain on any of the nobility supporting the throne. It has never happened—and will not last long."

Theoll spun and walked off, head high. Let Nosto assume the throne for a few days. If Lorens played some deeper game, the archbishop would receive the king's full wrath. If Lorens had fallen prey to a coup and had been kidnapped, let him rot in the Yorral Mountains.

Baron Theoll would be King Theoll and no one would have the power to depose him!

SIXTEEN

Lightning crackled overhead. Vered could not keep from ducking every time the sizzling strikes smashed into the softstone cliffs behind them and sent powdery orange rock showering onto their heads. He and Birtle Santon had ridden quickly and well to keep ahead of the slow-marching storm warriors. But if the magical warriors moved with ponderous steps, they never rested.

Even worse, Vered could not still the frenzied pounding of his heart. Just being pursued by the towering, misty, magical beings took its toll on his strength. Even worse, he worried about Santon's condition. The man's wound had opened twice on their headlong rush back into the canyon; the poorly healing gash also robbed Santon of his usual endurance. He wobbled in the saddle and almost fell. Only Vered's quickness had saved him from a nasty fall.

"You're turning pale," Vered said. "We'll have to find a place to rest."

"Rest? With the Wizard of Storms' entire cloud army nipping at our heels?"

"I wouldn't call it 'nipping,'" said Vered. "More like raining."

"Raining at our heels?" scoffed Santon, trying to present a brave front. "What a terrible thing to tell our grandchildren."

"Any children I have are bastards, just like me, and I'll tell them any damned story I please." Vered looked back over his shoulder. The storm warriors were at least an hour's travel behind. Dare they rest? "And I'd never be content with the simple truth. It's usually too dull to repeat."

"You embellish with the best," agreed Santon, "but there'll be no need for you to add to this tale."

"Caves," Vered said suddenly. "There must be caverns we can hide in. The softstone formations provide limitless reaches of caves."

"Dangerous caverns," said Santon. "The roof can collapse from even gentle movement of horses' hooves. I remember being trapped once when on patrol. We dashed into a cave to get out of a downpour. The echo of the horses brought down half a mountain on our heads. Ten of thirty never left our sanctuary."

Entombed. Vered shuddered at the idea. He did not like closed-in spaces. Darkness gave him no trouble, but when he could see the walls— touch them—and the ceiling was low and confining . . . He shuddered. He had been in jails only occasionally for petty crimes. Those few times had been too many for him.

Another blue-white jagged streak of lightning crashed into the stony wall above their head. A small avalanche of pebbles rained down on their heads.

"We can be buried outside or in one of them," he decided. "Pick one. This is your country, Santon."

"Mine? For a bent three-penny you can

keep it. I have no love for Claymore Pass or these cheeselike rocks."

Vered spurred his gray mare closer and got his arm around Santon once more. The older man tottered precariously in the saddle, and his complexion had turned a disturbing and ugly jaundiced yellow. Vered would have thought that the Wizard of Storms had ensorcelled his friend if he had not seen the slow progression of the disease from the cleanly bleeding sword cut to this sorry state.

"I've gotten turned around. Where's the sun? What direction are we heading?" Vered hesitated choosing an opening to enter.

"It makes no difference. There are no side canyons. We are trapped in this one as surely as cattle run down chutes to the slaughter."

"Stop trying to cheer me. I can stand only so much mirth at a time," said Vered. He urged his horse forward. The animal slipped on the pebbly slope leading to the cave mouth Vered had picked at random. He waited until Santon joined him before dismounting.

"Inside," said Santon. He clung to his horse, his good arm thrown around the roan's neck for support. Vered nodded and led the way inside. The only good he saw coming of this was the rock-strewn slope outside. It left no track for the storm warriors to follow and seemed to be of sharp-edged hard stone, unlike the cliffs above.

Vered scowled darkly and wondered if the storm warriors needed to track by sight. What awesome magic had the Wizard of Storms instilled in his creatures? Vered glanced at the sack containing the evilly glowing Demon Crown. Did the magical warriors sense this prize and follow no matter how they turned and dodged and hid?

"I still prefer to know where north is. It keeps me happy. A map and knowledge of north makes life safer."

"Safer?" scoffed Santon, settling down heavily just inside the entrance. "Not in these hills. The beasts living at higher altitudes keep it from being safe—as do the human warriors in the passes."

Vered said nothing about the cloud creatures flinging lightning as they stalked along the floor of the canyon outside. He stared out the opening, expecting them to appear at any instant. After a few minutes, he knew how ridiculous this was. What if he sighted them? He could do nothing. If the storm warriors passed by, fine. If not, they were no worse off than they had been fleeing before the deadly storm front.

"How do you feel?" he asked Santon.

"All right," Santon replied, his voice low. Vered knew his friend lied. He abandoned his sentry post at the mouth of the cave and rested his hand against Santon's forehead. The fever burned bright and stole away part of Santon's soul.

"I'll look deeper in the cave," said Vered. "We might have to retreat if they follow us."

"Storm clouds cannot exist inside a cave with such a low ceiling," Santon said, looking around. Vered had the feeling that Santon spoke without knowing what he said. If the Wizard of Storms' magical killers could exist under a clear blue sky, they could enter a cave.

He left his horse with Santon, more to keep the man occupied than for any other reason. Vered knew his dappled mare would not run away, not from inside a cave. He drew his short glass sword and ran the tip along the wall to mark his path. The cut caused fine dust to fall from the gash. The walls were more like chalk than granite, he noted with increasing uneasiness.

By the time he rounded a second bend in the wind-cut cavern system, Vered found himself in almost total darkness. He hesitated, holding back the irrational fear of cramped spaces that afflicted him. All he had to do was backtrack. He had marked the walls. It would not be difficult to trace his way back to light and Santon and the horses, even if he had to do so by feeling the walls. The cuts were obvious, even in the dark. Over and over he told himself this.

Vered stood for a moment, collecting his courage. His eyes adjusted to the blackness. He started to turn and retrace his footsteps when he saw a shimmering white ahead in the tunnel.

A soft voice beckoned to him. "I need you so. Come, my lover. Come to me!"

Vered's hand tightened around the hilt of his short sword. He needed to know everything about the cavern if he and Santon were to avoid the storm warriors outside and unsuspected unpleasantness within.

"Come to me," came the crooning, seductive voice. Vered's eyes had fully adapted to the darkness and the white patches moving ahead of him came into focus.

"Are there other phantoms in this cave?" he asked.

"Save me from this existence," the woman's voice pleaded. "I can do so much for you, if you will only help me. Help me!"

Vered stopped and stared. If the phantom had not shed gentle illumination on the cavern floor, Vered might have taken a fatal tumble into a deep pit. He tried to estimate the size of the pit and failed. Writhing about in it were scores of phantoms. The tenuous spirits intermingled their substance, parted, flowed upward like liquid, and then dissipated into showers of tiny white sparks. He tried to see if they reformed and could not do it.

"How many of you are there?" he asked his spirit guide.

"How many? I cannot say. Too many. As many as you want! For too long I have been trapped in the crevice between worlds. Free me. Free me!"

"I can't." Vered used his short sword to tap along the edge of the pit. "Are your bodies in this cave or have you just congregated here for some other reason?"

"I do not know. Something pulls me to this spot. How can I say when I cannot identify my own body?"

"You see the other phantoms?"

"Not really. I experience an edginess that I have assumed to mean others like myself are near."

Vered changed his estimate. Thousands of phantoms might be in the pit. The tension in the air might account for this phantom's feelings of nearness to others.

"There's nothing I can do. Believe me, I would if I could. There isn't!" Vered almost wanted to cry in frustration. He had been against aiding Ruirik Kulattian, even if that spirit helped them locate Lokenna, but seeing so many former humans in psychic pain had changed his mind. He *wanted* to help. His personal hell was being unable to.

"*Vered!*"

He spun at the sound of Santon's voice. Vered left behind the pit filled with its nebulous phantoms and hurried back along the tunnel.

For a brief instant he feared that he had gotten turned around and had lost his way, but the sight of the cave mouth reassured him that his sense of direction remained intact. Santon sat just inside the opening.

"What's wrong?" Vered knelt beside his friend. In the brighter light of day falling across Santon's face, Vered saw the progress of the disease. Santon had turned a jaundiced color that gave him more in common with the dead than the living.

"There. Look."

Vered gritted his teeth in anger. The storm warriors had found them. The five gray, puffy, billowing creatures stood in a battle formation at the foot of the slope. Lightning danced within their bodies and a trail of dampness leaking from their feet was their legacy to the barren, rocky countryside. What turned Vered liquid inside, though, were their red eyes. He saw the windows of hell in their eyes.

"We might be able to go deeper into the cave. I found a pit overflowing with phantoms."

"I am too weak to run. We must face them here."

Vered reached over and laid his hand on Santon's forehead. The wound burned with its own intense inner heat; fever took possession of the man's body.

"Can you even stand?"

Santon shook his head. "I tried. I can crawl. Meeting them in battle on my knees is not to my liking, but I will not surrender."

"They want the crown. We can give it to them. Will the Wizard of Storms be any worse a ruler than Lorens?"

"Alarice wouldn't want it that way."

"No," Vered said. Expediency might save

them—but what would happen to Porotane if they gave in this easily? Still, how could they hope to defeat magical warriors such as the five now facing them?

Vered gripped his sword and stepped forward. He threw up his hand to shield his face when a sheet of hot water rained down. Vered stumbled back and fell over Santon.

"What happened?" demanded Santon. "I cannot see the storm warriors. Is this a new attack?"

"There are only four. One has disappeared." Vered looked up into the cold azure autumn sky and saw a tiny storm cloud drifting over the far canyon wall. Between the mouth of the cave and the remaining magical creatures flowed a small freshet. He looked above onto the softstone cliffs to see where it originated. It began at his feet.

"The storm warrior exploded," he said, realization slowly coming to him. "Its body erupted and sent down a cascade of water."

"Hot water," corrected Santon. "I felt it."

Vered stared in mute amazement when another of the storm warriors exploded. The thick body of restless cloud seemed to harden just seconds before the body lost form. Arms, legs, and head vanished into an amorphous mass. The geyser of water spewing straight up into the air sent a second hot rain down on them.

The last thing that disappeared were the malevolent, glaring eyes.

The remaining three storm warriors began moving up the slope. The one in the center shared the fate of its two comrades.

"There are only a pair left," said Vered, not knowing what happened outside but taking heart in it. "You get the one on the right. I'll take the one on the left."

Before Santon could respond, the storm warrior on the right blew apart in a shower of hot water.

"You always were the lucky one. I've still got one to fight." Vered stepped just outside the cave, sword in hand and a curious calm on him. It always felt this way before battle. His nervousness vanished and he concentrated only on his opponent, ready to respond to any attack or react if his enemy gave an opening.

Lightning danced from one cloudy fingertip to another, then formed a blue ball and shot straight for Vered's head. He parried, as if his sword would defect such an attack. The impact of lightning against his glass sword knocked him back into the side of the cave. What astounded him most was that he still lived.

"The sword Alarice gave you," called out Santon. "The glass sword saved you."

Vered nodded. If he had carried a steel blade, he might have been reduced to a sizzling spot of grease on the rocks. But this did not give him a clue about how to fight the storm warrior.

"Here, uoo this." Santon cast his glass shield out to Vered. Never taking his eyes off the cloudy body of his opponent, Vered hefted the shield and settled it into place on his left arm. He deflected another powerful bolt of lightning with the glass shield, but the impact left him numb and dazed.

"What am I supposed to do?" he asked Santon.

"It's coming for you. Fight it!"

"How?"

Vered moved sluggishly, getting his feet set. He had the high ground but the storm warrior towered above him. A gust of wind blew him back, in spite of his firm stance. Lightning crackled around him. Water pelted his face and blinded him. He hid behind the shield and tried to use his sword on the storm warrior's legs. The blade passed through harmlessly, slicing only fog as it went.

As abruptly as the other four magical creatures had vanished, so did this one. The explosion sent Vered tumbling back into the cave, almost into Santon's lap.

"Your shield worked," Vered said, handing it back. Santon's grip proved too weak to hold it. Vered fastened it onto the man's left arm for him.

Vered got to his feet and stared at the wet patches dotting the rocky slope where the storm warriors had perished. It hardly seemed possible that minutes ago he had faced certain death and now all that remained were thin wisps of clouds in the sky.

"The shield helped," Vered said. "Something more worked against the Wizard of Storms' warriors."

Vered cocked his head to one side as the sound of horses' hooves echoed down the canyon. He moved back into the mouth of the cave and knelt beside Santon.

"Riders," he said. Santon nodded weakly. Sweat beaded his forehead and yellow pus seeped from the wound on his head. "Since we saw no one but Lorens' guard, it seems a safe guess that the royalists will soon be upon us."

"Lorens is a wizard," Santon managed to grate out between clenched teeth.

"You think he is responsible for destroying the storm warriors?"

Santon could do little more than nod. His

eyes had glazed over and he simply stared. No intelligence shone from his green eyes. Vered ran his arm around his friend and heaved, getting Santon into an upright sitting position. Santon was the heavier and Vered did not relish the task of getting him onto his horse.

Even if he did, where would they ride? Lorens had an entire company of guardsmen with him. A small smile flickered on Vered's lips. He had the remnants of a company. The storm warriors had reduced the wizard-king's ranks before coming after the Demon Crown.

Vered hoped that Lorens would ride past, continuing down the canyon in search of some trace of the crown. Those hopes were dashed when the king reined in at the foot of the slope where the storm warriors had formed their attack line. Vered watched in fascination as Lorens weaved about in the saddle. An officer reached over to support the monarch. Lorens impatiently waved off the officer.

Tiny patches of dirt began to glow. Like footsteps left by an unseen giant, the green-glowing spots moved up the rocky slope toward the cave. Vered heaved a deep sigh. Magic had found them. Only swords would get them free.

"Sword," he corrected, looking at his friend. Birtle Santon could not fight. He lay in a semicoma on the floor of the cave. Vered had never run from a fight in his life, but he would have now if an escape route had presented itself.

None did.

When the royalist troops began dismounting, Vered knew he was in for the fight of his life. The last fight.

SEVENTEEN

"Santon, get on your horse and ride deeper into the cave. We might be able to hide." Vered saw his companion slumped to one side, unable to move. The fever possessed him totally and robbed him of any strength. He had slipped into a coma.

Vered estimated his chances of getting Santon onto his horse and riding past Lorens' guardsmen. He cast out such a wild notion immediately. The battle array he faced would be too difficult to breach with such a tactic. A wild thought made him want to ride down the slope and try to fight his way through. They might overlook Santon or think that he had ridden on, hurrying deeper into the canyon. They would never consider a comrade in arms holding back.

The glowing spots moving up the slope like footprints of an invisible tracker told Vered such a ploy would never work. Lorens' magic sought the Demon Crown. The thought of returning the crown to the wizard-king came and went almost instantly. Vered would die rather than allow Porotane to return to Lorens' rule.

"Up there. Check the caves. They are near," came Lorens' voice. Vered stepped out and looked down the slope at the king. Two guardsmen had to support him. Vered knew that the young king had reached the limits of his own endurance. Countering the Wizard of Storms' magic warriors had drained him.

That worked for and against Vered and Santon. The commander of the king's personal guard would not be a fool. In a sortie such as this, he would not make any mistakes. Lorens could not direct him; he would not need it.

But with the king unable to command, that gave some sort of edge that Vered had to exploit. He looked from the exhausted king, along the pebble-strewn slope, to the area around the mouth of the cave—and higher.

The softstone showed dozens of holes carved by the incessant wind and rain. Vered saw huge cracks in the orange and yellow stone where water had seeped in, frozen, and caused even greater fissures to form. The cliff face above seemed poised to come tumbling down. All it needed was a little help—from him.

Vered sheathed his sword and scrambled up the treacherous cliff face. The holes cut by the elements provided ample foot and handholds. But he dared not place his entire weight on any one without first testing it. Too many simply crumbled under him and sent down betraying clouds of dust and rock.

"There!" came the cry. "On the cliff face. Archers, fire!"

Vered groaned. He had trouble enough climbing without poisoned and cruelly barbed war arrows digging into his body. The freebooter climbed faster, his grips slipping more often. He reached a dusty, narrow ledge and slid over the edge to lie flat as the first flight of arrows arched up seeking targets in his torso. Some penetrated the softstone and stuck. Others bounced off, rattling back down to the canyon floor. No matter what he did, it would have to be soon. The archers pinned him to the ledge. It would take only minutes for the other guardsmen to reach the cave and find Santon slumped and unconscious.

Vered grunted as he took out his short sword and drove it into a crevice at the edge of the softstone ledge. Twisting and straining, he levered the blade back and forth, shoving it ever deeper as he worked. When he worried that he might break off the glass blade, he began using it as a pry bar.

At first nothing happened. The rock remained obdurate and new flights of arrows sought out his precious body. But a few more seconds of work using his sword produced a grating sound. The sudden release of a huge portion of the ledge took him by surprise. Vered yelped as he fell with the ledge. Only quick reflexes saved him. He grabbed a rock spire and clung to it.

As his legs kicked futilely in thin air, he was conscious of what a fine target he presented to the archers.

No poisoned arrow buried itself in his back. From below all he heard were cries of pain and confusion. Vered twisted around and looked down. The miniature avalanche had kicked up a cloud of dust and masked the bigger rocks in his landslide. Although the guardsmen had not broken off their attack, they milled around in disarray.

"No!" he cried. Vered's anger flared and died, replaced by a feeling of loss. He had thrown the soldiers into confusion as he'd hoped. He had not counted on sealing the cave with his avalanche.

Birtle Santon lay inside the cave, unable to move because of his wound. Or worse, and Vered tried not to think about this, the rock slide had set off a cave-in. Santon might have found his eternal resting place under tons of the softstone.

"Vered," came a voice.

"Santon!" Vered jerked upright and almost fell from his precarious perch. "Is that you?"

"It is I, Ruirik Kulattian."

"What do you want, phantom? I have to find Santon. The slide buried him in the cave."

"There are soldiers below. They will capture you. You must not let them."

"I have to get Santon out. If that's what it takes . . ." Vered's mouth turned dry at the thought of turning himself over to Lorens, yet there seemed no other chance to rescue Santon. It would take an entire company of men to dig him out—and only King Lorens had the manpower to do it.

"You cannot," insisted Ruirik. "I have found the one you seek. I know where you can find Lokenna."

"It doesn't matter," Vered said.

"But my corpse! You promised. I have fulfilled my part of the promise."

"That's not what I meant. Santon has the Demon Crown in the cave. Finding Lokenna is pointless unless we can also give her the crown. She needs it as proof of her lineage."

"The crown is not buried," said Ruirik. "Neither is Santon."

"What are you saying, you vaporous fool? I know they're buried. I caused it!"

"Santon and crown are deeper within the mountain. This entrance is closed but your friend still lives."

"What do you mean, 'this entrance'? Are there others? Show me!"

The swirling white column of Ruirik's phantom moved along the face of the cliff, then vanished into one of the wormholes cut by erosion. Vered leaned out and tried to see where the spirit had gone. For his boldness he made himself target for an archer below. The arrow missed him by the span of a hand but Vered ducked back, legs locked around the spire and body pressing close. He scrambled up and found a ledge too small for easy travel. With the archer shooting one arrow after another at him, the way turned more dangerous than it should have been, but when he ducked in, Vered saw what Ruirik had found.

A rock chimney led downward. Without hesitation, Vered dropped into the narrow tunnel feetfirst—and instantly regretted his impulsive decision. The shaft twisted twice and turned black. The walls closed in on him, pressing his shoulders. A surge of irrational panic seized him when he felt unseen hands crushing in on him.

He screamed when the pressure around his body vanished and he fell in the velvet darkness. Vered landed hard on the cave floor, coughed from the roiling cloud of dust, and tried to get his bearings. The chute had turned him around. He had no idea in which direction lay the clogged cave opening. For several seconds, he simply sat on the floor and got nose and eyes clear.

"Santon?" he called. "Where are you?" His words echoed. No human response came.

The sound that did reach him chilled him. It was not human. What evil mountain beasts made their lair in such caves he could not imagine, but Santon had mentioned many at higher levels that even well-armed men avoided. In the dark he had no chance.

"To your right lies Santon and your horses," came Ruirik Kulattian's voice. Vered jumped nervously.

"I heard strange sounds."

"Your horses are not pleased with being trapped inside the cave. The walls muffle and distort sound. I remember." Ruirik's voice trailed off, then came back, stronger. "I remember. When I was alive, I remember being in a cave such as this."

"But not this one?"

"How can I say?"

"Lead me to Santon." Vered stood and reached out, his hand against a wall. When the dancing white mist that was Ruirik Kulattian's shade appeared, Vered followed slowly. He did not trust the phantom to steer him away from pits and other potentially dangerous traps. For the phantom, such no longer posed a threat and twenty years of neglect dulled even inbred reflex.

Vered's hand touched something warm and round and alive. He held back his cry of shock, then explored further. A smile slowly crossed his lips. He patted a horse's rump. Whether it was his gray mare or Santon's steed, he could not say. Just finding a familiar form in the darkness relieved much of his fear.

"Santon? Where are you?"

"Here," came a weak voice. "Let Ruirik guide you."

The phantom led Vered to his friend's side.

In the dim light cast by the phantom, Vered saw Santon's gaunt face.

"He's found Lokenna," Santon said. "Our mission nears an end."

"We go nowhere while you're ill. I need to find some medicinal plants and make pastes and potions to get your fever down."

"Lokenna. Get to Lokenna and give her the crown."

"I'll not abandon you. Certainly not in here with phantoms floating everywhere."

"There are others here?" demanded Ruirik. "Is my corpse nearby? Please! I remember a place such as this. You must search the tunnels and find out!"

"Being with someone so single-minded can be boring," said Vered.

But he spoke only to himself. Santon had passed out.

To Ruirik, Vered said, "Is there another exit from these caves, other than the way we entered?" He did not want to abandon the horses and did not think he could get Santon up through the narrow rock chimneys and small air vents. They would leave together, or perish together.

"There are many."

"You're not being very helpful," Vered said. "Which one takes us out—and as far from the soldiers as possible?"

Ruirik Kulattian did not reply immediately. Agitation showed in the foggy cloud of his being. "I think you lied. You are not hunting for my body."

"We told the truth, but you knew our other problems. The Wizard of Storms sent his warriors after us. Lorens trailed us using magic. The guardsmen want the Demon Crown back. These

are complications which slowed us drastically."
He refrained from mentioning how close to
death Birtle Santon was. The phantom might
take this as retribution for their supposed slack-
ening of effort in finding his moldering corpse.

"This cave looks familiar. I remember it."

"Do you remember this one in particular or
one which looked similar?" demanded Vered.

"I cannot say."

"Santon can. He was one of your compan-
ions who survived. He knows these mountains
better than anyone else living," Vered lied. "We
need to heal him so we can get on with finding
your damned body."

"Without him the task is impossible?"

"Absolutely," said Vered. "I cannot touch
the Demon Crown without dire consequences
befalling me. Consequences worse than mere
death." He swallowed hard at the idea of being
left alone with the magical device. Its attraction
for him would prove fatal. Without Santon to
stand between crown and him, Vered knew he
would succumb and don the Demon Crown.

How long would he survive? A day? Vered
doubted it. Lorens was directly of the royal
blood line and it had wrecked him in the span of
a few months.

If he could not endure its silent cry for even
this short a time, Vered knew he could never
make use of the information Ruirik Kulattian
had about Lokenna's whereabouts.

"You remain my best hope for passing beyond this vile half-existence," said Ruirik. "I will
aid you this one last time. Then you must show
me your determination to complete your part of
our agreement."

"Done," said Vered.

Ruirik's phantom shimmered and turned as

insubstantial as the flickering polar lights that veiled nighttime winter skies. Vered cried out to the spirit. "Stop, wait. You . . . your substance mingles with that of other phantoms. I cannot tell which is you and which is . . . someone else."

"There are others here? I *felt* presences."

"One shade told me there is a powerful attraction to this cave. Do you feel it?"

"No," said Ruirik. He formed into a mockery of a human being. "I find it difficult to control my shape for very long at a time. The strongest places are those where I can become almost human again. This is not one of them."

Vered took this as proof that they needed to search further for Ruirik's mortal shell. The other phantoms came here sensing some link with their former life. For Ruirik that bond lay elsewhere.

Vered tied his friend belly-down over his horse and then walked through the dark cavern, believing he travelled through infinite night. The closed-in feelings came and went, and always he was wrong. When he was positive that the walls were just inches from his face, he tried reaching out and found only void. At other times, when he felt as if he strode through airy spaces vaster than all Porotane he bumped into the softstone walls.

And always he saw the fluttering forms of the phantoms. He had thought that there were hundreds in the cave. He tried counting and estimated thousands. They skirted the edge of the immense pit where the female phantom had tried to lure him into her service. Again he listened to the plaintive cries for release, and again his heart went out to the phantoms. But he could do nothing.

He was not even sure they could help Ruirik Kulattian.

Vered shouted with joy when he saw the faint light of day down a side corridor. "Ruirik, here. A way out!"

"The opening is small. The horses might not be able to squeeze through."

"But I can. I need to feel wind on my face and see sky. Blue sky!" Vered shoved his head through the small opening and inhaled deeply. The musty odor from the cave vanished as cool, fresh mountain air replaced it in his nostrils. Even more promising, Vered saw growing an arm's length away two of the plants he needed for Santon's poultice. He plucked the leaves from the lacy green plants and settled down just inside the tiny hole.

"We rest for a while," he said. "I need to attend to Santon."

"This will cure him?"

"Perhaps. I don't think he will recover quickly with only mend-leaf and wild grayberry, but it is better than nothing. These will bring down his fever, even if they do little for the other diseases rampaging through his body."

Vered carefully prepared the potion and applied it to Santon's wound. The man moaned softly, shaking his head as if to tell Vered to stop. Vered worried about Santon's breathing. Blood had rushed to head and feet and further impaired healing.

"He bleeds," said Ruirik.

"The poisons flow from the wound," said Vered. "That is not what I'd intended, but it is good." He crawled back to the tiny hole and pulled in more of the mend-leaf. Balling it up and crushing it, he applied a fresh wad of pulp to Santon's head.

When his supply was exhausted, Vered returned to the hole and wiggled as far through it as he could, hand groping for the plants growing nearby.

He yelled when a rough hand seized his wrist and pulled. "Captain, I got one of the bastards!" the soldier yelled.

Vered struggled to break free and get back into the cave, but the guardsman's grip was too strong.

EIGHTEEN

Vered struggled to pull himself free from the guardsman's grip. He was too tightly wedged into the small opening to do more than wiggle futilely like a fish on a hook.

"Here. I have one. Over here!" the soldier cried.

Vered's shoulder began to ache from the strain. With his left hand he fumbled for his dagger, but even if he drew it he would be unable to use it. His body blocked the hole.

Vered blinked, thinking that his eyes were deceiving him. The rock in front of him began to shimmer and move. The movement ceased but the commotion outside grew.

"A phantom!" came the soldier's angry cry. For a brief instant, the grip slackened. Vered twisted, his sweaty skin slipping from the soldier's hold. Getting his feet around to where he could brace himself against the rock helped. Using legs and shoulder, Vered pulled the soldier toward the small opening. When a scarred, ugly face appeared, Vered used his dagger. Blood gushed from the gash he opened just under the guardsman's left eye.

As suddenly as he had been seized, he was

released. Vered tumbled back into the cave, staring out at the angry, injured soldier.

Just beyond the soldier a pillar of shifting white gauze caught the light of day.

"It's all right, Ruirik," Vered called. "I'm free."

The phantom whirled around its vertical axis and reentered the cave to appear beside Vered. Ruirik had enough strength to appear almost solid and definitely human.

"Others come. He summoned no fewer than ten. You must hurry."

Vered drew his short sword and cut at the soldier's hands as the man tried to pull away rocks and debris around the small hole. Such a tactic delayed; Vered knew that when the others arrived they would soon open the hole and pour into the cave.

"I'll cut your liver out!" the guardsman promised. "You cannot get by me. You will join your vaporous friend, mark my words!"

"It appears that I have already marked your ugly face. That is enough good work for a day." Vered backed off when the soldier bellowed incoherently.

"Is it wise to anger him?" asked Ruirik Kulattian.

"Of course not, but it gives me some small satisfaction." Vered backed from the opening, rubbing his shoulder and glaring at the soldier. He turned and ran back to where Santon lay. The thick, yellow pus still drained from the head wound but the man's color had changed for the better. No longer the jaundiced yellow, his complexion was now a pasty, almost deathly white.

"Santon, can you ride? We have found trouble again."

Green eyes flickered open. Before, they had

been glazed and unfocused. Now they centered on Vered. "How can we be in trouble? There aren't any women in these parts."

Vered grinned. "Since I haven't found any, there are none. But we must ride. They might not be able to move enough rocks to get in through that small hole but there must be other ways out—and in."

"Ahead," said Ruirik. "That direction." A misty arm pointed down a side tunnel.

"Narrow," said Vered, not liking the tightness of the fit. "And the roof is low. We can't ride."

"I'll make it. I have to."

Vered helped Birtle Santon to his feet. The man was hardly able to stand, but by linking his immensely powerful right arm through the reins and over the saddle, he was able to stumble along, the roan supporting most of his weight.

"It is a shame you cannot simply move in a straight line," said Ruirik. "We could be out of the mountain within minutes."

"I prefer to do things slowly," said Vered. He winced at the grinding noises behind them. The soldiers worked with too much energy on that tiny hole. With Santon unable to move any faster, an able-bodied squad could overtake them in minutes.

"I do not recognize this cave," said Ruirik, "but the rock is familiar."

"It's everywhere in these demon-cursed mountains," said Vered. "No reason you shouldn't recognize it. Besides, you've been wandering the Yorrals for twenty years. I'd think everything would look familiar after a decade or two."

"It's not like that. Phantoms are drawn to

points of power. Some remain, fearing to leave, thinking their bodies are near. I always had the feeling that mine was hidden away, yet accessible."

"I don't see how you think we can find it when you haven't."

"Years vanish behind me unaccounted for," Ruirik said sadly. "Time means little when you are robbed of body and peace. Concentrating becomes more and more difficult, too. And always the cold seeps in and steals away something of your humanity."

"And you cannot see your own body," finished Vered. He was not impressed with the phantom's litany of woe. He had troubles of his own to cope with.

He halted to check Santon. The man nodded weakly. Vered urged his balking horse forward, toward a dim dot of light that grew until it became a jagged opening in the side of the mountain. With some trepidation, Vered peered out. He expected to see Lorens' troops arrayed for an ambush.

"This is on a different spur of the canyon than where the soldier grabbed your arm," said Ruirik. "They might find this spot, but only after a full day of travelling."

"We cut under—through—the mountain?" Vered shuddered. He was just as happy having done it without knowing tons of rock were poised above his head, ready to collapse. As long as he thought about other matters, he could survive. Comments like this brought back to him the perilous nature of their trip through the caverns.

"A new path, Santon. Sunlight. We can breathe the air. We can get away from Lorens' troops!"

"I recognize this valley," said Santon.

"We rest for a while. I see more mend-leaf. And there's a scrubby crackle bush with enough dry berries hanging on it to make my special poultice."

"I can use a break," said Santon, sinking down, back against the rocky mountainside and face turned to the sun. Vered worked quickly to make the healing poultice and applied it to Santon's head.

"That stings," complained Santon. "But it's moist and cool. I like that."

"Your fever's broken." Vered no longer worried about Santon's survival on this score, but he continued to worry about Lorens' soldiers scouring the Yorral Mountains. The king would not lightly give up the hunt for the Demon Crown.

Vered shivered as if he were the one with fever when he thought of the Wizard of Storms' magical warriors exploding. Lorens might not have received the full training of a wizard but he controlled spells potent enough to destroy the storm warriors.

"It's as if I had left this valley only yesterday," said Santon. "So beautiful and yet it proved so deadly."

"You're not just caught up in a fever dream?" Vered scanned the deceptively serene, phantom-infested valley. It appeared no different from a dozen others they had searched in their hunt for Ruirik Kulattian's corpse.

"Yon tall mountain peak. The one split into a rocky trident, though you cannot tell that from this angle. How can anyone forget that triple peak?"

"Easily," said Vered. Then he paused. Something in his friend's voice cautioned him that this was not a subject for joking. "What happened there?"

"The brigands impaled a captive a day on one of those peaks. Needle-sharp points at the top. They'd put their victim on a blanket, with hands tied behind the back, and begin tossing him twenty feet and more into the air. Eventually he would fail to come down on the blanket and would land on one of the trident points. It is difficult to tell from here, but the peaks are almost pure iron. The elements have forged them into weapons aimed at the sky." Santon closed his eyes and seemed to shrink in on himself as memories assailed him. "Weapons aimed at the sky and many of my former comrades in arms."

"A good reason to dread this place," said Vered.

"Dread? Hardly. I came to think of it as a haven. The brigands did that to let us know that they were beyond our reach. But we were beyond theirs, too."

"A fortress?" guessed Vered.

"We fortified an old abandoned mineshaft near here. The brigands never penetrated our outermost defense perimeter, though our losses were great."

"Did all your forces use it as a base?" asked Vered.

Santon turned and stared at Vered. "I know what you are thinking. It is possible that Ruirik would be taken there if he lay in a coma. But so many died in other places scattered throughout the Yorral Mountains."

"My body?" perked up the phantom. "Do you know where it is?"

"You said this cave looked familiar. The inside of one rock prison looks like any other to me. You wouldn't have been too alert, either," said Vered.

"You know where this fortress lies?" Ruirik's phantom spun and whirled in excitement and sent off tiny streamers of white mist.

"Less than a league down the valley, if my bearings are right," said Santon.

"There is another matter to attend to first," cut in Vered. "Where is Lokenna? You said you found her. We're trying to recover your body. You've got to trust us with your knowledge."

"No!" cried Ruirik. "If I tell you, then you'll never try to find this fortified mineshaft. This is my last and best hope of escaping my sorry existence!"

"We have come this far in your behalf," said Santon. "There is no way of knowing if you're lying to us. You might be luring us on."

"I have found Lokenna." Ruirik Kulattian dissolved into an amorphous shape of everchanging tendrils and columns. Slowly, he tightened into a glowing white sphere and then reformed. "Very well. I take the risk of my life."

"Some risk," muttered Vered, "considering that you're already dead."

"Lokenna lives in a village known as Fron."

"Do you know where this is?" asked Vered of Santon.

The grizzled, pale man nodded slowly. "It is not more than a day's travel off the main track through Claymore Pass. I remember it as a miserable little town that got burned to the ground by brigands at least once a month. I never knew why any of the inhabitants stayed."

"She is in Fron," insisted Ruirik. The phantom lost shape once more, hovering over their heads, as if waiting to see what they would do next.

Santon heaved a deep sigh, then forced himself to his feet. "The air renews me as much as your fine potions. I might be up to riding for a few minutes."

"For Fron?" asked Vered.

"For the fortress. We promised Ruirik to continue our search."

"Thank you!" came the long, low sigh of gratitude from the phantom. "You are honorable men."

"Stupid ones, too," said Vered. "Lorens is not going to stop hunting us." He scanned the sky for suspicious cloud formations. "I doubt that the Wizard of Storms will leave us in peace, either. Too many people want that accursed crown."

"Then it behooves us to hurry," said Santon, trying to get into the saddle. He tried twice and failed. "Give me a hand. I'm still weak."

"Don't let the nag run away with you," Vered said, hoisting the heavy man into the saddle. Vered brushed off his hands and stared at the tatters flapping on his back. "What a descent from high fashion. Look at me. The cave dust, the fights, everything has reduced me to rags befitting a beggar."

"Are we any more than that?" asked Santon.

"No, more's the pity." Vered swung into his saddle and started in the direction Santon indicated.

They rode for ten minutes, rested, then rode for fifteen before Santon straightened in the saddle. The man's face flushed and looked almost normal.

"There," he said softly. "There is our haven. Let us hope that brigands haven't taken it for their own since the days King Lamost held the Yorral Mountains in his grip."

Vered and Santon rode slowly up a weed-overgrown path. Vered saw where battlements had been placed in earlier days. Weather and occasional landslides had erased much of the fortifications. He looked up and saw where snow formed during the long winter months. A spring thaw would bring avalanches that would sweep clean boulders larger than any used by the soldiers in that bygone era of King Lamost.

"The entrance," said Santon. "Some heavy rock fall, but not enough to seal it permanently, I think. You might be forced to do some hard excavation."

"A pleasure," Vered said sarcastically. "Who wouldn't want to dig open still another hole in the ground so we can bury ourselves alive?"

Vered explored the area and found the shoring on the tunnel mouth in surprisingly good condition. The rocks blocking the entrance were too large for him to move alone, but a brushy area farther north drew his attention.

"What did you find?" asked Santon.

"The bushes are blown away from the rock. Unusual." Vered explored and found a large fissure. "I think this has opened up since last you were here."

"There are quakes of some intensity. None struck when I was on patrol, but the older veterans had tall tales to spin around campfires of the mountains themselves moving."

Vered tugged and cut and toiled to clear the fissure of dense undergrowth. An hour later, he indicated that Santon should follow him inside with the horses.

"A tight fit again," observed the older man, "but the horses are getting used to it."

"I'm glad someone is." Vered closed his eyes and tried to think of open spaces, of clean air and blue skies—the very things he left behind to entomb himself under still another mountain.

Mind unsettled but resolve firm, Vered entered. He found the going easy. In less than a minute he stood in a wide gallery dimly lit through the fissure.

"The main chamber," said Santon, joining his friend. He tethered the animals near a stone trough filled with pure, clean water. "An artesian spring feeds it year round," Santon said. He bent and drank of it himself, then washed away some of the trail dirt. "Still as refreshing as I remember."

"What else do you remember of this mausoleum?" asked Vered. White patches of phantoms drifted through the tunnels. "This is another spot where the spirits congregate."

Santon walked slowly, getting his bearings. "There. Down that tunnel is where the infirmary used to be."

Vered preceded him, sword drawn. The darkness closed in around him until he was forced to stop.

"Too dark."

"Then we'll need light." The sudden flare dazzled him. Santon had found a torch that burned fitfully, even after so many years. "We'd make our recruits bundle together rushes from a lake an hour's travel up the valley. They never understood why we insisted on rushes from that particular lake."

"They've lasted."

"Aye. We knew quality then."

Vered turned to the low, keystone-arched entrance to a room and felt light-headed. "You knew quantity, also."

"A moment, if we are going exploring." Santon unslung the rucksack containing the Demon Crown and hoisted it over his good shoulder.

"Why take it? The horses won't run off with it."

Santon looked at him for a moment, then said, "We wouldn't want to be split up in the caves. These tunnels are extensive and confusing."

Vered started to protest. Santon doubted his resolve about denying the crown's lure and did not want to tempt him. Before the words formed on Vered's lips Santon pushed him aside, holding the guttering torch high. The almost-smokeless torch illuminated a room filled with tiers of crude beds hewn from the living rock. Hundreds had died on those beds.

And the bodies had not been removed for burial.

"Retreat must have come quickly," said Santon.

"Or death. What was the fate of this fortress?" Vered forgot about the crown when faced with such magnitude of death.

"Abandoned. I never learned why. I was on patrol when we got orders to return to Porotane." Santon walked forward. "We never learned the details of the rout. I always thought the brigands overwhelmed us."

"Could it have been an epidemic that caused Lamost's change of heart in maintaining power in the Yorrals?"

"Aye. Let's hope, if it was disease, that it has died out over the years." Santon walked along the tiers of rocky death beds, looking at the corpses. "They are well preserved. The temperature is right and the cave is dry."

"Most seem to have taken severe wounds," Vered said, almost in relief. If plague stalked these soldiers in a bygone day, it might still hunt the unwary. Proof of war injuries reassured him that some other explanation for Lamost's hasty withdrawal was the correct one.

"Have you found my corpse? I sense great power here. A . . . an ineffable sensation rising from the middle of the mountain. I cannot describe it."

"Describe yourself," ordered Vered. "What did you look like in life? Any armbands or bracelets or rings that might help us?"

"Such would be stolen," said Santon, shifting the pack holding the Demon Crown into a more comfortable position on his back. "Even among comrades, there is the feeling that the living are better off with wealth than the dead."

"That is something I can agree to," said Vered.

"The steel foot," said Ruirik Kulattian.

"What?" Both men turned and stared at the phantom. So much energy had infused the spirit that he appeared to be a living human being. Only the faint white glow betrayed the truth.

"I had a steel foot. My left foot was crushed by a wagon more than a year before I died. A bladesmaster fashioned a hollow foot for me. I strapped it on and could walk with scarcely a limp."

"Fine," said Vered. "Rise!" he called. "All you corpses, get up and walk around. We want to see who doesn't limp—much."

"Vered, hold your tongue." Santon settled

down, resting against a stone table. His hand shook as he held the torch. Vered took it and continued the inspection while his friend rested. Never had he seen such a variety of ways to die. He poked through the rags hanging on a few of the corpses, looking for signs of a steel foot or name tags or other identification.

"It appears that these were left since none could be identified," he decided. "Lamost might have ordered the retreat but none of these unfortunates could be named, so they were abandoned." He shivered again. This wasn't as much an infirmary, then, as it was a mortuary for the unknown.

Vered used the tip of his sword to push back a blanket. A sergeant's sigil still gleamed after thirty years in the torchlight. The glass sword poked down further. Vered couldn't tell the cause of death from the body. He ran the edge of the sword along the legs. Then he tapped and heard a hollow ringing.

"Sergeant Ruirik Kulattian," he called. The phantom whirled up and stood beside him, a misty apparition that added to the light cast on the body. "Is it likely you kicked ass with this steel foot?"

"What?" demanded Ruirik. "What are you saying?"

"Look well. Might this be your body?"

"I . . . I see nothing. Of others, I see them well enough, though many appear as if through a veil. But I see nothing where you're pointing. This isn't a cruel joke, is it?"

"Santon!" Vered waited until his friend joined them. "Look this one over. The steel foot might have proven all the clue we needed."

"A sergeant, from the insignia. There's no way to match phantom with facial features."

"A front tooth!" cried Ruirik. "I was missing a tooth in front."

"Left or right side? Upper or lower?"

"Lower. But I . . . I cannot remember which side."

"Right?" asked Vered. He had pried open the jaws and ruptured long-dried tendons. A single tooth was missing from the jawbone on the lower right side.

"It's been too long. I cannot remember. Pieces flood back but so much is missing. I am confused. The world turns vivid colors around me and swirls. There has never been a time like this for me."

Vered and Santon exchanged glances. Santon nodded slowly, then said, "We may have found your body, Ruirik."

For a long minute, the phantom said nothing. Then in a voice so low that neither man could listen without straining, "Dare I believe this? You do not torment me?"

"Did you speak truly when you said Lokenna resides in Fron?" demanded Vered.

"I did. There is nothing for me to gain by lying."

"We'll consecrate a grave for this body and name you in the burial ceremony, Ruirik. We might have found the wrong body. This might not be yours."

"I have nothing to lose by the ceremony," Ruirik said.

Vered said nothing. If they consecrated a grave and named the wrong man, some unknown soldier would be doomed forever to existence as a phantom. Vered took a deep breath and let it out slowly. But the risk was small. No one had sought surcease for those who had died in Claymore Pass twenty years ago. The future would not bring in others who would care, either. One unknown man might be doomed to walk the world as a phantom but Ruirik Kulattian might also be freed.

Vered and Santon began construction of a rock cairn at the far end of the room. An hour later, Vered said, "That's good enough for a prince. Let's begin."

He went to fetch a flask of water from the trough. Ruirik dogged his steps, the apparition fluttering around him like a swarm of misty white flies. Vered returned to find that Santon had bundled up the body in a saddle blanket, leaving only the hands and face exposed.

"I'll do it," said Santon. "Although I never knew him, he might have ridden beside me as a comrade."

Santon began the mumbled prayer of leave-taking, dropping water on each of the corpse's fingertips, finishing with single drops on each of the hollowed eyesockets and where lips would have been if they had not mummified over the years.

"The saints are merciful and will carry Ruirik Kulattian, Sergeant of Scouts for King Lamost, to a better existence." With that Santon stood and backed away.

Both men jerked around when a sudden shriek cut through the heavy silence in the mine-fortress. The cry started as one of pain and climbed in intensity . . . and altered as it went. It ended as a shout of sheer joy.

"I am free!" Ruirik Kulattian exulted.

Vered covered the corpse's face with the blanket and began stacking the rocks atop the body—Ruirik's body. That brief cry had proven that they had properly matched phantom with body.

"Rest well, friend," Vered said, backing from the grave.

"He will," came a soft whisper, more like the wind through tall trees than a human voice.

"Alarice!" cried Santon.

"Thank you. There is one less troubled phantom because of you. But you must hurry."

"Wait, Alarice, don't leave. I want to—" Birtle Santon reached out with his good hand but found only emptiness. The Glass Warrior's phantom had existed for the span of two heartbeats and no more. She had again appeared and left.

"She wants us to go to Fron," said Vered. "That's where Lokenna is and that's where we can get rid of the Demon Crown."

"She could have lingered a few minutes," Santon said, his voice weak and his back bowed.

Vered stopped and cocked his head to one side, listening intently. Santon heard the sounds, too, and stiffened.

"Lorens! He has again found us!"

Vered heard the clank of steel weapons rubbing against stone. Lorens' guardsmen forced their way through the narrow fissure. The soldiers' cheer when they found the horses chilled Santon to the bone.

They had come so far only to be trapped within the fortress!

NINETEEN

"*No!*" screamed the Wizard of Storms. Kaga'kalb fell back, hands to his head. Blood spurted from a tiny wound on his temple. He staggered and dropped to his knees, rain pounding the barren plain around him. His eyes lifted to the monstrous, black-bottomed cloud above him. From this thunder cloud had sprung his storm warriors.

Kaga'kalb wiped the blood from the wound and smeared it on his robe. Determination replaced the surprise he'd felt. It had been so many years since any opposed him.

It had been many years since he had strayed from the Castle of the Winds and meddled in the internal affairs of Porotane.

He rose on shaking legs. He thrust out his hands and concentrated. Killing Lorens' soldiers had proven more satisfying than he had thought. But this was not his only reason for conjuring the storm warriors. He had sensed the presence of the Demon Crown and had directed the five cloud creatures to retrieve it, but something had gone wrong. One of the warriors had . . . ceased to be.

Kaga'kalb shrieked again. A new wound appeared on his temple. Both spurted blood. He touched the wounds and uttered a healing spell, but the tiny punctures refused to stop bleeding.

"Who opposes me? Who dares?" he bellowed.

A third storm warrior was destroyed. Kaga'kalb closed his eyes and let his senses merge with that of a warrior. The world shimmered as if seen through a veil of desert heat, but the deadly green glow told him that the crown he sought was near. He directed his storm warrior toward it. A shale slope led up to the mouth of a cave—and within the cave the Demon Crown sent out its silent message of power.

A fourth wound exploded on his forehead. Wind whipped about the Wizard of Storms and caused him to rock to and fro. He struggled to keep his balance, to remember where he was. Part of him inhabited the remaining storm warrior and the part of his being that was *him* stood battered by a thunderstorm of his own creation.

"The crown," he moaned out. "I will have it! But who kills me?"

He turned, his eyes seeing the castle and its lofty spires of precious gemstones—and his eyes also seeing a rocky canyon in the Yorral Mountains, not far from the track that mortals called Claymore Pass.

"Lorens," he said, not sure which vision proved truer. Kaga'kalb blinked. The towers of his castle vanished and he saw clearly through the storm warrior's glowing red orbs. "Lorens, you have powers I did not recognize."

He lifted a cloudy arm and pointed. Lightning from five fingers lanced forth, cremating five of Lorens' guard. The others scattered, leaving an empty battleground. Kaga'kalb sneered. Such cowards! They dared not face the power of a storm!

He turned and began striding upslope, intent on the faint but distinctive power emanating from the Demon Crown. A mortal emerged from the cave and slashed at him.

Kaga'kalb yelped in surprise. No mere blade cut at his cloudy leg. A blade fashioned by the Glass Warrior caused a twinge. He stepped back and glowered at the impudent mortal. Could this be the thief who ripped the Demon Crown from Lorens' brow? It hardly seemed likely, yet he showed courage lacking in the royalist troops.

Power built throughout Kaga'kalb's arm. He pointed his hand. Lightning blasted out to remove this annoyance. Again the accursed glass blade protected the mortal. Kaga'kalb started to use a different form of magic when pain surged within his head.

He staggered and . . . dissipated.

Tumbling through space, Kaga'kalb held his head. Blood oozed between his fingers from five different cuts. He smashed hard into the barren plain stretching before his Castle of the Winds. The rain laved his face. Lightning blasted down to touch his fingers, renewing him, reassuring him of his power. Kaga'kalb blinked twice and saw only the spires of his domain.

Five storm warriors had been destroyed.

"Lorens, your power is far greater than I anticipated. Even without the Demon Crown you show promise." Kaga'kalb wiped the blood from his forehead and stood. "You show promise that must be snuffed out. You will destroy Porotane and that must never happen!"

The Wizard of Storms walked slowly into

his keep, thunder rumbling down the slopes and across the Uvain Plateau.

"Sire, you are pale. Let us summon a chirurgeon for you. There is one only a day's travel down the River Ty."

"Silence, fool." Lorens struggled to sit upright and failed. The sight of the Wizard of Storms' powerful magical warriors had unsettled him, but the spells had come to his lips unbidden. He had remembered his lessons well! Patrin would be pleased with his pupil, had he survived to see this day.

But the cost had been great. Destroying one storm warrior had been simple. The next had proven ten times harder, and the third ten times harder still. By the time he destroyed the fifth, Lorens had become so drained that he had fallen from his saddle. Only a lieutenant had prevented him from injuring himself severely.

"They are near. I feel them. What has happened?"

"Sire, we lost them in the maze of tunnels."

Lorens worried that he would be unable to conjure the Spell of the Ten Trackers that had proven so useful before. It was a difficult spell to control and he was so tired. So tired, so tired.

"Sire?"

Lorens awoke with a start. He had begun to drift. He dared not do that. The Demon Crown. He had to recover it before anyone learned of his secret and hasty departure from Castle Porotane. That fool of a double he had left behind would not convince many should he try to hold a royal audience. And Lorens did not trust him to remain in chambers as he had ordered.

A fake king wearing a fake crown. Lorens snorted in contempt.

"What's happened?" he repeated.

"We've lost them. The thieves exited the cavern and are in the next valley over. Our scout saw them from the summit."

Lorens glanced up the steep cliff face. The softstone had proven treacherous. Two of his scouts had tried climbing that slope and had fallen to their deaths. He had not held out any hope for the third—but his luck had to change. It had to. So much had gone wrong.

His hands rubbed the place where the Demon Crown had rested. How empty he felt without the magical crown. He needed it. Why send scouts to do work he could do magically in the wink of an eye? And what went on while he was away from the castle? Plots, to be sure. But who sought his death?

Theoll? The conniving little baron would stop at nothing. But how did he work his perfidy this time? Lorens almost burst into tears at the depth of his ignorance. He had to know. And Dews Gaemock and Dalziel Sef? Their siege might begin soon. Where were their troops? He needed to know it *all!*

"The crown. I need the crown." Tears leaked from his eyes and ran down his cheeks. He was too weak to wipe them before they left dirty streaks on his face.

"The valley is accessible through a narrow pass. We can ride all day and be there soon, Sire."

"It is awful being blind."

"Sire?"

"What?" Lorens tried to concentrate but his mind drifted. The dissipation spell used against the storm warriors had left him no reserve. His puffy eyelids drooped and his head sagged forward until his chin rested on his chest.

"Should we pursue? All of us?"

His heavy snores gave the officer the only command he was likely to get. The King of Porotane slept so deeply that he might have fallen into a coma. More than one in his guard touched dagger or sword, thinking how easily a tyrant could be removed.

Lorens awoke with a start. He looked around and tried to remember where he was. His dreams had taken him back to his simple quarters in the City of Stolen Dreams. Patrin had been disciplining him for an infraction. Storm warriors had closed in and he had destroyed them, but a woman's face had floated above and had mocked him.

Lorens shivered. She had worn the Demon Crown. He had tried to touch it, to force her to return it and she had mocked him. Lorens struggled to remember who she was. She had seemed familiar, yet a stranger.

His throbbing head felt as if it would split open at any instant.

"Sire, we have followed their spoor to an abandoned fortress."

"A fortress?" Lorens sat up, curiously weak. Separating dream from reality proved difficult for him. "The Castle of the Winds?"

"Sire?" The officer glanced around. The others with him shrugged and averted their eyes. "No, Sire, this is a mine that had been converted into a fortress. One of my sergeants claims it had been built when his grandfather patrolled these mountains for your father, King Lamost."

"What are you telling me?" Lorens could not puzzle out his guard commander's words.

"We believe that the two thieves we chase have entered the fortress. The main entrance is blocked by fallen stone, but our tracker has discovered where they entered. A crevice recently opened by a quake leads inside."

"They are within that mountain?" Lorens pointed. Some small spark of the tracking spell he had cast so long ago remained in force. Tiny phosphorescent footprints marched directly for the fissure his commander had mentioned.

"It might be an ambush, Sire."

"What do they want inside an ancient fortress?"

"We do not know, Sire. They cannot hope to stand off our full might, even inside such a fortress."

Lorens tried to think of all the chances he took entering this deserted fortress. His head hurt too much. His hands shook and he could not stand upright without becoming giddy. The use of his few powerful spells had taken much from him and he tried not to show it in front of his officers.

When he had used the Demon Crown he had seen how few in Porotane—and his army— were loyal to him. All spoke highly of his father and vowed loyalty to the throne. Therein lay the troubles Lorens saw brewing. The soldiers swore their loyalty to the throne and not to him personally. In an instant they would turn against him if they saw the chance to put another in power.

Lorens tried to conjure just a small spell and found that he could not. The tracking spell continued working on its own, as if it had become a thing alive.

"Follow the footprints inside," he ordered.

"And you, Sire?"

"Where do you think I'll be?" he said, a sneer curling his lip. "I'll be in the front with you."

The guard commander shook his head slightly, as if not believing his ears. "Very well, Your Majesty. So shall it be." The officer bowed low, backed away, and then went to pass the order along the ranks of men anxiously waiting beside their horses.

For several seconds Lorens fought down his rising gorge. Had he done the wrong thing? The soldier expected another order. What? Why shouldn't a king lead his men? Did the officer know this was an ambush and only sought to lure him in?

Again tears of rage and frustration formed in the corners of Lorens' eyes. He *needed* the crown. Now more than ever he needed it. And it had been stolen by the ruffians hiding in the fortress.

"Forward!" Lorens took up the officer's cry and rode to the fissure. The glowing footprints he had conjured led inside. He followed their track, the first into the dark crevice. Only the pressure of men behind him kept Lorens walking forward. He imagined swords thrusting at him from every cranny. Arrows launched from deep inside the cave. Creatures beyond his most tormented dreams lurching up to devour him.

But he walked on. He dared not show cowardice.

It came as a relief when he entered a large chamber and was able to wave his men on past to scout the area.

"Sire, we've found two horses," reported his lieutenant. "What do we do now?"

"Search. Find the rogues who rode them."
Lorens glanced at the dim magical footprints on
the floor and saw with no pleasure that they
faded away. The Spell of the Ten Trackers had
finally weakened and vanished. He made futile
passes with his hand to renew it. No spell
worked, even the simplest. He was too drained.
Destroying the Wizard of Storms' tiny army had
proven too taxing for his limited abilities.

"The dust is disturbed. Footprints lead
down this tunnel," came back the report.

Lorens watched as the guard officer effi-
ciently positioned his men if this proved to be a
trap. He knew so little of such things, yet he had
to issue a command. He was King of Porotane
and kings commanded.

His lot would be easier with the Demon
Crown set at a jaunty angle on his head. Lorens
rubbed his temples, almost feeling the crown
resting there again.

"Are there other exits?" he asked.

"Sire, we don't know without extensive
scouting. None of my soldiers has been here
before, although many repeat tales told them by
their fathers and grandfathers."

"Torches. Light torches and advance."

"The smoke might blind us."

"No light to see by, will be your downfall."

"We can see by the light shed by the phantoms, Sire. There are hundreds flitting about
inside this mineshaft." The officer ran his hand
along a roughly hewn wall, his blunt fingers
tracing a played-out vein of gold ore.

Lorens started at this notion, not having
seen the hundreds of phantoms when he entered. He stared at them and heard faint, plaintive cries for mercy.

"Will any of the spirits offer us assistance?

They can find our quarry much easier than we can."

"Doubtful, Sire. They promise anything in exchange for release. We cannot trust them."

"No, we cannot trust them. Any of them," said Lorens. It came as a mild shock to him that he didn't even know this young lieutenant's name who commanded his company of personal guards. When he had worn the Demon Crown, there had been no need for attention to such details. He had been able to see everything, no matter where it lay in the kingdom. Plots were laid bare and each person in the castle revealed all, whether they knew it or not.

"No side tunnels. They went directly to the infirmary," came a shouted report that echoed along the broad rock corridors. "We can get them now."

"Do it, Commander," he ordered the officer. "I want them and what they carry."

A war cry from the throats of twenty men rose. Swords clanking, armor creaking, shields scraping along the walls, the soldiers began their attack.

Lorens followed as fast as his debilitated condition would allow. But strength poured into him. It would not be long now. The Demon Crown would return to his royal head where it belonged!

TWENTY

"Break another bone," ordered Archbishop Nosto. The cleric stood impassively, watching as a well-muscled, sweating Inquisitor applied more pressure to the arm of King Lorens' double. The ersatz king screamed in agony as the complicated iron rods and pulleys tightened and snapped the vulnerable bones in his forearm. Jagged white bone protruded through the flesh.

The pain did not loosen the impostor's tongue.

Baron Theoll knew that there was nothing to be gained from this brutality—as far as the Inquisitor was concerned. He looked not at the heretic impostor Nosto tortured but at the assembled lords and ladies of Porotane. They watched from galleries and the main floor of the royal audience chamber. Once orchestras had played here for the amusement of the gathered nobility. Now only pain from the Inquisitor played its ugly song down the narrow chamber.

None dared speak out against Archbishop Nosto, yet none supported him, either.

In that lay Theoll's road to the throne.

His dark eyes moved slowly, studying reactions, guessing at alliances and loyalties. When he stopped at a plain, almost mousy brown-haired woman with an intense expression on her face, he shivered slightly with expectation.

Lady Anneshoria lacked the qualities so many in the court possessed. None would single her out for beauty or grace, and only Theoll recognized in her the drive and ambition to seize the throne. Her quick mind worked on new and ever more devious plots.

Baron Theoll could use her. In a way, he even admired her. But never would he turn his back on her.

His attention came back to Nosto. The archbishop straightened his shoulders and glared at the captive dangling in chains. "You will now be put to the Question. Have you strayed from the True Path in deed or thought?"

"No!" shrieked the victim.

"Evidence points to this being a foul lie. Are you a heretic? Do you have intercourse with demons?" New pressures were applied to the kingly double's body. More important bones broke.

"It is the belief of the Inquisition that this impostor has usurped the throne from the true King Lorens. A search of Castle Porotane is now being conducted to determine the fate of our king."

"I am innocent. He came to me. I lived in a small seacoast town, and he sent his agents to me. He is our king!" the poor wight screamed. "He *ordered* me!"

"Who is this mysterious *he* of whom you speak?" Archbishop Nosto asked in a deceptively mild voice. Theoll saw the cleric's hands trembling with anticipation of another lie. "Is it a demon who summoned you? It was! Admit it!"

"No, no!" The impostor struggled feebly in his chains. "The king ordered me. I am his loyal servant. He ordered me to impersonate him while he ventured into Porotane on a vital mission. He goes among his subjects for reasons of his own!"

"What mission could this be? He spoke of no such trip to me." Archbishop Nosto's logic continued along its inexorable course. King Lorens had said nothing about leaving the castle, therefore he had not left voluntarily.

"I know nothing of our dear king's motives. I am loyal. I obeyed his command."

"You thought to usurp power. But you are not capable of such a thought, are you?"

"No!"

Theoll closed his eyes for a moment. The interrogation now took a familiar course. Nothing that Lorens' double said would exonerate him.

"Of course not. Then you admit that a demon commanded you?"

"No, it was King Lorens!"

"Lorens is no demon. You speak treason— or heresy. Which is it?"

The victim gave up all hope. His lips rippled as if they had an obscene life of their own. "Treason," he said in a weak voice.

Theoll nodded. The choice was good. Archbishop Nosto would never rest until a confession was pulled from the man. Admitting to treason presented the lesser of two painful deaths.

"Continue interrogation of the traitor," ordered Nosto. "Find what has happened to our rightful king."

"He's dead!" shrieked the impostor. "I killed him. I did it to seize the throne for myself!"

Theoll hoped that would end the farce. Nosto made a small gesture of benediction and the torturing Inquisitor dropped the knotted cord around the man's neck. A quick tug sent the man's tortured soul to be judged by the saints—and, Theoll knew, Archbishop Nosto thought that the lost soul would be found wanting and doomed forever.

The baron waited for the announcement he knew would come. He tried not to smile when Nosto called out in his booming bass voice, "King Lorens is lost to us. The kingdom is rife with heresy. Too many, even within these castle walls, stray from the True Path."

Theoll jumped when Anneshoria sidled up next to him. Her voice was low. "You have done well, Baron. Nosto is going to announce himself king."

"I? Surely, Lady Anneshoria, you cannot think I had anything to do with this? The Inquisition is responsible for uncovering the impostor and returning us all to the True Path."

"Whatever you say, Baron." Anneshoria smiled slightly and moved away. Theoll appreciated her diplomacy, even if she stood a full head taller and insisted on peering down at him.

". . . there is no other choice left me," said Archbishop Nosto. "I am installing myself as king-regent to help everyone seek the True Path and remain on it."

This announcement took many in the audience chamber by surprise. Theoll noted those who seemed shocked. They could be dismissed totally from any future power struggle. Those who seemed annoyed or those with expressions of disgust or shock formed still another power bloc he would have to court. They would be his stepping stone to the throne—and Archbishop Nosto would be the bridge.

"By the saints, I now ascend the throne of Porotane to act as king until the true heir can be restored—and the kingdom is once again returned to the True Path."

That final condition made Theoll smile. Let Lorens return. Archbishop Nosto would not relinquish the throne because Porotane would never achieve the moral and religious purity the cleric demanded. Even a saint would be hard-pressed to live up to standards Nosto demanded of nobles and peasants.

Only an internal struggle would remove Nosto. Or a clever assassination. Baron Theoll wondered how long it would take before someone drove a blade into Nosto's back. It would be amusing, he thought, if it happened while Nosto was seated on the throne.

The new king began barking orders concerning the disposal of the traitor's body. A wistfulness came to Nosto's words. He would have preferred that Lorens' double had confessed as a heretic. Baron Theoll slipped away. He cared little for the preparations for a formal coronation or the insincere congratulations from the nobles assembled. He had work to do.

"Is this all you can tell me?" shouted Theoll. He rocked back to strike Harhar but the jester cringed away, feigning fear. Harhar—Efran Gaemock—had endured much at this sadistic noble's hand, and he would endure much more to learn of the intricate plots running rife in Castle Porotane.

"Truly, Baron, there is no more. None at all!"

"There must be opposition to Nosto. Look at the way the others cower when he walks by!"

"They fear him, Lord, just as they feared King Lorens."

"Lorens used the Demon Crown."

"And Archbishop Nosto uses the Inquisition."

Theoll fumed. Efran studied him closely. Theoll wrestled with the problem of which was the more powerful tool for maintaining position on the throne of Porotane. Efran had his own ideas. Efran thought that he, like Theoll, would have preferred the crown, but Nosto used his position as head of the church to good advantage.

"What of Anneshoria?" Theoll asked.

"I can find nothing about her to indicate opposition to Nosto."

"Lies!" Theoll paced restlessly, hands clenched behind his back. The diminutive baron worked through the possibilities open to him. He could risk assassinating Nosto himself, but that left him open to countercharges of being against the church. That created more problems than it solved. Better to allow another to kill Nosto, then step in to fill the power void before real struggle developed.

A rap on the door interrupted Theoll's scheming. He turned from the jester and flung open the door. Efran Gaemock expected to see Commander Squann or another of his personal guard.

Lady Anneshoria stood in the doorway, demurely dressed in a high-collared plain gown. A small smile crinkled the corners of her full-lipped mouth.

"Baron, how good of you to see me."

"He granted no audience for this evening,"

spoke up Efran, wondering if Theoll worked to trip him up—or if the baron had no dealings with Anneshoria.

"Ignore him, Lady. Do come in." Theoll bowed slightly, the angle indicating the difference in their ranks. He made the gesture for a minimum of politeness, not as deference to a superior. Efran saw Theoll tense and start to grab her by the throat when she returned the bow in exactly the same degree.

She afforded him equal rank.

Efran settled down in one corner of the room, eyes alert. Such a meeting meant that strong forces combined in the castle. With luck, he could negate both and leave the gates open to his brother. Dews still carried on the siege, even though the castle's supplies would take them through the long winter with ease. Only by continuing the siege into the planting season could the rebels hope to bring Theoll and the others to their knees.

Anneshoria glanced in the fool's direction. "Get rid of him."

"Permanently?" joked Theoll.

"As you see fit."

Theoll motioned Harhar from the room. Efran Gaemock did not want to leave but his playacting as a jester required him to obey. He somersaulted and cut capers and tried to force the woman to relent.

Efran saw nothing but iron in her brown eyes. He left Theoll's quarters without further argument. In the corridor outside, Efran frowned. None of Theoll's guards were present. He explored and found the entire section of the castle empty of patrols. Was Anneshoria going to kill Theoll?

He squatted in the hall and worked on the

problems of power. He decided that the woman sought an alliance, not a death. She had removed Theoll's guards as a precaution against being overheard. If it had been anything more, she would have brought guards of her own— and Efran would be dead, also.

He slipped along the deserted corridor as quiet as any phantom drifting in the dead of night. Efran found a secret passage favored by Theoll and slipped inside. Quick, knowing steps took him through the maze of narrow walkways and past peepholes until he came to a secret panel within the secret passage.

A spring lock yielded to his patient tinkering, and he crawled on hands and knees to a point where he could spy on Theoll and Anneshoria. Efran had labored for months building and concealing this spy hole but had not dared use it before this moment.

A single mistake now meant the siege would drag on—and new rulers might destroy Porotane even more quickly than if Archbishop Nosto remained seated on the throne.

Efran Gaemock pressed his eye to the hole and listened intently.

"You leave me no choice, Anneshoria," said Theoll.

"I intended nothing less than to force you into supporting me."

"The plan is a good one, but I wish you had been more circumspect in execution."

"Damn caution!" the woman flared. Efran tried to follow her restless movement around the room but the field of vision through the spy hole was too limited. She moved like Theoll, pacing and gesturing.

"I had considered an alliance with you."

"With yourself on the throne as undisputed monarch," she said.

"Of course," Theoll said, smiling.

"This way is better. We rule jointly. In no other fashion could I ascend the throne." Anneshoria paused. "I refuse to be your harlot."

"Consort was the term I had in mind," said Theoll.

"We rule as equals."

"Of course," Theoll agreed. Efran heard the undertones in both nobles' voices. Neither trusted the other and each would betray their temporary ally at the first chance. But whatever scheme Anneshoria had put into motion, Theoll had gone along with it.

Did the baron have to agree or did he merely find it expedient to do so? Efran wished that he had heard the details.

"Is it done?" asked Theoll.

"Where would the jester have gone after I chased him from the room?" Anneshoria's tone caused a cold lump to form in Efran's belly. The part of the plan he had missed was to be revealed anew—and he did not like the turn it took.

"Possibly to the throne room. Possibly he would have roamed the corridors trying to gather further intelligence for me."

"Intelligence from Harhar?" Anneshoria's bitterness and contempt burned Efran's ears.

"What better source? Many speak freely in front of a fool. How can he betray them?"

"Is that your secret to power, Theoll?"

"Harhar has had his uses."

This simple statement from the baron sent Efran scrambling away from the spy hole. A dozen different plans formed and died in his head before he got back to the empty corridor. Not even slowing to close the secret passage panel, Efran ran directly to the king's audience chamber.

The tight knot of guards immediately outside the door alerted Efran that Anneshoria's plan had been put into action already. He dodged before any of the guards saw him and ducked into a small room that opened into another directly behind the throne. Efran peered out at the few men and women assembled at the foot of the dais. Their expressions mingled horror with relief.

Efran slipped unnoticed into the chamber and edged around to one side, using the tattered, threadbare tapestry to conceal himself.

Seated serenely on the throne was Archbishop Nosto, his hands folded across his lap. A heavy lance protruded from his chest. Small rivulets of blood that had seeped around the barbed head had dried and no longer flowed. Nosto was well dead.

Efran Gaemock took a deep breath and strained to hear what those assembled at the foot of the throne were whispering among themselves. Repeatedly he heard his name.

"Harhar did it. The jester! Imagine!"

Others supported this wild claim. Efran began working his way back to the anteroom. Sweat ran from every pore in his body by the time he was again safe within the confines of the room. He had not murdered Nosto. Anneshoria had dressed someone in a jester's outfit and *he* had killed the archbishop-king.

But who would believe such a tale?

Efran shook his head and fastened a headband so that it kept both lank black hair and sweat from his eyes. He took his rattle and twisted the handle. A wicked short-bladed knife came free. Efran used the sharp-edged weapon to cut the bells from his costume. Where he headed he did not want to betray himself with a jingle or a ring.

More guards had entered the corridor. Efran's heart felt as if it would explode; he forced himself to calm. Waiting for the opportunity to grab a solitary guard almost caused him to go wild with frustration. But the chance came and he moved swiftly and well.

One hand reached around the guard's face and strong fingers pinched down on nostrils to shut off breathing and stretch the neck taut. His other hand—the one with the knife—worked across the throat. A tiny ribbon of scarlet appeared. Efran dragged the dying guardsman into the anteroom and quickly stripped him of his uniform.

Efran allowed himself a slight smile at the irony of the situation. The guardsman owed his loyalty to Anneshoria and wore her uniform. She had put him in an untenable position; it seemed fair that she might get him out of Castle Porotane alive.

Dressed in the ill-fitting uniform, Efran Gaemock strode into the corridor appearing more confident than he really was. It had been too long since he had fought knife to knife, hand to hand. His battles had used a more subtle weapon since the months since Duke Freow had lain dying, the victim of Theoll's insidious poisons.

Efran made his way to the courtyard and the stables. "Make way for the royal courier!" he cried. The stableboy jumped, awakened from a nap.

"What is it?" the youth demanded.

"A message is to be sent. I ride to the rebel camp with an ultimatum. Dews Gaemock surrenders or the full might of Porotane is brought against him."

"How's that going to make him surrender?" the boy asked, confused. "We already do what we can against the rebels."

"You dare question the King of Porotane?" bellowed Efran. The stableboy cringed back.

"No, no!"

"A horse. Get me your finest steed. I must ride like the wind this night!"

"You can't leave the castle till dawn," the youth said. "Orders from King Nosto."

Efran cursed under his breath. He had wondered if the accursed archbishop had sealed the castle to prevent a mass escape from his Inquisition. He had.

Efran decided against further argument. He half turned, then spun, the whiplike action of his body driving his fist with irresistible force against the stableboy's belly. The youth buckled. Efran brought up a knee and caught him under the chin. When the stableboy went down, he did not stir.

Efran saddled and rode to the massive gates. He knew no one would open them during the night—and especially not with orders from the new king to the contrary. He reined his steed around and guided the gelding to a side gate where a pair of soldiers dozed. One looked up, eyes still fogged with sleep.

"Urgent orders from the king," Efran said softly, not wanting to wake up the other soldier. "There is a fire burning just outside the wall. I'm to investigate."

"The only fires outside are rebel campfires," the soldier said. "And you know the standing orders."

Efran saw the insignia on the guardsman's uniform and smiled. He leaned down from the saddle and beckoned the soldier closer, showing him a matching sigil on his sleeve. "Lady Anneshoria sends me on a special mission— one unknown to the king. If you need to know more, you must ask her."

The guard swallowed hard, his head bobbing up and down as if it were on springs. "You should have said so. Remember me to the lady, and thank her for her charity to my poor family. Sergeant Disso is always willing to please."

"Sergeant Disso," repeated Efran. "The name will not be forgotten in my report. Keep a sharp watch. I'll return in an hour's time."

"Aye, and good luck to you."

Efran nodded and urged his gelding through the small gate and into the open. Let Disso wait the hour. In that time Efran would have ridden to his brother's camp and would be safely away from the intrigues of Castle Porotane.

The promise of hot food in his belly and the first safety he had known in months kept him warm as he rode through the chill autumn night.

TWENTY-ONE

"The horses!" cried Birtle Santon. "We've got to get to them."

"Too late for that," Vered said. "I can't see in the darkness but I can hear. There must be a dozen or more guardsmen working their way down this tunnel."

Santon cursed the demons, the saints, himself for his weakness, Lorens for following so tenaciously, then began anew missing no one for his cursing. He finally stopped when he realized it was doing no good. To escape, they would have to act.

"I'm not sure how long I can run," he told Vered. Every muscle in his body had turned to water. Standing gave him no difficulty but exertion robbed him of strength quickly. He swung the rucksack containing the Demon Crown into a more comfortable position for carrying. The only stroke of luck they'd had was his insistence on not leaving the accursed crown behind with the rest of their gear where Vered might be able to slip back and touch it.

"Your fever has broken," said Vered, "and the mend-leaf has had a chance to work."

"I can't swing my ax very well." He hefted the heavy battle-ax that had once seemed to weigh nothing in his powerful grip. Now it required effort to lift to eye-level.

"We can't ride because they have our horses," said Vered, "and we can't fight because you're still weak from infection and I'm bone-tired from piling stones and burying Ruirik. That leaves only one course for us."

"Hide?" asked Santon. This didn't strike him as a good solution to their problem. Someone had used powerful spells to destroy the storm warriors. Any wizard able to conjure and control such power would be able to find them quickly.

"Subterfuge."

"Be quick about it," said Santon. "I *feel* them getting closer." Tiny sounds of the soldiers moving through the mountain-fortress tunnels echoed and magnified. He knew the guardsmen walked carefully, trying to make no betraying noise. That so many pebbles were kicked and blades rattled meant a full squad—or more—came after them.

"I wish the elements had been kinder to the uniforms," complained Vered. He pulled the rags off one corpse and began donning it over his own dishevelment. "Hold the torch low so that shadows are cast on my cheeks and forehead."

Santon did as he was told. The sight before him was ghastly. Vered had transformed himself into something unreal—and possibly undead. The phantoms wailing and moaning and fluttering around the tunnels were unnerving. Vered produced outright panic when he spun into the tunnel and waved his arms.

"Aieeee!" he shrieked. Santon knew what to expect and still jumped. The gasps and pounding of heavy boots against the rock floor told that the charade had the desired effect on the soldiers.

"Now what?" asked Santon. "The lure of the Demon Crown is too strong to keep Lorens at bay with a bit of arm-waving and shouting."

"Now we run. Come along. Let's hope that we've bought more than a few seconds of time to hide in these tunnels."

Santon followed his friend through the rocky passages as quickly as he could. The torch cast an ever-shifting, shadow light that gave birth to illusions. Santon jumped nervously several times at nothing more than a rock formation limned strangely. As he walked he tried to remember what he could about these abandoned mines, of how King Lamost had turned them into a fortress.

"Vered, wait," he called out. "We'll find ourselves in a dead end if we continue along this tunnel. We want to go . . . north."

"Make it sound as if you know what you're saying. Confidence, even false, is what I need to bolster my spirits." Vered turned and pointed down a crossing tunnel. "That's north."

"How can you be so sure?"

"I'm not. But I take my own advice." Vered started off at a pace too fast for Santon to maintain.

Panting harshly, Santon did his best to keep up. Soon he had to rest. Sweating and tired, he sank down and let the cool tunnel wall support his back. Santon worried over how little he remembered of the fortress. There had been special features to keep the royalist troops from being trapped. But what were they? Escape routes, undoubtedly, but where did they start— and end?

"It's too bad we had to abandon the horses.

They served us well and deserved better than being given over to Lorens' soldiers," Santon said. "But it might be for the best. It doesn't appear as if we'd have been able to ride them." The ceilings in these tunnels had lowered considerably. When he walked he could lift his shield and drag it along the rocky juts from the roof.

"They mined extensively," said Vered. "I see evidence of it in the stoops leading to either side. This is the main tunnel and must lead somewhere."

"It would do little good to have escape routes that required you to crawl on your belly," agreed Santon. "At one time over five hundred soldiers were quartered here."

Vered laughed softly. "An interesting sight, five hundred armed and armored men wiggling about in the dust trying to get free of this giant tomb."

"Don't make it sound so final. The sappers would have designed exits for the soldiers to leave on horseback and on foot, not on crawling on their stomachs."

"Engineers always design to please themselves," said Vered. He stood and explored further along the tunnel. He called back, "This might be an exit tunnel, though. New cuts have been made in the rock."

"How new? The fortress has been abandoned, except by phantoms, for twenty years."

When Vered didn't answer, Santon heaved himself to his feet and went to look at his friend's discovery. Santon went cold inside when he saw the bright marks on the rock.

"Metallic," said Vered. "Can it be from picks and shovels?"

"Look at the spacing." Santon reached out.

With the fingers on his powerful hand outstretched, he barely covered the long gouge marks. "That is left by a mouth. Those cuts are made by iron teeth."

"Teeth? Absurd. What manner of creature . . ." Vered's words trailed off.

"Aye, a rock worm. From the height above the floor, the worm must be as tall as you, Vered."

"Don't joke."

Santon was not joking. Their problems had grown with this discovery. Lorens' soldiers wanted what Santon carried in the rucksack. The pale green glow had increased, even through the cloth sack. Santon looked at the torch Vered held and saw that its usefulness was reaching an end. It would soon burn to the handle. Santon took out the glass box containing the Demon Crown and opened the lid.

The glow illuminated their way in a manner even eerier than that of the flickering torch.

"We'll have to move on," said Santon. He hadn't rested adequately but the sight of rock-worm gnawings added urgency to their flight. Better to die from running than to be eaten by worms while he rested.

"Did rock worms live in the fortress when it was occupied?" asked Vered.

"I remember nothing of them, but I spent little time here. Mostly, I patrolled Claymore Pass and camped rather than returning to this base."

"Have you ever seen one?"

"Never just one. They live in nests. Chambers filled with huge numbers of them. They gnaw through rock getting what nutrition they can from it. Aye, I've seen them and wish that I had not. They move slowly but are difficult to kill." Santon shuddered. "Their strong jaws enable them to bite through even the strongest armor with a single snap of their jaws."

"Remind me to never invite a rock worm to any of my formal dinners. It wouldn't do having them eat the flatware—and never noticing it wasn't the appetizer. The other guests would surely complain."

Santon felt a growing uneasiness as they walked silently along the tunnels. His memory of the layout had failed him. The best they could hope for was not to become utterly lost or blunder back into Lorens' troops.

The worst Birtle Santon refused to consider.

"How long before Lorens whips his men into pursuit?" asked Vered.

"You gave them a fright, but they are the best he has in the castle. The king's personal guard isn't composed of cowards."

"I looked a sight, didn't I?" Vered chuckled. He stopped in the middle of the tunnel and performed a slow turn to show off the rags dangling from his body. "They must have thought I was a corpse come back to life."

"With so many phantoms around, the guardsmen were ready to run, whether they realized it or not."

Santon joined Vered in a laugh at the expense of Lorens' guard. The laugh cut off suddenly when they entered a junction with a larger tunnel. Not a hundred paces down the tunnel strode six of the soldiers they made light of.

Santon kept walking, then grabbed Vered and spun him around. Vered hadn't seen the guardsmen. In a low voice Santon said, "They'll be on us in seconds. What are we going to do?"

"The same thing as before. It worked once, didn't it."

"The torch is out. All we have is the crown." Santon held it at arm's length. The pale green glow wasn't strong enough to cast a shadow on Vered's face as the torch had done.

"Might not be a good idea using it, anyway," said Vered. "They know what they're looking for. When they see it, in the hand of an animated corpse or not, they'll come for it."

Santon looked down the corridor they traversed. Only darkness lay ahead. "They're coming slowly, checking each side tunnel. We might have time to escape down this one."

"Do we have any other choice?" Vered paused for a moment, dropping to hands and knees and smoothing the rock dust on the floor to erase any sign of their passage. He did not do a good job.

"Come on. There's no time to do it right. They'll be here before you can completely hide our trail."

Santon walked as fast as he could. His legs trembled with every step and he found it increasingly difficult to hold the glass box with the Demon Crown at arm's length to light their path. He even considered letting Vered hold the box, but discarded this wild notion. Vered could not fully control himself in the crown's presence. The addictive lure of the Demon Crown's magic had made itself apparent, not only in Vered but in Lorens' behavior.

"They've found our tunnel," said Vered. "I can feel the vibrations through the walls. They've stopped. They're discussing it. They'll be sending men after us any instant."

"You're imagining that," snapped Santon.

"You can't make out anything by a few rock vibrations."

"They have an army after us, Santon. Put your ear to the wall and listen."

Birtle Santon stopped and found a flat spot where he pressed his ear. "That's not the sound of footsteps," he said, his voice choked. "That's the noise a rock worm makes when it is eating."

"Ahead? Or off to one side?" demanded Vered.

"How can I know? But you may be right about the soldiers following us. There is another, sharper sound that drowns out the rock-worm munchings."

"Die on a sword tip or a rock-worm fang. What a choice," grumbled Vered. "I have no wish to die dressed like this. I had something better in mind. A stately robe of red silk with embroidered patterns in gold thread, perhaps. Certainly in bed. I had even thought to have a pair of nubile young ladies to help ease me from this world. And a few—"

"Enough!" Santon's temper flared. "We've got to get away from both rock worms and soldiers. How?"

"Keep going," suggested Vered. "What can we lose if we are in as deep trouble as you think."

Santon wondered about Vered. At times he was morose and pessimistic. At moments like this, he seemed flippant and even cheerful. It might be nothing more than a way of hiding his fear. Santon knew that Vered did not like closed-in spaces, yet his friend showed no hesitation in entering increasingly narrower tunnels.

Did one fear drown out another? And were they all hidden by his cheerfulness?

Santon decided he would ponder this later. After they escaped the tunnels and Lorens and the rock worms.

The greenish glow cast by the Demon Crown wavered and Santon almost missed the motion ahead of him on the rocky floor. He danced back, dropping his shield to protect himself from the fangs that ripped at his legs. Metallic teeth bit into the glass shield and slipped off, leaving only scratch marks.

Vered bumped into him. "What—" When Vered saw the rock worm on the floor, he pushed Santon to one side and swung his short sword with surprising accuracy in the narrow tunnel. The glass tip cut across the worm's throat and left a shallow gash. The worm reared like a snake and struck.

Santon gasped. The worm's speed was greater than he had remembered, but Vered was faster—or luckier. The rock worm impaled itself on the point of the man's sword, the entire end vanishing into the worm's gaping, tooth-filled mouth.

"Twist it," cried Santon. "Twist it and get it out of the worm's mouth. They use acid to dissolve the rock they eat."

Vered regained his balance and jerked his glass sword from the worm's mouth. The arm-thick, pebble-scaled creature fell to the floor, lifeless.

"How long is it?" Vered asked, crouching down. The worm's body vanished into the wall. A hole hardly larger than the creature's body had been carefully gnawed through solid stone.

"Who cares? The soldiers are gaining on us. And worms are not solitary creatures. There will be more around. Close."

Vered said, "Seldom do I admit that you are

right, Santon. This time is an exception." With an almost prissy step, Vered got around the dead rock worm.

Santon had gone ahead, advancing cautiously, the crown lighting his way. His caution kept them from plunging into a pit filled with wriggling rock worms. The pale light cast by the Demon Crown revealed thousands of the creatures. They had eaten away the tunnel and surrounding rock to form a hole fifty feet deep.

"No chance of crossing that," said Vered. He tapped the rocks in the wall as if this might betray a new worm hole.

"Don't," said Santon. "That might attract them."

Vered didn't question his friend. He edged away from the wall and stood in the center of the narrow passage. Santon saw the fear of enclosed spaces beginning to work on Vered. Gone was the joke from his lip and the sparkle in his eye.

"We can get around them. There is a ledge circling the pit. If we move slowly and keep quiet, we will make it."

"What's on the other side?" asked Vered, eyeing the ledge with increasing fear.

"Who knows?" said Santon. "But we do know what lies behind us." The echo of guardsmen's bootsteps emphasized his claim.

Santon began the dangerous circuit around the pit. The worms writhed, hidden in shadow and darkness, only occasional glints from the Demon Crown's glow casting back from metallic teeth. Santon wobbled slightly as he moved. His weakness told on him. Even worse, he had to hold the crown, balance his battle-ax, and carry his shield. With one hand useless, the right hand had to do the job of many.

"Are you all right?" he called out to Vered.

"Just fine," came the shaky answer. Vered looked as pale as he had when the fever was at its peak. Anyone blundering upon them at this instant would have been hard-pressed to tell who was recovering from a seriously infected wound and who had been healthy.

"There!" came the cry. "There they are! And they have the Demon Crown!"

"Soldiers," Vered warned needlessly.

"I'm moving as quickly as I can," said Santon, but the battle-ax impeded his progress. He stopped and tucked the glass box containing the crown under his left arm. A quick movement brought the ax up and into his grip. Santon slipped the leather thong from his wrist. He turned on the ledge and saw the first soldier groping with his sword in an attempt to reach Vered.

The soldiers hadn't seen the pit filled with rock worms. Their attention focused on the crown.

Santon changed that situation with an adroit toss of his ax. The heavy blade twisted over and over in darkness and appeared as if by magic in the guardsman's chest. By some quirk of luck, he did not topple into the pit. He sank to his knees.

"Hurry, Vered. Hurry, before the others get around him."

Even as he spoke, Santon saw the guardsman behind the one dying from the ax strike working his way along.

"Kick him off the ledge," ordered an officer, still in the tunnel. "He's dead."

"He still lives," protested the guardsman behind his comrade.

"Do as you are ordered! King Lorens must recover the Demon Crown!"

Santon reached the new tunnel mouth and slipped inside. He spun around and held out his good hand for Vered. He clamped on his friend's wrist and pulled the man into the tunnel with a single powerful tug.

Vered dropped to his knees, sweating and shaking.

Santon checked the ledge. They might have to make a defense here, unless his gamble had paid off.

It had. The commotion on the ledge drew the rock worms. They surged up from their nesting place in the pit and attacked the dying soldier. The one behind yelled in fear when he saw the worms. His abrupt reaction cost him his balance—and his life. He tumbled into the pit, screaming until an iron-fanged rock worm ripped out his throat.

The guardsmen were diverted. Santon put his good arm around Vered and pulled the man to his feet.

"Come on," he urged. "We've got to find a way out of here."

"But where? What direction are we going? The walls. The roof. It's all closing in on me."

Santon kicked Vered hard enough to make the man cry out in pain. "You've got our only weapon. You bring up the rear and keep a sharp lookout for the soldiers." Santon's stern tones forced Vered to concentrate on something other than his morbid fear. Vered nodded and swallowed hard, his eyes still wild but his body set and coming back under control.

Santon's exhaustion kept their pace slower than he would have liked, but he did not stop to rest. He knew he might never rise again if he succumbed. As important, he did not want to give Vered the chance to dread the ever-narrowing tunnel.

When he did not think he could go on another step, he saw a small pinpoint of light. Santon hurried on, almost stumbling as he went. A cave-in had blocked an exit. Only a hole the size of his fist remained at the top of the larger mouth.

"We're still trapped," said Vered, "but we can see where we're going. Let me by. You rest and I'll get us out."

Santon let his friend begin to work. Vered's panic now fueled his actions in a useful endeavor. Rock and debris flew back from the hole until Vered had a space almost as large as his shoulders cleared.

"I see sky outside. It . . . it's sunrise! How long have we been inside this accursed place?"

"Keep digging. Your shoulders might clear but mine never would," Santon said. His broad shoulders required another foot of space to clear.

"Wind. There's a hint of winter in the wind." Vered babbled as he dug.

The refreshing breath from the outside renewed Santon's strength.

"How much farther?" he called to Vered.

"Not far. Another few minutes of digging, that's all."

Santon turned when he heard a scraping noise. He barely lifted his shield to deflect the downward cut of a sword. The impact knocked him staggering, but he managed to keep the glass shield up and between him and the pounding, slashing weapon.

"What's going on back there?" came Vered's querulous voice. "I'm killing myself and you're—"

"Vered!" Santon's warning came in time. The smaller man had pulled back through the opening and had settled down on the rocky slope. When he saw the troubles facing his friend, he scooped up his sword in time to deflect the thrust of a second guardsman.

"Where did they come from?" Vered demanded. He kicked out and caught his opponent squarely under the chin. The blow knocked the soldier back and gave Vered time to get his feet under him.

"I don't know!" Santon hid behind the shield and bulled his way forward. The soldier did what he had hoped he would; he tried to come over the top of the shield with his sword. This left his legs exposed. Santon's powerful right arm circled the soldier's legs and pulled them out from under him.

Shield pinning the sword arm down, Santon drove his knee into the guardsman's exposed midriff. A hard fist to the side of the head crushed his temple and ended the battle. Santon stood, seeing that Vered had gutted his opponent.

"They came on me with no warning," he explained.

"Just like the others?" asked Vered. Coming down a side tunnel were at least four bouncing torches and dozens of shadows. "How many do you think?"

"Too many." Santon grabbed his opponent's sword and scrambled up the rocky slope and began wiggling through the opening Vered had enlarged. His shoulders scraped rock and left skin behind but Lorens' approaching soldiers added speed to his flight.

Santon tumbled out into dawn.

Behind him came Vered, clawing and kicking to get free. They stood and stared at the opening. On the far side a soldier entered the small crawl space to come after them.

"You've got the crown?" asked Vered.

"It's never left my side," Santon said, patting the rucksack with the Demon Crown in it.

"Good."

Vered kicked a large stone and caused a minor landslide. He worked his way up the slope above the opening and began working in earnest. Within minutes rock tumbled down in a steady blanket.

Vered joined Santon at the base of the hill. Avalanches both small and large continued from his activity.

"That will plug them up for a time."

"And it'll cover us if we don't get out of here." Santon saw several ledges of rock that trembled as they were undercut by rock sliding down the hillside.

"We should be on horseback," complained Vered. "But we are alive. That's what matters."

"We're alive and we know where Lokenna is," added Santon. "Truly, it is *that* which matters most."

They started on foot to find the village of Fron and the other heir to the throne of Porotane.

TWENTY-TWO

"May all the demons eat you alive!" raged King Lorens. His guard commander tried not to show fear. He failed in the face of his monarch's towering wrath. "Losing them in the mine was foolish. Your squad almost had them."

"Sire, please. I have explained that. Part of the squad had been killed."

"Rock worms, or so you say."

"Worms," the lieutenant said, his face stony. The king might not believe the report, but it had happened. His best men had fallen to their deaths in a pit filled with metal-toothed monsters.

"The squad that found them hadn't run afoul of . . . rock worms." Lorens' tone was sarcastic. Nothing had gone right during the past two weeks. Nothing. He was surrounded by fools and worse. The incompetence of his troops turned in his gut like a rusty blade.

"They took my men by surprise. We expected only attack from the thieves, not from rock worms. Before reinforcements could arrive, the thieves had slipped through the hole and escaped."

"You've told me all this. They brought the

mountain down and crushed another four of
your valiant men. Yes, yes, you've said all this. It
does not explain why days have passed since
these catastrophes and you have still not found
their spoor."

"Winter winds blow off the Yorral Mountains, Sire," the lieutenant said. "Their trail is
covered by thin snow. Even worse, my finest
trackers perished within the mine."

"Excuses. All you offer is more reason for
me to question your ability to lead my elite
guards!" Lorens' voice almost cracked with
strain.

"Sire, if you could again conjure for us.
Your tracking spell—the phosphorescent footprints—could lead us to them quickly. You are a
wizard without peer. Conjure for us and we will
fight to the death!" The lieutenant wanted to spit
out the bad taste forming in his mouth from
these lying words, but he saw his king's anger
and had to turn it aside. Lorens had become
more vicious with every setback—and he took
out his rage on innocent guardsmen.

Lorens did not answer immediately. He
dared not tell the officer that he had tried to
again conjure the Spell of the Ten Trackers.
Each casting had been weaker than the prior
one. Something or someone blocked his every
attempt to cast *any* spell.

Lorens wondered if this was some subtle
revenge brought down on his head by the Wizard of Storms. Destroying the five storm warriors had required both skill and daring, but he
had not been able to properly form a spell since
then. It was as if his powers drained daily,
leaving him weaker both physically and emo-
tionally.

Lorens hid the tears forming in his eyes. It

would not do to let his lieutenant see his weakness. The soldier already hated and feared him. This combination made for more efficient service—as long as the ruler was strong enough to use it. Lorens had begun to doubt himself and, as a result, felt his ability to command slipping away.

Everything would have been different if those two ruffians hadn't stolen the Demon Crown. His hands rubbed along his temples where the potent magical crown had once rested. How easy it would be for him to rule Porotane with it. Simply cast forth his senses and *know* what others did and said, even in their most private moments. That was the source of true power.

Lorens pulled his long, thin cloak around his body as the cold mountain wind tried to snap it away. Winter would soon blanket the upper peaks and begin creeping down. He had less than a month before even Claymore Pass closed with heavy wet snows drifted higher than the spires of his castle.

Lorens continued rubbing his temples, as if this would return the Demon Crown to its former resting place. Nothing had gone right. Nothing. His personal guard had been reduced by half. Those the storm warriors had not slaughtered had perished within the old fortified mine.

Rock worms. Superior fighters. Lorens believed none of it. His guard commander lied to cover his own incompetence.

If he only had the Demon Crown he would know!

A commotion from the camp perimeter brought Lorens around. He frowned when a figure bundled in rags was brought before him.

"Sire, he claims to be your servant."

"I have no servants with me." Lorens scowled at the groveling figure dressed in brown and black motley. The man did appear familiar, but Lorens did not recognize him. He had left all his servants in the castle.

Lorens' lips sneered. The double he had placed on the throne enjoyed all the benefits of the monarchy, while the true king suffered the elements and outrageous fortune in the field.

A grimy face tipped up. "Mighty King Lorens, how is it you cannot remember your jester Harhar?"

"Harhar?" Lorens stared in disbelief at the fool. "It is you. But how did you find me? Why did you leave the castle?"

"It is under siege, Majesty. Theoll sits half-assed on the throne after assassinating Archbishop Nosto. And Lady Anneshoria shares the other half of the throne with Theoll. Together they duel and rule, and they are cruel to this fool, O my king!"

"What are you saying? How did you know I was gone from the castle?" Lorens glanced over at his guard commander. The officer stood impassively but Lorens detected the undercurrent of interest. Had the officer betrayed him? Few had known that he placed a double on the throne. The commander of his personal guard had been one.

Harhar huddled against the wind, his tattered clothing doing little to protect his thin body. Lorens made no effort to help him. All he wanted was information.

"How did you learn that I had left Castle Porotane?"

Efran Gaemock, speaking once more as

Harhar, related all that had happened, leaving out only the part about Anneshoria making it appear as if he had murdered Archbishop Nosto.

"Those traitors," whined Lorens. "How dare they do this to me? It's not fair!"

"No, Sire, it isn't. But what has brought you so far into the Yorral Mountains? And why did you not know of these terrible things happening in the castle?" Efran studied the guard commander, not Lorens, for the truth. From the stiffness in the officer's posture and the fleeting emotions of disgust and fear, Efran guessed that they had been unable to recover the Demon Crown. If Vered and Birtle Santon had stolen it, they remained free with it.

Efran's opinion of the two rogues rose.

And a new plot formed in his fertile brain. His brother and Dalziel Sef had failed to intercept Lorens as the king raced north on the mission to find the crown. Sef had been unwilling to commit more than a handful of troops to a hunt of the Yorral Mountains when so many were needed to keep the siege of the castle in place against constant forays by cavalry. Dews had agreed and, reluctantly, Efran did, too. Now the situation had changed. Lorens' forces were decimated by . . . what?

Efran would have to find out what had reduced the ranks of the palace guard to such an extent. Two ruffians had not done it. With ample reinforcements, the rebels could seize Lorens and force him to abdicate. And the Demon Crown might even be found.

The two main symbols of power in Porotane would be under rebel control. Efran knew the effect on the populace and the nobility. The civil war would end.

Efran frowned. The war between rebels and royalists would end, but the war between Dalziel Sef and the Gaemocks would begin. Efran did not have to conjure a spell to know that Sef wanted the throne for himself. All either of the brothers desired was stable and just rule.

"Find them. Find them and get me back the crown!" whimpered Lorens.

Efran blinked. The tone used by the king showed him to be nearing the limits of his control. Defeating a man such as this would take even fewer troops than he'd anticipated.

"Find them," muttered Lorens, wandering off. The commander of his personal guard hurried off, leaving the jester huddled in the snow. A smile crept across Efran's lips. It would be only a matter of time before he sent a message to his brother.

Dews Gaemock would capture the King of Porotane and end the war that had ravaged the country for too many decades.

"What do you mean the patrol has not returned? Of course they will return." Lorens stood and shifted his weight from foot to foot. His expression was not that of a confident ruler. His indecision radiated like the warmth of a fire.

"They are more than two days overdue, Sire," said the commander of the guard.

"But it's been over a week since those ruffians eluded us in the mine. How can this be?"

"I fear the patrol has deserted, Sire."

Efran cocked his head to one side. He had been telling bad jokes to cheer Lorens when the commander had entered the drafty tent with his report. This news cheered Efran greatly. He had released a message-carrying spite-wren upon learning of Lorens' bad luck. A day of flight had gotten the message to Dews. Another day's preparation and three of hard riding would bring a fighting force to the perimeter of the king's camp.

Dews Gaemock might have encountered the patrol and dispatched them. Efran gloated. The end for this petty tyrant neared.

"Deserted? Impossible. No coward dares leave the service of his king!"

"There is another possibility, Sire. Brigands still roam these hills. Ionia's forces are reputedly aligned with the rebels. She might have joined battle with our men and defeated them."

"Defeat? Never!"

"Sire," the guard commander said tiredly, "Ionia sends armies through Claymore Pass. A small patrol could never stand against such overwhelming numbers."

"It might have been the doing of the Wizard of Storms," muttered Lorens. "He hates me. He sends his storm warriors against me."

Efran listened closely. He had not been able to get a decent report from any of the guardsmen about that day when the five cloud-bodied demons had attacked. He hardly believed that Lorens had driven such powerful magical creatures off with spells of his own conjuring, but none denied it. What would the reclusive Wizard of Storms want from a petty tyrant like Lorens?

Even as the thought crossed his mind, Efran knew. The Wizard of Storms sought the Demon Crown. No other bait could lure the wizard from his mountain fastness. Had the Wizard of Storms already captured the crown? If he had destroyed the patrol, why hadn't he also destroyed the main force? Efran Gaemock did not think the wizard was likely to toy with Lorens, especially if the young king had vanquished five storm warriors.

Efran decided that the Wizard of Storms did not move against Lorens—yet. The loss of the patrol had little to do with the wizard. Desertion was a distinct possibility. Sudden storms might have trapped them in the higher passes. Even Birtle Santon and Vered might have killed the soldiers. Did one of them wear the Demon Crown? Efran worried more and more about that.

He and his brother fought to keep one tyrant using the Demon Crown off the throne. Efran did not want to work against another.

"Sire, there is a signal from the mouth of the southernmost canyon."

"The patrol!"

"No, Sire," said the lieutenant. "They would return from the east. These are unidentified riders."

"Ionia's troops?"

Even as the question passed Lorens' lips, the cry from the most distant sentry rolled through the camp. "Rebel forces! Dews Gaemock's soldiers!"

King Lorens and his guard commander flew from the tent. Efran waited a few minutes to be sure that no one returned unexpectedly, then examined the detail maps the king had spread on a low table. The canyons were marked with tiny dots showing the positions of the sentries. Efran hastily duplicated the map on a sheet of thin paper, then folded it and put it into his pocket.

The officer knew his tactics well. Dews would fight long and hard, even against the few remaining soldiers in the camp, if he did not learn soon of the enemy disposition. Efran ducked outside the king's tent and caught the full bite of a winter gust in his face. Squinting, hot tears burning against his frostbitten cheeks, he made his way against the incipient blizzard to where he kept the pitiful bedroll they had given him.

In the center of the blanket something moved. He reached in and pulled out a second spite-wren. The small bird shivered against the wintry weather.

"You'll soon be warm and fed, my little friend," Efran soothed. He stroked the small brown bird's red-tinged topknot as he affixed the map to the bird's leg. "Fly quickly to your mate. She awaits you with my brother."

The bird seemed to stagger. As it took wing, a gust of wind caught it. The tiny brown spite-wren beat its wings faster and blended in with the blowing white snow.

Efran turned to pull the threadbare blanket around his shoulders and found a pair of boots. He looked up until he came to the lieutenant's glowering visage.

"A good day to you, Commander."

"I'd wondered about you, fool. At times you seemed too alert, but I never knew. Until now. What message did the bird carry to the rebels?"

"Why, nothing. I just lost my dinner. Such a tiny thing, but fresh fowl is—" Efran's hand reached into the folds of his motley and found the handle of a tiny dagger. As he spoke he moved so that his thrust would be accurate.

He used the full power of his legs to drive

upward, the dagger aimed for the officer's heart.
The lieutenant jerked back and stumbled; Efran
missed his target and the knife point skittered
along the front of the man's uniform. A ragged
gash appeared and turned bloody, but the officer began shouting for help from his comrades.

Efran's hand clamped over the man's
mouth. The dagger struck downward, seeking a
more deadly berth than it had found before. The
commander fought but he had not expected
Efran's strength, skill, or swiftness. He had
faced a jester whom he had thought a spy.

He had found a warrior—and death.

Blood sizzled and hissed as it drained from
the lieutenant's neck into the snow. Efran
Gaemock rose, gore-covered blade in hand. No
one had seen him kill the officer. He wiped off
the dagger and went to find King Lorens.

The swirling snow blowing down off the
heights obscured the battlefield. Efran tried to
make out the struggling figures and finally gave
up. He had to believe that the bird had faithfully
carried its message to Dews and that his brother
had used the information to get past the king's
guard. There wasn't any other way the rebels
could have penetrated this quickly into the heart
of the camp.

"King Lorens, where are you?" Efran
called. Only howling wind and death cries
reached him. He blundered through the blind-
ing wet snow, then recoiled when a phantom
fluttered past. Was this from a recently slain
soldier or had it lingered for years in the pass?
Efran did not stop to inquire.

In the tent once more, he brushed off the
snow and looked for the king.

"Not here." Efran started to go back into the increasingly inclement weather, then stopped. Let Lorens come to him. He could wait in relative warmth and comfort. He sat down, dagger in hand, and stared at the tent flap as it snapped in the wind.

A dark figure appeared, silhouetted against the blowing snow. Efran caught his breath and held it. His hand tightened on his dagger as he waited to confront Lorens.

The flap jerked back and the figure entered. Efran sank back into the chair and sighed. "You can get yourself killed doing that, Dews."

"Efran! I found you!"

"You make it sound as if I'd been lost."

"We've taken the camp. Your map led us past their strongest points. The flank commanders tell me that Lorens' soldiers are in rout. They're running for their lives."

"What of Lorens?"

"I'd hoped to find him here." Dews sat beside his brother. "We'll scour the camp. He can't get far in this weather."

"I want him alive. We can use him as a lever to force the castle's surrender."

"What? Why would Theoll surrender because we hold the king? Or Anneshoria? She is even worse than the baron. They'd drive a knife into his back faster than I would!"

"The countryside still lends some small support to a king of the royal line. If the people give up the fight, the castle will fall."

"Aye, convincing the people that I'm not just another power-hungry tyrant seeking the throne has been hard."

"Allying with Dalziel Sef has made it even more difficult, I'd wager," said Efran.

"The truth is, I had no desire to leave him in command of the siege, but I did not think that Theoll would surrender easily."

"I'm glad you came personally."

"The crown?" asked Dews. "Had Lorens recovered it?"

"No."

The brothers sank into silence. Occasional loud clanks of steel against steel died and were replaced by the howling wind off the Yorral Mountains.

Ten minutes later, a rebel forced his way into the tent, barely able to stand against the wind. "Dews, we're in control. Everyone has surrendered. Do we put them to death?"

"No!" both Efran and Dews shouted simultaneously. Dews motioned his brother to silence. "We need their support, not their death. Treat them well and try to see that they don't freeze—but don't coddle them, either. They're not the enemy, but they are our prisoners."

"What of Lorens?" asked Efran. "Did you find him?"

The rebel shook his head. "Nowhere to be found. We'll keep looking, but the storm's getting worse. Some of the men're saying that the Wizard of Storms sent it to bedevil us."

"Keep looking for Lorens," ordered Dews.

Efran stared into the white wall just beyond the tent opening. Were they right? Did the Wizard of Storms send this as a warning?

He shook off the notion. They had achieved a great victory this day. Lorens had been routed —and he would be found soon and put into chains. Dead or alive, it did not matter. The petty tyrant would never again sit on Porotane's throne.

Efran Gaemock just wished that he could feel more positive about this victory.

TWENTY-THREE

"I don't need to ride. I don't *want* to. My ass is getting sore. You ride for a while, Vered." Birtle Santon shifted on the horse and glared at his friend. Vered walked a dozen paces ahead. He stopped and turned, shaking his head.

"You still haven't fully recovered."

"It's been more than a week since we buried Lorens in the mine."

"Buried? Trapped is more likely. Inconvenienced is most likely of all."

Santon grumbled and cursed under his breath. Vered spoke the truth. Even if their small avalanche had buried one or two guardsmen, the rest remained unscathed within the mine-fortress. All they had done was force Lorens to retreat, find another way from the mine and continue the hunt for them.

In that, Santon reflected, they had been lucky. They had come out of the fortress in an inaccessible valley. Lorens would lose days finding them. Or perhaps he had lost them totally. Santon could hope, even if he did not truly believe this.

Finding the horse wandering riderless had been another stroke of fortune for them. But

Santon felt whole again. He need not be treated like an invalid and given special privileges when his friend was obviously tired of hiking. An occasional throbbing in his head was the only remaining trace of his infection. Even the gash had begun to heal, although it looked as if it would leave a ragged white scar.

"The wind's getting colder," complained Vered.

"All the more reason for you to ride and let me walk. Save yourself for the steep passes."

"Steeper than this one?" Vered shook his head in amazement. They had crossed Claymore Pass' main track and headed south by west down a miserable rut of a path. Every notch in the mountains had seemed higher than the last, especially to a man walking.

"I cannot remember the village Ruirik mentioned, but it may be a new one. Fron is not a name to forget."

"Nor is it one to remember," said Vered. He turned and pulled his cloak tighter around his body. The wind caught the rents and further destroyed the garment. He finally gave up and continued the slow climb into still another rocky pass.

"It will be if he spoke the truth. Lokenna awaits us. I feel it," said Santon.

"Your hot air doesn't reach this far. Come closer before gusting out your fantasies."

Santon chuckled. Vered had been in a morose mood of late, in spite of their good fortune. A week without sighting Lorens' guard, almost a week of travel with this fine horse carrying a considerable burden, the end of their quest known. What more could he want?

"The storms worsen. We should find shelter for the night," said Vered.

"Winter comes quickly in the Yorral Mountains."

"This is a strange storm. It centers on the peaks to either side of the road, if any dares call this stony rut a road."

Santon turned in the saddle and looked at the far-flung peaks in the mountain range. Vered's sharp eyes had again found what he had missed. A few of the loftiest purple-cloaked mountains sported a fluffy white crown of clouds. Most were sharp and clear in the pure autumn air. Only the two ahead of them drew the full wrath of a storm.

As Santon watched, the violence locked within the thunder clouds burst forth. Lightning shattered pieces of rock from either side of the pass and sent boulders tumbling down to block their path. Black tendrils began to dip from the underbelly of the storm, turbulent and billowing with unnatural life.

"We ought to take cover now," said Santon. "It might do us no good. That storm." He swallowed, his mouth suddenly dry. "That is another of the gifts sent us by the Wizard of Storms."

"May all the demons take him and devour his flesh!" cursed Vered. He reached out and caught the horse's reins as Santon passed him. Vered led the horse to the side of the road where a scrubby mountain copperwood grew. Santon swung from the saddle and landed heavily. His legs yielded under the strain and he began to doubt himself.

While he rode, he felt fine. The slight exertion of dismounting robbed him of his strength. As much as he hated to admit it, Vered was right. He had yet to recover fully from the fever.

"Tether the horse. We should go scouting,"

Santon said. He flexed his right arm and re-
joiced in the power there. His left carried the
glass shield as if it were nothing more than a
feather. But his legs! They worked like lead
weights, numb and ponderous.

He and Vered worked their way up the
hillside, reaching the crest and peering down
into a small ravine. The trailing wisps of dark
cloud touched not a hundred paces from them.

"The saints have blessed us with luck,"
whispered Vered. "We would have ridden into
them if we hadn't seen the storm cloud."

A half dozen of Lorens' guardsmen had
prepared an ambush on the trail. Their trap
turned against them. The pillar of cloud stuff
began to swirl and turn and whip about, sending
out small fist-sized clouds randomly. Each of the
tiny clouds sprouted arms and legs and a head
with eyes blazing red hate.

"Storm warriors. The Wizard of Storms has
sent his minions after us!"

"Or against Lorens. The magical warriors
attack the guardsmen, not us."

Santon watched in mute fascination as the
storm warriors took form and moved to attack
the human soldiers. The patrol leader had positioned his men to command the road; they were
cut off from their horses. The men fought val-
iantly but the lightning bolts caught them if they
attacked, cut them down if they ran, and blew
apart their hiding places if they did not move.

In less than a minute only smoldering bodies remained. The individual storm warriors
lifted their arms and sent down a torrential rain
that diminished them. When only tiny puffs of
cloud were left, these were sucked back up into
the thunder cloud above. The only evidence of
battle lay with the victims.

"Can the cloud sense us?" wondered Vered. He craned his head back and peered at the peaks above them.

"The Wizard of Storms directs his army in some fashion. That was not an accidental attack."

"A wizard never works by chance alone," agreed Vered. He shifted and looked around, waiting to see if more of Lorens' soldiers appeared.

"The Wizard of Storms must want the crown," said Santon. "But can he use scrying spells to find it?"

"Let's hope not or the cloud will rain down on us. What should we do? Continue or turn back? I'm not in favor of staying here—not with *that* over our heads."

Santon stared at the underside of the black cloud and had to admit his own rising fear of it. He could best any man in single combat. With shield and ax—or even the puny sword he still carried—he feared no one. But wizards fought with weapons both unseen and unstoppable and all the more fearsome because of that.

"We ride on. With luck, we can pick up spare horses and ride the faster."

"Agreed." Vered already dashed forth, intent on the small corral the soldiers had fashioned for their mounts. Vered took the three sturdiest and fashioned travel packs from the provisions the soldiers would no longer need. By the time he finished, Santon had ridden up on the rapidly tiring animal that had served them so well during the past week.

"We can't leave the mare," said Santon.

"Didn't intend to," answered his friend. "Dismount and ride this one. We'll use your mare as a spare. We ride till one tires, then switch. That ought to get us into Fron before *we* tire."

"Too late," said Santon.

"And you were the one who was all healed," said Vered as he swung up and settled into the saddle. "This is a fine mount. Only the best for the king's guard—and us!"

With that he put his heels into the horse's flanks and turned the gelding uphill toward the pass.

The rest of the day they rode, stopping only to change horses every hour. By nightfall, they came to the top of the pass and looked down into a small lushly green valley still protected from the winter gusts they had fought.

"A lovely place," said Santon. "But is it Fron?"

"There is no way to tell from here. Down to the village and inquire, though it must be Fron. How many villages can there be in this remote area?"

Vered turned, straightened in the saddle, and asked of Santon, "Do you feel it, too?"

Santon nodded. His heart beat more rapidly and he had the eerie feeling of being on the brink of a great and wondrous discovery. The only sensation comparable in his life was when he had seen Alarice for the first time. He had known there was something special about the white-haired Glass Warrior.

There was something special about Fron— and it came from goodness, not evil.

They rode slowly into the village. A few men, going home from a day preparing their fields for winter, waved and hailed them. They returned the greetings but did not stop until they came to a small inn.

"I need ale," said Vered. "I need more than

that, but I'll start with ale," he amended hastily as he dismounted.

Santon held the rucksack containing the Demon Crown. The green glow had changed subtly. Before, after Lorens had worn it, the green had been that of corrosion and corruption. The hue had become brighter, purer, and in some fashion he could not put words to, *cleaner*.

"We should find Lokenna."

"Santon, you'll be the death of me. She has lived here for almost twenty years. Do you think she will run off on the very day we arrive? A few minutes to relieve our trail-thirst is all I'm asking."

"Very well." Santon climbed down, stiff but not as weak as he had been earlier. He tucked the rucksack under his left arm and followed Vered into the small tavern.

A burly man scowled at them as they entered. He called from behind the small, well-kept, and polished bar, "What's your pleasure?"

"Ale. Four mugs to start."

"There's more of you coming?" the man asked, his scowl deepening.

"Only the pair of us," said Vered, "but our thirst is greater than any two men's!"

Santon dropped the rucksack behind him on the floor to concentrate on the ale brought over by the innkeeper. He drank deeply and savored its fine malty taste as it slid smoothly down his gullet. "Good ale," he complimented.

"Make it myself."

"Excellent," agreed Vered. He finished his first and began to drink the second when he stopped and slowly lowered the flagon.

Santon turned to see what caught his friend's interest. He smiled broadly. Vered had good taste in women. Neatly dressed in a simple peasant blouse and green skirt, she was tall, lithe, and lovely. A bit too tall for his taste and much too thin, but still possessed of an inner radiance that outshone mere physical considerations.

"My wife," the innkeeper said, as if daring them to dispute it. Under different circumstances, Vered might have. How an ugly ape of a man like the tavern owner could marry such a fine woman would have provoked hours of hot debate—and fights.

"Can we have two more?" called out Vered, more intent on his drinking than the apparent mismating.

"Bring the empties over," said the innkeeper. "And the wife'll get you some food. You have the look of being on the trail all day. Travel in autumn makes you hungrier than any other time of the year."

"And then some. Thank you, good sir."

Vered returned with the foamy flagons as the woman placed a platter of cold cuts and a small loaf of bread on the table.

"I hope you enjoy this as much as you have the ale," she said. Santon stared at her openly now, wondering at such beauty in this hidden mountain village.

"If you've prepared it, I'm sure it will be splendid," said Vered, his eyes bold on the firm swell of her blouse and the trimness of her waist.

"A flatterer. I've been warned about men like you," she said, her smile robbing it of any disapproval.

Santon reached for the meat and bread, deftly cutting a slice of bread with his dagger before using the tip to flip the meat onto it. He stuck the dagger in the wood table and picked up the bread and meat when the woman passed behind him.

"Hold there!" he ordered. "Don't—" His words cut off in mid-sentence as the woman opened the rucksack and took out the glass box containing the Demon Crown.

The green glow almost blinded him.

"So pretty. May I touch it?"

She took the crown from the box and held it. She wobbled slightly, then smiled. "It is unlike anything I've ever seen."

"It's yours, Lokenna."

"What?" She turned and stared at him in astonishment. "How did you know my name?"

Santon and Vered exchanged looks. Their quest had ended. They had found the second royal twin.

"The Demon Crown is the property of the rightful heir to the throne of Porotane."

"But I . . ."

"Let us be the first to pledge our fealty, Queen Lokenna."

Unbidden, Lokenna placed the Demon Crown on her head. The glow filled the room with gentle light and Birtle Santon's heart with gladness. With Lokenna he felt the crown had found its proper owner.

CONAN

☐ 54260-6	CONAN THE CHAMPION	$3.50
☐ 54261-4		Canada $4.50
☐ 54228-2	CONAN THE DEFENDER	$2.95
☐ 54229-0		Canada $3.50
☐ 54238-X	CONAN THE DESTROYER	$2.95
☐ 54239-8		Canada $3.50
☐ 54258-4	CONAN THE FEARLESS	$2.95
☐ 54259-2		Canada $3.95
☐ 54225-8	CONAN THE INVINCIBLE	$2.95
☐ 54226-6		Canada $3.50
☐ 54236-3	CONAN THE MAGNIFICENT	$2.95
☐ 54237-1		Canada $3.50
☐ 54256-8	CONAN THE RAIDER	(Trade) $6.95
☐ 54257-6		Canada $8.95
☐ 54250-9	CONAN THE RENEGADE	$2.95
☐ 54251-7		Canada $3.50
☐ 54242-8	CONAN THE TRIUMPHANT	$2.95
☐ 54243-6		Canada $3.50
☐ 54231-2	CONAN THE UNCONQUERED	$2.95
☐ 54232-0		Canada $3.50
☐ 54252-5	CONAN THE VALOROUS	$2.95
☐ 54253-3		Canada $3.95
☐ 54246-0	CONAN THE VICTORIOUS	$2.95
☐ 54247-9		Canada $3.50

Buy them at your local bookstore or use this handy coupon:
Clip and mail this page with your order.

Publishers Book and Audio Mailing Service
P.O. Box 120159, Staten Island, NY 10312-0004

Please send me the book(s) I have checked above. I am enclosing $_____
(please add $1.25 for the first book, and $.25 for each additional book to
cover postage and handling. Send check or money order only—no CODs.)

Name _____

Address _____

City _____ State/Zip _____

Please allow six weeks for delivery. Prices subject to change without notice.

PHILIP JOSÉ FARMER